He wished she was naked, and thanked God she wasn't

He couldn't swallow, couldn't think or move or speak. Could only want.

She didn't move or speak either, but just watched him warily. Some kind of hero, she'd called him in that scornful, disappointed tone. Neither his absence nor her shower had improved her opinion of him, if that look was anything to judge by.

But he could change it—if he touched her, if he kissed her, if he tried. He could make her forget he wasn't the man she wanted him to be, at least for a few hours, but then she would go back to being disappointed and he—he would be tempted to try to be that man. That hero.

Dear Reader,

November is full of excitement—vengeance, murder, international espionage and exploding yachts. Not in real life, of course, but in those stories you love to read from Silhouette Intimate Moments. This month's romantic selections will be the perfect break from those unexpected snowstorms or, if you're like me, overeating at Thanksgiving (my mother challenges me to eat at least half my body weight). Oh, and what better way to forget about how many shopping days are left until the holidays?

Popular author Marilyn Pappano returns to the line with *The Bluest Eyes in Texas* (#1391), in which an embittered hero wants revenge against his parents' murder and only a beautiful private investigator can help him. *In Third Sight* (#1392), the second story in Suzanne McMinn's PAX miniseries, a D.C. cop with a special gift must save an anthropologist from danger and the world from a deadly threat.

You'll love Frances Housden's *Honeymoon with a Stranger* (#1393), the next book in her INTERNATIONAL AFFAIRS miniseries. Here, a design apprentice mistakenly walks into a biological-weapons deal, and as a result, she and a secret agent must pose as a couple. Can they contain their real-life passion as they stop a global menace? Brenda Harlen will excite readers with *Dangerous Passions* (#1394), in which a woman falls in love with her private investigator guardian. When an impostor posing as her protector is sent to kidnap her, she has to trust that her true love will keep her safe.

Have a joyous November and be sure to return next month to Silhouette Intimate Moments, where your thirst for suspense and romance is sure to be satisfied. Happy reading!

Sincerely,

Patience Smith
Associate Senior Editor

Please address questions and book requests to:
Silhouette Reader Service
U.S.: 3010 Walden Ave., P.O. Box 1325, Buffalo, NY 14269
Canadian: P.O. Box 609, Fort Erie, Ont. L2A 5X3

MARILYN PAPPANO

The Bluest Eyes in Texas

Silhouette®

INTIMATE MOMENTS™

Published by Silhouette Books

America's Publisher of Contemporary Romance

SILHOUETTE BOOKS

ISBN 0-373-27461-0

THE BLUEST EYES IN TEXAS

MARILYN PAPPANO

brings impeccable credentials to her career—a lifelong habit of gazing out windows, not paying attention in class, daydreaming and spinning tales for her own entertainment. The sale of her first book brought great relief to her family, proving that she wasn't crazy but was, instead, creative. Since then, she's sold more than forty books to various publishers and even a film production company. You can write to her at P.O. Box 643, Sapulpa, OK, 74067-0643.

To Wanda Strain, my mother, who, like Lexy,
understands the value of family.

I know you think a lot of what you tried to teach me
went in one ear and out the other, but all the important
stuff took. Thank you for that, and for the example
you've shown us of love, grace and strength.
Whatever I've got, I got from you.

Chapter 1

Bailey Madison. Three weeks ago Logan Marshall had never heard the name; now he was so damn tired of it that he'd prefer to never hear again. Everywhere he went, people mentioned her—*Bailey Madison's looking for you. Did that Madison woman ever find you? What does Madison want with you?*

He'd had no clue until he'd found out that she was a private investigator in Memphis, Tennessee. There were only three people in the world who might have any interest in finding him, and he wanted nothing to do with any of them. He just wanted to be left alone to carry out his work, but Bailey Madison was making that damned hard.

He was sitting on a stool at the bar in a shabby tavern outside Pineville, Texas. The place attracted a clientele so rough that Manny—the owner, bartender and bouncer—had never been able to keep a waitress for more than a week. Decent folks kept their distance; even the sheriff put in an appearance only for the occasional homicide.

But Bailey Madison had come wandering in the night before. He shook his head at the utter stupidity of it. Even an out-sider could take one look around and know she didn't belong. The only reason she'd escaped unharmed was because she'd mentioned his name and Manny had taken it on himself to es-cort her safely back to her car. But he was complaining about it now, not because he wanted thanks for what he'd done but because he wanted to be sure she wouldn't come around again.

"I can't be having no woman kidnapped, murdered or worse around here," he was saying as he chewed the toothpick clenched between his teeth. "Especially no respectable woman from elsewhere."

Logan's first impulse was to ask what could be worse than murder, but he knew the regulars at the bar. He couldn't imag-ine the woman who would willingly let any of them touch her. For any woman with standards, rape very well might be worse than death.

"You gotta talk to her," Manny went on. "Make her under-stand she don't come back here no more."

Logan didn't *want* to talk to her. Whatever she wanted, whether it was some misbegotten relative wanting to contact him or a lawyer for some recently passed misbegotten relative, he didn't care. The only people he gave a damn about knew how to find him. The rest could go to hell and take Bailey Madison with them.

But he couldn't leave her alone to fumble all over the place, blabbing his name and drawing attention to him wher-ever she went. He had a job to do, and the last thing he needed was attention.

So maybe it was time to make her acquaintance, to persuade her to forget all about him. If money couldn't do it, threats prob-ably could. He was very good at making threats and equally good at carrying them out. His promises carried weight because he'd never failed to deliver.

He swallowed the last of the beer in his bottle, then slid to his feet. "I'll talk to her, Manny. Did she say where she's staying?"

The bartender shook his head. "Prob'ly in town. She say she be back."

Of course she would. "If she comes back, let her take her chances with Leon." According to Manny, it was Leon who'd taken the strongest liking to her the night before. The guy was six and a half feet tall, over three hundred pounds, tattooed and pierced and believed wholeheartedly in taking what he wanted. One go-round with him and Bailey Madison would never go snooping where she didn't belong again.

If she survived.

Manny must have had the same thought, because he scowled at him. "If she comes back, I'll deliver you to her myself."

"Gee, thanks for the loyalty." After tossing a few bills on the bar, Logan walked outside into the bright sunshine. The bar, named Thelma's, though no one could remember a Thelma ever connected to the place, wouldn't open officially for another few hours, so if this newest problem did make good on her idiotic promise to return, it would be a while. He could drive into Pineville and take a look around or he could get some sleep to make up for last night's late hours, then park himself at a table inside and wait for her to show.

He settled for town and slid behind the wheel of his 1968 Plymouth GTX. Pineville was small, with only one motel and a couple restaurants. If Bailey Madison was there, she wouldn't be hard to find.

It was four miles along the two-lane highway into town, one for every year he'd lived there. He'd come back for only brief visits in the past fifteen years, but nothing had changed. The same businesses were still open, and the same old men still sat on the sidewalk in front of the feed store, rehashing the same old stories. The same sheriff who'd arrested him when he first arrived in town was still in office, still worthless and still hostile, and the same bars shared their Saturday-night customers with the same churches come Sunday morning. Nothing had changed.

Except that Sam and Ella were gone.

And it was his fault.

The motel was located on the opposite side of town, set off

the road a few hundred feet, a run-down place whose only sav-
ing grace was the distance to the next motel. People too tired
to drive another sixty miles stayed there, shelling out twenty-
five bucks for a room that smelled like sixty years of travelers.
The place was clean, but all the polish and air fresheners in the
world couldn't hide the fact that it was also worn and thread-
bare, a last resort.

The only car in the parking lot belonged to the owner, the
daughter of Ella's cousin three times removed. She didn't blame
him for Ella's death; she would tell him what he needed to know
if he just went inside and asked.

He didn't.

Another slow drive through town revealed only business as
usual. There was no strange woman walking down the street—
tall, pretty, nice body, according to Manny—and no Tennessee
tag adorning any of the cars. Maybe Manny had guessed wrong
and she'd taken a room in a nicer motel an hour away. Maybe
her promise to come back had merely been idle talk. Maybe
she'd moved on to create trouble someplace else.

Instead of heading back to the motel to talk to Ella's cousin's
daughter, he turned north off the main street and headed out of
town. He'd traveled this road hundreds of times—on foot, on
the motorcycle he'd bought with the earnings from his first job,
in a rental car on his occasional visits back…and once in a fu-
neral procession. That had been one of the two worst days of
his life. Considering that at the time he'd still been in the Army,
fighting in the war in Iraq, that was saying a lot.

A mile and a half out of town he turned onto a hard-packed
dirt road and followed it into thick woods. The countryside here
was a world apart from the West Texas town where he'd grown
up and the Iraqi desert where he'd spent more than a year and
the Afghani mountains the year before that. Everything here
was green and overgrown; all the rich color and smells were
home to him.

Sam had been a farmer, Ella a farmer's wife, and they'd had
some hopes of making a farmer out of him. They had encour-

aged him to join the Army after high school; Sam had done it and claimed it made a man of him. But instead of coming home to the farm after his enlistment, Logan had decided to sign up for another three years, then another, and by then he'd been well on his way to a career. They'd worried about him after 9/11 and prayed for him when the war started, and they'd been proud of him.

No one else in his life had ever been proud of him.

And to repay them, he'd brought their killer into their home.

He stopped at the gate where the road narrowed to one lane. The house wasn't far—up a rise, sitting in the middle of a clearing, with the barn out back and untended fields on three sides. This was probably the first time in a century that the fields had gone untilled, but Logan had never become a farmer. Even if he had, he couldn't work *this* land, couldn't live in *this* house.

The gate was open, listing drunkenly to one side. He couldn't remember ever seeing it closed. There was no livestock to keep in, no strangers to keep out—that had been Sam and Ella's philosophy. Even the sturdiest of gates wouldn't have kept their killer out—not when Logan had invited him right up to the supper table.

Hands tightening around the steering wheel, he drove through the gate and up the final rise. Like the town, the house was unchanged from the last time he'd seen it. Two stories, painted white, a porch with rockers. It was small enough to fit in one wing of the house where he'd grown up, but it had been more a home to him than anyplace else. He hadn't known fear in this house or need or violence. Just love and comfort.

And great sorrow.

There *was* one thing different—the car parked in front of the house. It was one of those imports that passed as a midsize sedan these days. Like millions of other cars on the road, it was red, dusty and unremarkable…except for its Tennessee tags.

What the *hell* was she doing there?

He parked behind her car, blocking it in between his own vehicle and the stone flower bed in front. He got out and pushed the door up but not shut, then crossed the yard to the porch.

The front door stood open, as it always had on a warm day, with an old-fashioned screen door to keep out pests. It obviously didn't work against pests of the two-legged variety. It squeaked a bit when he eased it open, then slipped inside. After listening a moment, he heard the creak of a floorboard upstairs and headed in that direction.

He could find his way through the house blindfolded. Ella had never bothered to rearrange anything. She'd had too many other things to do—helping out on the farm when needed, cooking, cleaning, sewing, taking care of the church and the family and the occasional stray teenage boy. Who had the time to worry whether the couch looked better here or there?

He moved stealthily up the stairs, automatically stepping over the ones that creaked, bypassing the half-moon table at the top and avoiding the chest at the corner that visitors always stubbed their toes on. When he reached the room that had once been his, he stopped silently in the doorway.

The woman—tall, pretty, nice body—stood at the window, one of his high school yearbooks open in her hands, using the sunlight to get a better look. So this was Bailey Madison. Who was she? What did she want with him? And what the hell was she doing in Sam and Ella's house?

Time to find out. Leaning one shoulder against the doorjamb, he folded his arms across his chest and said softly, dangerously, "Come on in, Ms. Madison. Make yourself at home."

Startled, Bailey choked off a shriek and nearly lost her grip on the annual as she spun toward the door. She hadn't heard a sound—no car driving up, no footsteps on the wood floor, no creaking on the stairs. Just, one minute she'd been utterly alone and the next Logan Marshall had appeared out of thin air.

She had no doubt the man standing so casually in the doorway *was* Logan Marshall. Not only did he bear a strong resemblance to the yearbook photo she'd been studying, but there was an even stronger resemblance to his brother, Brady. He was a few years younger, a few years harder and missing Brady's incredibly sexy mustache, but other than that, the features were the same. Black hair, dark skin, straight nose, sensual mouth and incredible eyes. Startlingly blue, a surprise in the midst of all that darkness.

With a rush of relief that slowed her pounding heart, she closed the yearbook, marking her place with one finger. "Jeez, you startled me."

He didn't move a muscle—didn't come into the room, didn't smile, didn't ease that harsh expression at all. He just stood there looking at her, all dark and intense and making her feel cold despite the sun shining in the room. "I wonder why. Because you've broken into a house where you don't belong? Because you're snooping through a stranger's belongings? Or because, as the saying goes, curiosity killed the cat?"

She swallowed hard. She was about ninety-nine percent sure he was just trying to intimidate her…but that one percent niggled at her. No matter how much he looked like Brady, he wasn't. He'd lived an entirely different life that very well might have turned him into an entirely different person. While Brady was good, honest and decent in spite of his upbringing, it wouldn't surprise anyone if Logan was exactly the opposite.

She opted to believe—to pretend to believe—that the tone of voice and the soft words *were* merely an intimidation tactic. Straightening to her full height of five foot seven, she took a few steps toward him, right hand extended. "I'm paid to be curious. My name is Bailey Madison. I'm a private investigator and I've been hired to find you."

He ignored her outstretched hand and pulled the yearbook away instead, flipping it open to the place she'd marked. It was the senior class photos, and right in the middle of the right page was his. Logan James Marshall. He looked so young in the picture but, at the same time, decades older than the kids around him. Life hadn't been kind to the Marshall boys growing up, and it showed.

Dropping the yearbook on the nearby dresser, he circled around her. She resisted the urge to turn with him, to avoid turning her back to him for even an instant, but she did watch, first over one shoulder, then the other. She knew he was checking her out, knew what he would see—that her jeans and T-shirt fitted too snugly to provide cover for a weapon of any sort, that nothing of any consequence could be tucked inside her pockets, that her cell phone was clipped to her waistband. She had a couple weapons—one in the purse she'd left downstairs, another in the car—but at the moment she was unarmed…except for her favorite boots, with pointed toes and three-inch heels, and the moves her self-defense instructor had drilled into her.

Completing the circuit, he stopped at the door again, then held out his hand. "Can I see your cell phone?"

She unhooked it from her jeans and was in the process of offering it when abruptly she drew back. "Why?"

"Because I need to call the sheriff and report a burglar."

She hid the phone behind her back with both hands as if that could somehow stop him from taking it. Her face growing warm with a blush, she swallowed hard again. "I haven't taken anything." It was a weak excuse, and sounded it.

"But you did break in."

The crimson in her cheeks deepened. "I, uh, yeah, I did…manipulate the lock just a little."

"Why?"

Because there was no way she could excuse the fact that she *had* broken in, she chose instead to fall back on what they called Charlie's Rule back at the agency: the ends justify the means. It was so much bull, and she'd argued it with him repeatedly, but her opinions didn't carry much weight when Charlie was the one who always got the big cases while *she* spent most of her time doing research on the computer. "Because you're a hard man to find."

"Maybe that's because I don't want to be found."

She acknowledged that with a shrug. "A lot of people don't want to be found. That's why private investigations is a thriving industry."

"Why are you looking for me?"

Back in Memphis, when she was spending long, long hours on the computer and the telephone, tracking down every Logan Marshall in the country, she'd figured she would be straight-forward with him when she found him: *Your niece hired me to locate you, she wants to meet you, let's head to Oklahoma.* She'd known he had run away from home when he was fifteen, that he'd had no contact with any of his family since then, but she'd thought, as she usually did, that honesty was the best policy. After all, his problems had been with his parents, not his brother, and nineteen years gave a kid a chance to grow up, to forgive and forget.

Then she'd begun getting leads on him and had given up the phone and the keyboard for face-to-face interviews with people who knew him, and discovered that to this day he denied the existence of a family, including his brother. He wasn't likely to welcome the opportunity to reconnect with Brady or to meet his nieces with open arms, so she'd looked for leverage…and found it.

"It's not a difficult question." His sarcasm drew her from her thoughts. "Why are you looking for me?"

"I want to talk to you about your family."

"I don't have any family." The dismissal was delivered with the perfect timing, the perfect level of disinterest to suggest that he was telling the truth.

"Denying them doesn't make them cease to exist. Your parents, Jim and Rita Marshall, are still the powers-that-be in Marshall City, Texas. Your brother, Brady, is living in Buffalo Plains, Oklahoma, with his wife and daughters—Lexy, who's almost sixteen, and Brynn, who's almost one."

"Damn," he said, his tone so mild it robbed the word of any meaning. "And here I'd been hoping they were all rotting in the ground someplace."

Bailey stiffened, her shoulders going back, her nerves tightening. She couldn't care less what he thought of his parents—based on what little she knew of them, she would also wish they were dead—but Brady and the girls were *her* family, and no one messed with her family without taking her on, too.

"Which of 'em are you working for?"

"Lexy." She bit off the name, silently daring him to say anything about the niece she adored more than anything. She would see just how disdainful he could be with her size-nine, pointed-toe, three-inch-heeled boot in his throat…*after* she'd eliminated the possibility of his ever having children himself.

"You must be some P.I.," he jeered. "Working for a kid."

She gave him a smug, ugly smile. "I found you, didn't I?"

Ten seconds ago she would have said he couldn't have gotten any unfriendlier. But in the blink of an eye, his demeanor turned so cold, so dangerous, that a chill danced down her spine. Though he didn't move closer, the intensity radiating from him invaded her space, raising goose bumps on her arms, and made her want desperately to take refuge far, far away. "Like I said, I don't have any family. I left that bunch nineteen years ago and I've thanked God for every day they weren't in my life. I don't want *you* in my life either. Tell them you couldn't find me. Tell them I didn't give a damn. Tell them I'm dead. Just get the hell out of here, leave me alone and forget you ever heard my name, or you'll be sorrier than you can imagine. Understand?"

She did. She believed he could make her damn sorry. There was such anger in his eyes, such rage in his soft voice. If she didn't know at least part of the reason, she'd be quaking in her boots. But she did know. And she'd made a promise to Lexy. She *always* kept her promises.

Confident that he'd scared her off, Logan turned to leave the bedroom. She let him get a step or two outside the door before she spoke. "I can't do that." She was proud—and relieved—that her voice was strong.

He went motionless in the hallway, and once again the intensity came off him in waves. Slowly he turned to fix that icy blue gaze on her.

She'd read somewhere that the most dangerous people were those with nothing to lose. Looking into his eyes, she believed Logan Marshall thought he had nothing to lose.

"I promised Lexy I would bring you to Oklahoma to meet her."

"She's better off not knowing me."

"Probably. But she's fifteen. Family's very important to her because she never really had any until this last year. And you can behave like a civilized person for one weekend."

"And how do you intend to get me there for a weekend?"

"Threats. Coercion. Handcuffs. At gunpoint." Then she smiled tightly. "Or maybe I intend to make a deal with you."

The derision that had entered his expression at the mention of handcuffs and a gun faded as his gaze narrowed on her. "What kind of deal?"

"You learn a lot about someone when you're looking for them. For example, I learned that you're looking for someone, too. You go to Oklahoma, make nice with your brother and your nieces for a weekend…and I'll help you find him."

Logan would give a lot to turn around and walk out of the house, but he could no more walk away from the promise of information than he could stop breathing. Much as he hated it, she had the upper hand and there was nothing he could do—at the moment—but deal with her.

He moved farther into the room. Though she wanted to back off—he recognized that scared-little-bunny look in her eyes—she held her ground, at least until he settled against the dresser, his ankles crossed, his arms folded over his chest so he wouldn't be tempted to wrap his fingers around her slender throat and squeeze the information out of her. "Who is it you think I'm looking for?"

She pulled the ladder-back chair from the desk where he'd spent too many hours trying to understand algebra and chemistry, sat down and primly crossed her legs. While she gathered her thoughts—or constructed her bluff?—he took stock of her.

She wasn't particularly tall—a good six inches shorter than him—though with Manny topping out at five foot four, pretty much everyone seemed tall. She was probably somewhere around his age and she was lean rather than slender. She carried some muscle under those tight clothes—her upper arms were well defined and so were her long, strong legs. And she was pretty, her pale brown hair streaked with gold, her hazel eyes solemn, her mouth shaped in a nice cupid's bow. He always noticed pretty women, though he rarely did anything about it. In some cultures where he'd spent time, too much notice of a pretty woman, and a man could wind up missing vital parts.

Bailey Madison had looked at him a couple times as if she would be happy to remove those parts herself.

Finally, her hands clasped together over her knees, she spoke. "Let's make the deal first. Will you go to Oklahoma to visit your brother and his family?"

Logan had lived more than half his life in Texas, first in the town that bore his family name, then in Pineville, but he'd never once been tempted to cross the Red River into the neighboring state. He had no intention of doing so now unless the trail he was following led there. But that didn't stop him from giving her the answer she wanted, albeit grudgingly. "If I have to."

"Tomorrow?"

"No. When I've finished what I've started."

"What you've started is taking a long time. I'm talking about one weekend. You can be back in Texas and on MacGregor's trail by noon Monday."

At least she wasn't totally bluffing—she did know he was looking for Pete MacGregor. But a lot of people knew that. Whether she could help him find Mac…that was what counted.

"This Lexy person has waited fifteen years. A few more weeks or months isn't going to hurt her. Besides, if I go now, what's to stop you from saying Monday, 'Oh, sorry, I lied, I don't know anything'?" Just as he'd lied. He wasn't going anywhere near Brady or his family. They really could rot in hell for all he cared.

She drew a breath before answering. "The man you're looking for is Peter Alan MacGregor. He was born October 11, in Chicago. He set a record for suspensions from school before he finally quit in eleventh grade and he had quite a juvenile arrest record before he joined the Army and straightened up. He was on his second enlistment when he got sent to Iraq, where he was wounded in an ambush on his convoy outside Baghdad. He came home on convalescent leave and spent two weeks in this house with Sam and Ella Jensen. A week before he was scheduled to report to duty again, he killed the Jensens, stole seventy-eight dollars and their pickup and disappeared, and he hasn't been heard from since."

Inwardly Logan flinched at her matter-of-fact recital of events—so unemotional and damned cold. Sam and Ella had taken Mac in because he'd had no place else to go, because they were generous like that. They had respected him for serving in the Army, had been grateful to him for the dangers he'd been willing to face in the war and they'd felt it was their duty as patriotic Americans to welcome him home. They'd nursed him, opened their house and their hearts and their lives to him, and he'd repaid them by stabbing Ella seven times with her own kitchen knife, by beating Sam to death with a piece of firewood. All for seventy-eight freakin' dollars and a pickup that wasn't worth much more.

And it was all Logan's fault.

Logan's wrong to set right.

"You could have picked up all that from the newspapers," he said harshly. Mac's crimes and Sam's and Ella's lives distilled into a few columns that gave just the facts.

"I did pick up all that from the newspapers," Bailey admitted. "It's the other things I learned that should be worth a trip to Oklahoma for you."

"What other things?"

She smiled that taut little smile again. "Want to talk while we drive north?"

Sure. When hell froze over. "Give me one piece of information about Mac that isn't common knowledge."

Though she considered it for a moment, he had the impression she already knew which piece she would offer. "He has a brother."

He shook his head. "He didn't have any family." That was one of the things that had brought the two of them together. Neither of them had had parents who cared whether they came home from the war alive or in a body bag; there had been no brothers, sisters or cousins sending letters and care packages and no wife or family to go home to when they were wounded. Sure, Logan had had Ella and Sam...but it hadn't been the same as real family. It was stupid and illogical and it shamed him, but it just hadn't been the same.

She shook her head, too, chidingly, her hair swaying around her shoulders. "Saying you don't have family doesn't make it true. You're proof of that."

"Mac was an only child—"

"Of his parents' marriage. His mother had been married before. When she left her first husband for the bright lights of Chicago, she left her son, too. Mac's half brother." The chiding was on her face again when she looked at him. "The man murdered an elderly couple who'd taken him into their home. Do you really think he was above lying about his family?"

Of course not. Mac had no scruples, no morals, no honor. He didn't deserve to live. But Logan intended to take care of that soon enough.

"Do you know this brother's name?"

Bailey nodded.

"Are you going to tell me?"

"Once we've reached an agreement about your going to Oklahoma."

"With what you've already told me, I can track him down myself."

"You can, but it'll take time. He wasn't much easier to find than you were. So...when do we leave?"

"I'll go as soon as I've found Mac."

She started shaking her head before the sentence was half out and didn't stop until he was done. "You're not being reasonable."

His chuckle sounded harsh in the room. "I don't have to be reasonable. We have a deal."

"Not yet."

Just like that, his brief, ugly humor dissipated. "Look, Mac is wanted by the Army for desertion and by the local authorities for murder—both crimes punishable by death. The longer he manages to hide, the harder it's going to be to find him, and he's already got one hell of a head start. I can't screw around and make nice with some kid I didn't even know existed before today because that's what *you* want. Get your priorities straight or stay the hell out of my way."

Outwardly she appeared unaffected by his anger. She was cool, calm, serene as she studied him. Finally she stood up. "All right. We'll find MacGregor first. But as soon as we've turned him over to the authorities, then we go to Buffalo Plains. Deal?"

"What's with this 'we'? You'll tell me everything you know, and *I'll* find Mac."

She smiled faintly. "That wasn't my offer. I said I would *help* you find him, not leave you to do it on your own. If I do that, who knows where you'll go when it's all over? Probably anywhere but Buffalo Plains."

Logan ignored the insult to his integrity, especially since, at the moment, he didn't have any. "I don't need a partner."

"I'd say you do. I've learned more about Peter MacGregor in a few weeks than you have in six months. Of course, if you really don't want me tagging along for the next few weeks, there's a simple solution—meet Lexy this weekend. Then I'll go back to Memphis and you can do whatever you want."

His scowl made it clear what he thought of her suggestion. He had enough anger and guilt in his life right now without adding Brady to it. Maybe someday he'd be ready to forgive. But he was no closer to that day now than he'd been nineteen years ago.

She closed the distance between them with a few steps and offered her hand once again. "What do you say, Logan? Do we have a deal?"

He looked at her hand—narrow, uncallused, the fingers long and slender, the nails neatly rounded and painted white on the tips. Hostilely he raised his gaze to hers but didn't take her hand. "I'd rather deal with the devil."

"And here I thought you *were* the devil," she murmured.

She refused to lower her hand, so grudgingly he took it, processing warmth, softness, in the seconds before he released it again. "We have a deal," he agreed. As he turned away, he muttered, "One you'll live to regret."

He was walking through the door, his right hand clenched in a fist as if he could erase the memory of the contact, when she softly answered, "More likely you will."

He smiled bleakly. No doubt she was right. *If* he lived, he would definitely regret it.

Chapter 2

Bailey followed him downstairs. He stopped in the hallway, looking to the kitchen at the back of the house, where her purse was visible on the table through the open door, then at the living room to the side. She wasn't surprised when he turned into the living room. According to the newspaper stories, Pete MacGregor had killed Ella Jensen in her own kitchen, leaving her frail body crumpled in a pool of blood. There were no signs of violence visible in the room—she'd looked for them—but there was a feeling there... And if *she'd* felt it, how much worse was it for Logan, who'd walked in on the scene with all its horror?

She went into the living room, homey and welcoming in an old-fashioned way. Lace doilies decorated the tables, a lap quilt was folded over the back of the couch and an oval braided rug covered much of the wood floor. When she'd first arrived, she'd studied the knickknacks that filled the flat surfaces, as well as the framed photographs that decorated the walls, focusing on one picture in particular. It was the same one Logan was looking at now—taken in the yard out front one sunny afternoon, him in his Army uniform; a tall, thin man with white hair and thick glasses on one side; a petite, delicate woman in a long skirt and apron on the other. Ella's hand was resting on Logan's arm, Sam's on his shoulder, and they looked proud, all three of them.

Any idiot could guess that Logan blamed himself for their deaths and that he wanted justice. He had resources the local sheriff's department lacked—notably time and money. Where the Jensen murders were only a small part of the sheriff's investigative responsibilities, Logan could dedicate himself to nothing else and had ever since leaving the Army six months ago.

She sat down in a worn wooden rocker, sinking into the ruffled cushions that lined the seat and the back and set it rocking. Each backward glide caused a floorboard to creak. It wasn't annoying, though, but rather comforting, like a soft snore or a tuneless whistle.

Finally he turned from the photo, looked around, then moved to the nearest window. There he brushed the lace curtains aside to lean against the sill, his hands resting on the wood on either side of him. "What do you know about Mac's brother?"

"His name is Escobar. He lives near the border and he owns a ranch there."

"What's his first name? Where near the border?"

She smiled. "I'll tell you that once we're on our way."

His corresponding smile was everything a smile should never be. "Aw, you don't trust me?"

"Not as far as I could throw you."

The smile came again. "Remember that," he said—warned—before he pushed away from the windowsill. "Let's go."

He was halfway to the door before she made it out of the chair. She hustled to the kitchen to grab her purse, then reached the porch about the time he hit the sidewalk.

"Hey," she called. "I can pick a lock to open a door, but I don't have a clue how to pick one to lock it."

He didn't break his stride. "Just press the button in. It'll lock when you close it."

She found the button he referred to on the inside knob, pulled the door up, then checked it. It was locked, though without the promise of much security. But even the most impregnable dead bolt in the world wouldn't have protected the Jensens—not when their killer had been a guest in their home.

Logan was impatiently waiting next to his car, a pair of dark glasses hiding his eyes, when she walked out. "Get your gear."

"I can drive—"

"You want to take two cars? Fine. Tell me where we're going in case we get separated on the way."

It was a perfectly reasonable request under normal circumstances, which these most certainly weren't. No doubt if she gave him an honest answer, he would slash her tires or take her keys, then drive off and leave her in his dust. She would be lucky if she ever caught up to him again.

"I was suggesting that we leave your car here and take mine," she said politely.

He looked at her car, and the disdain returned to his expression. "No, thanks."

"It's a perfectly good car," she protested.

"Uh-huh. I bet it gets good mileage, has a half-assed stereo system and tops out at about eighty miles an hour. No way."

She treated his car to the same disdainful look. "And I bet this guzzles gas like water, has a stereo that can blow out your eardrums at fifty paces and doesn't even have air-conditioning."

"Get your gear or stay behind," he warned.

"Fine. Let me drive."

The look that crossed his face fell just short of horror. "Nobody drives my car."

"Make an exception."

"Why? You afraid I'm gonna leave you by the road first time we make a bathroom stop?"

That was exactly what she was afraid of. She hadn't told him much, but it was enough to send him in the right direction, and he seemed just the type to leave her stranded in the middle of nowhere.

Her jaw set grimly, she went to the car, retrieved her backup pistol from the glove compartment and slid it into her purse, then returned. "My 'gear' is at the motel in town. We'll have to stop there."

The entire car literally rumbled with power when he started the engine. She settled into the passenger seat, purse in her lap, Logan just inches away, and wondered just how big a mistake she was making.

A short while later she got at least part of an answer to that when he almost stopped at a stop sign, then turned west onto the main street. She twisted in the seat to face him. "The motel's the other way."

He didn't respond.

"Damn it, Marshall—"

That made him glance her way. "Hey, don't blame me because you weren't prepared."

"It wouldn't take me five minutes to pack!"

"You can buy new clothes."

"I don't want new clothes!"

When his only response was a shrug, she folded her arms across her chest and coldly said, "I want to pick up my clothes. If you don't turn this car around *right now,* I'm not telling you one more damn thing about Pete MacGregor."

The tires squealed as he jammed the brake to the floor and steered to the side of the street. "Then get out. I'll find this Escobar on my own."

"I'll call him. I'll warn him about you."

His demeanor turned icy again. "You wouldn't."

Of course she wouldn't. People should suffer the consequences of their actions, which meant Pete MacGregor should spend the rest of his life in prison…or die. She would never help a killer escape justice.

But while Logan might suspect that, he didn't *know* it.

"Are you sure of that?" she asked. "Sure enough to put me out here? Sure enough to risk blowing your best chance at finding MacGregor?"

It took every bit of strength she possessed not to squirm under the intensity of his stare. Just as she'd been earlier, he was about ninety-nine percent certain she was bluffing, but that one percent worried him. He wasn't going to call her bluff. Not this time.

An instant after she reached that conclusion, he glanced in the rearview mirror, then peeled out in a tight turn that left skid marks on the road and drove back through town to the motel. Pulling up in front of the room she pointed out, he scowled at her. "Five minutes."

Smiling sweetly, she reached across, cut off the engine and snagged the keys before he began to guess what she was doing. She hopped out of the car, slid them into her jeans pocket, then headed toward the room.

She was hastily stuffing clothes into the suitcase open on the bed when he appeared in the open door. She'd come for four days this trip and had brought enough clothes for seven. What could she say? She liked being prepared.

He didn't cross the threshold but stood smack center in the doorway and watched silently. No doubt he had some mental clock counting down and he would smugly let her know when five minutes had passed. She fully intended to be done before then.

After cramming everything into the suitcase that had come out of it, she zipped it, then grabbed a tote and went into the cramped bathroom, scooping makeup and toiletries inside. With that bag over one shoulder, she retrieved her laptop from the bottom dresser drawer and slung the strap over the other shoulder, then hefted the suitcase from the bed. A glance at the bedside clock showed she had seconds to spare.

"I'm ready," she announced.

Finally Logan moved out of the doorway, but not to head for his car, as she expected. Instead he approached the bed, nudged the rumpled covers back with one booted toe, then bent to retrieve something from the floor. Bailey looked at the scrap of coral lace dangling from his finger and told herself she wouldn't be embarrassed. Lingerie was a fact of life. He'd probably seen as much of it as she had. She wouldn't snatch the tiny filmy panties away from him and hide them as if doing so could erase them from existence.

She took the garment from him in a calm, controlled manner, stuffed them in an outside pocket of the suitcase, then pushed past him with her load to head for the door.

"And here I would have figured you for white cotton," he murmured behind her.

She pretended not to hear.

She strode to the rear of the car, fished out the keys and unlocked the trunk, then blinked. It was quite possibly the neatest car trunk she'd ever seen—spare tire out of the way, tool kit snugged into a corner, duffle bag tucked into another corner and gun cases neatly side by—

Gun cases. Two obviously held pistols; the other two were for longer guns. He didn't intend to take any chances with MacGregor. And why should he? The man was a murderer. If he could kill that sweet old couple for nothing, he wouldn't think twice about killing someone like Logan, who presented far more of a threat to him.

But logic aside, the weapons made her uncomfortable. Sure, she carried a gun—two of them at the moment—but strictly for self-defense. She'd never shot anyone and never would unless there was absolutely no other choice. But going looking for someone armed to the teeth—that was more like hunting, tracking prey, making the kill.

A dark hand suddenly appeared in her line of sight as Logan lifted her suitcase into the trunk, settling it next to the gun cases. He slid the tote bag from her shoulder and fitted it into the space next to it, then made room for the laptop case. Finally he closed the trunk, then held out his hand for the keys.

She started to hand them over, then hesitated. "You *are* planning to turn MacGregor over to the authorities when you find him, aren't you?"

For a long time he gazed at her, but thanks to those damn glasses, she couldn't see anything but a dim reflection of herself. Not that it mattered—even if she'd been looking directly into his eyes, she still wouldn't have seen anything he didn't want her to see. Finally his mouth relaxed from its grim set long enough to form an answer. "I'm not a cold-blooded murderer."

Relief eased over her. She dropped the key ring in his palm, then opened the passenger door, sliding inside. The sun-warmed leather of the seat went a long way toward easing the chill the guns had created inside her. He'd served honorably in the Army and received commendations for his heroic actions in the war. Heavens, he was Brady's *brother.* Of course he wasn't a murderer.

But he also blamed himself for the deaths of two people he'd loved dearly. He wanted justice, needed vengeance. Even she, with no emotional involvement in the case, could make the argument that killing Pete MacGregor where he stood was indeed justice.

But it was pointless to worry about his intentions now. Before he could even be faced with the choice, they had to find MacGregor. She had to keep him from ditching her or from disappearing before he'd kept his end of the bargain. Those were her worries.

MacGregor was his.

Wind rushed through the car, keeping the temperature comfortable even though they were driving directly into the setting sun. Logan's skin felt raw, as if the slightest touch might send sensations skittering all the way to his brain, and his throat was parched. If he was alone, he would have music blasting from the CD player, adding its own vibrations to those already supplied by the engine and the road, but with Bailey sitting there all prim and pissy, he figured adding music would only get him more complaints.

She hadn't spoken since that question as they'd stood at the back of the car. *You are planning to turn MacGregor over to the authorities when you find him, aren't you?* Fair question. A lie for an answer. He intended to kill Mac—maybe painfully, maybe slowly or maybe he would just put a bullet in his brain and be done with it. Whatever his choice, the bastard would never hurt anyone again when Logan was finished with him.

And then…then he had no clue what he'd do. The past year had turned his life upside down. He'd lost the only two people who mattered, had given up his career to track down their killer, had turned his life over to that obsession. Once it was over, what reason would he have to live? What would he do? Where would he go?

Not to Oklahoma. Not to Brady and his kids.

He'd never imagined his brother having kids. Whenever he thought of Brady, it was always in the past, as if he'd never aged beyond the seventeen he was when Logan left home. His parents had frozen at the point in his memories, as well. As if they had all died and only Logan had survived.

He couldn't have been so lucky.

They'd reached Dallas in time for evening rush hour. Now, with the major part of the city behind them, he exited the freeway and pulled into the parking lot of a motel that advertised clean rooms and low rates. There was a gas station on one side, a burger place on the other. What more could they ask for?

"We're stopping?" Bailey asked when he cut the engine under the awning that shaded the motel entrance.

"I'm tired."

"But I can dr—" She broke off, no doubt remembering their earlier discussion. "Get one room."

He opened his mouth to make a smart-ass remark, but she cut him off. "With two beds."

"Aw, damn. And here I was hoping…"

She didn't even grace that with a scowl.

Inside the lobby the cute clerk came on to him even though she had a good view of Bailey waiting in the car. He was accustomed to that, though it had been a long time since he'd taken anyone up on her offer. He would get interested in sex again sometime. He just didn't care about it now.

She gave them a first-floor room at the back, away from the highway noise. After getting only a few hours' sleep the night before, then dealing with Bailey today, he was so damn tired that even the Texas Motor Speedway couldn't keep him awake.

They left their bags in the room—all three of hers plus his duffle—then at his suggestion, walked next door to the burger restaurant. After standing in line to place their order, they found a table away from the plate glass windows that radiated heat from the sun and sat down to wait for the pimply kid behind the counter to call their number.

On the drive it had been easy not to talk—too much noise through the open windows. Here in the relative peace of a restaurant where business was slow, he could have just as easily remained silent. When he chose, he was good at it. This time he didn't choose.

"You don't sound like you're from Memphis."

Bailey was playing with the paper wrapper she'd stripped from her drinking straw, flattening it between her fingers, then folding it into neat patterns. At his comment, she glanced up, then crumpled the paper and tossed it onto the table. "I'm not. I grew up in Kansas."

"The great flat state." He didn't wait for agreement or argument. "How'd you end up in Tennessee?"

"I had just graduated from college and spent the summer before law school working for a law firm. I liked the P.I.s they contracted with and thought their job seemed a lot more interesting than the lawyers'. So I forgot about law school, put in some applications and got hired in Memphis."

"That must have thrilled Mom and Dad."

"Actually Mom didn't care either way. She just wanted me to be happy. And my father…was dead. He just would have wanted me to be happy, too."

He'd heard some parents were like that. If pressed, he would have said that Jim and Rita had just wanted him for their own entertainment. Neither of them had had a paternal bone in their bodies, or if they had, it had long since been broken, the way they'd broken more than a few of *his* bones. Truthfully, though, Brady had gotten most of the fractures. It had taken them a while to realize that there were plenty of ways to inflict pain without risking the kind of injury that attracted the attention of the authorities.

He wondered idly who they'd taken their rage out on once Brady had left home. It was probably too much to hope that it had been each other.

Steering away from that line of thought, he refocused on Bailey. "Are you a good enough P.I. that you attract clients in other states or are you so lousy that you have to go looking for business in other states where they don't know you?"

Her smile was small and sarcastic. "The agency is good enough that they don't have to go looking for business at all. It finds them."

"Then how did you wind up working for a kid in Oklahoma?"

She toyed with one of the stack of napkins that had come with their drinks, folding it, creasing it with one long, slender finger, then smoothing it flat again. Finally she pushed it away and met his gaze. "Lexy's my niece," she said reluctantly, as if it might make a difference.

Did it? It certainly explained her willingness to threaten, coerce and blackmail. This wasn't just a professional intent on keeping her promise to a client but an aunt determined to make her niece happy, which would make her harder to shake once Mac had been taken care of.

Harder. Not impossible.

The pimply kid called their number over the loudspeaker, and Logan left the table to pick up their tray. After a stop at another counter to add tiny paper cups of ketchup, he returned to the table, passed her food to her and unwrapped the foil paper around his hamburger.

So her sister was married to his brother. That made them almost…nothing. Hell, he didn't even admit to having a brother. He sure wasn't claiming Brady's family, and by rights, his wife's family didn't even exist in Logan's world.

Except Bailey did exist. She was all too real and all too big a pain.

"Is there anything you'd like to know about Brady and the girls?" she asked, her tone cautious as she dipped a thick-cut French fry in ketchup.

"Nope."

"You know, he might be able to help you with this search. He's the under—"

"Which part of 'nope' did you not understand?"

"Come on. A smart man accepts help when he needs it. This is a tough job to try alone."

"I'm not alone," he pointed out dryly. "I've got you."

That made her fall silent for a while, long enough to eat half her hamburger and most of the fries. Then she looked at him again, wearing the expression he was coming to recognize as her stubborn, not-gonna-give-up look. "Aren't you at all curious about him? About how he left home? About where he's been and what he's done these past nineteen years?"

"Nope."

"I don't believe you."

"Oh, gee, that hurts my feelings."

"He's your *brother.*"

"Like that means something. These are good burgers, aren't they?" He dipped the ragged edge of his hamburger in ketchup, then took a big bite. Food was one of the few pleasures he'd found since returning from the war. Endless months of MREs—the prepackaged "meals ready to eat" that were the mainstay of combat troops' diet—and the periodic hot meals they were served while in camp had left him craving old favorites like pizza, hamburgers and doughnuts. He'd lived off junk food for the last six months and could probably do it for the rest of his life.

Being the stubborn, naive type, Bailey didn't get the message that he was through with the conversation. "It means something to Brady."

He slowly chewed another bite while scowling at her. "You've got a sister."

"Three, actually."

"And you're just the best of friends with all three of them."

"We're close."

"Goody for you. You wanna be best friends with 'em, fine. It's none of my business. I don't wanna be best friends with Brady, and that's none of your business."

Her cheeks flushed a pale pink. "I just don't understand—"

"You shouldn't mess with things you don't understand."

"What about your nieces? Aren't you the least bit interested in them?"

He considered that while he polished off his burger. He'd never been a kid-friendly person, not even when he was a kid himself. Back then, pain, shame and the fear of discovery had kept him and Brady from getting close to other kids. As he'd grown up, he'd come to view kids as nuisances best kept at a distance. They started life crying, smelly and needy, before turning into a whiny, troublemaking subhuman species. Given a choice, he would never deal with anyone younger than eighteen. At least by then, they'd reached the point where they stood a chance of becoming a real person.

His silence brought a bit of hope to Bailey's expression that he dashed when he finally answered. "No. Not the least bit."

She scowled at him as she crumpled her wrapper with enough force that she was probably imagining it was his throat. "You're a jerk—you know that?"

"A jerk," he repeated, amused. "Now *that* really hurts my feelings. Is that the best you can come up with?"

Shoving her chair back so hard it would have fallen if not for the table behind them, she stood up, then leaned toward him. "No. You're a selfish, self-centered, rude, cold-hearted, unfeeling bastard who doesn't deserve to have someone like Brady, Lexy and Brynn in his life. You could go straight to hell for all I care, but I made a promise to Lexy, and you made one to me, and by God, we're both going to keep them or I'll kill you myself."

With that, she turned on her heel and strode to the door. He watched her go as he finished his fries. If he was lucky, she would find her way back to Pineville, pick up her car and get the hell out of his life.

But he hadn't been lucky in a long time.

He wasted another ten minutes before clearing his table and heading for the motel. As he rounded the back corner, the first thing he saw was Bailey, sitting on the sidewalk outside their room. It was hard to tell from her stony expression whether she'd cooled down. Not that he cared. Traveling with an unwanted companion was tough. Having her too pissed off to talk to him, though, just might make it bearable.

He unlocked the door, went inside and left it standing open. He was pulling back the covers on the bed nearest the door when she finally came inside.

"It's not even eight o'clock," she commented.

"You can tell time. Good."

"You can't be going to bed before eight o'clock."

He bunched up the bedspread to one side, then untucked the sheets from under the mattress before facing her. "I got about three hours' sleep last night and I've been dealing with a major pain in the ass today. I'm tired. I want to sleep. You can watch TV or read the Good Book—" he gestured toward the battered Bible on the night table "—or twiddle your thumbs. I don't care. Just whatever you do, be ready to leave first thing in the morning."

She yanked the pillows free of the spread on the second bed, mashed them against the headboard, then plopped herself down and switched on the television.

After securing the locks on the doors, Logan emptied his pockets on the nightstand, including his car keys. Bailey's gaze instantly went to them, then away. Would she hide them as soon as she judged he was asleep? Probably. It didn't matter. If he left her, it would be someplace a hell of a lot more remote than Dallas.

He kicked off his shoes, peeled off his T-shirt, then stripped to his boxers. When he turned to slide between the covers, he heard a gasp that started loud, then choked off, as if she'd clamped her hand over her mouth. Scowling, he turned to look at her and saw that was indeed what she'd done.

He held her gaze a long time, daring her to ask, but she swallowed hard, lowered her hand and said nothing. Satisfied, he eased into bed, shut off the lamp on his side of the center table, rolled over and went to sleep.

Bailey kept the sound on the television low so it wouldn't disturb Logan, but she couldn't concentrate on the show. He'd undressed so casually—something of a surprise considering that they were practically strangers while at the same time not surprising at all considering what an ass he'd been. She'd been trying not to watch—not an easy task when he was all smooth brown skin and hard, sinewy muscle—but when he'd turned his back to her…

His back was striped with scars, some no more than thin, pale lines, others thickened and white. They'd stretched from side to side, from shoulder to opposite hip, some disappearing beneath the waistband of his boxers, and they'd looked…horrible.

She could think of only one way to get scars like that: torture. He'd been beaten with a strap of some sort, beaten until his skin was torn, raw and bloody. Her first thought was the war—the enemy wasn't known for treating prisoners humanely—but he hadn't been taken prisoner. Besides, these were old scars, existing prior to his time in the Army.

Which left his parents as the most likely source. That explained his hatred for them, his utter lack of interest in whether they lived or died. But why did he hate his brother? God forbid, had Brady taken part in the abuse?

She didn't believe it. Wouldn't. Couldn't. She'd watched her brother-in-law with Hallie and with the girls. He was far too gentle, too good a soul. He *protected* people. He didn't hurt them.

More likely Brady had been the favored son, the elder who could do no wrong, and Logan resented him for that. She'd read enough about child abuse to know it was sometimes like that—the parents would single out one child for all the punishment, all the rage, while treating the others the way loving parents should.

It was the only explanation she could come up with.

Nearly two hours had passed when a yawn shook her out of her thoughts. She shut off the television and rose from the bed, lifting her suitcase into the space. Usually she slept in a tank top and panties, both so skimpy they were only a step up from being naked. Tonight she dug a T-shirt from the bag, then took it into the bathroom along with her tote bag.

She combed her hair, washed off her makeup, moisturized her face, then changed into the T-shirt. It was about four sizes smaller than she would have liked and eight or ten inches shorter, but unless she developed a fondness for sleeping fully dressed, it was the best she could do. Hesitantly she returned to the bedroom, slid hastily beneath the covers, then reached to turn out the lamp.

For a long moment she lay there, leaning on one elbow, the other hand stilled on the switch, her gaze fixed on Logan's keys. It wasn't likely he would leave her there. Surely his preference would run to some West Texas town miles from nowhere. Still, that one percent doubt made her switch off the lamp, then scoop up the keys and slide them under the covers with her. He would probably be smugly amused at this proof that she didn't trust him, and she was getting tired of his smugness, but better safe than sorry, right?

She'd settled on her side, the key ring looped over one finger and tucked under the pillow that supported her head, and was concentrating on slow, even breaths when a gravelly voice came out of the darkness.

"You counting on me to be gentleman enough to not root through those covers for my keys?"

Damn. She would have sworn he was asleep. "A gentleman would be the last thing I'd mistake you for," she replied, keeping her own voice quiet in the darkness. "I'm counting on waking up if you do start rooting."

"You make me sound like a damn pig."

"I was merely using your word. Besides, sometimes you act like one."

His chuckle was mild. "Any other insults you want to add?"

"I'll let you know as they come to mind." She tucked the covers under her chin, making a tight little cocoon for herself, then plumped the pillow under her head. It would be best to end the conversation right there, to close her eyes and pretend to sleep until she actually drifted off. She doubted he would object.

But she didn't close her eyes or let things drop. "Those scars on your back...did your parents give you those?"

This time there was nothing light about his chuckle. "The only thing they ever gave me that mattered."

"I'm sorry."

"Yeah. Sure."

She couldn't take offense at his dismissal. An apology was such a little thing, and coming from a stranger, it meant nothing. Nothing could make right what his parents had done to him, except possibly knowing that they would suffer for it in hell.

She listened to his steady breathing for a while. With anyone else, she would take it as a sign he was asleep. With him, assuming anything was likely to prove that trite old saying about making an ass of you and me.

As the bedside clock rolled over to eleven, Bailey was convinced she would never fall asleep, but the next time she glanced at it for confirmation, it read six thirty-three. She was about to turn over and snooze again when her gaze slid past the clock to the other bed. Logan was dressed in jeans and a dark T-shirt, his jaw was freshly shaved, his hair was damp from his shower and he was watching the morning news with the volume muted.

There was something incredibly disconcerting about the

fact that he'd been up and about while she'd lain sleeping, dead to the world. It made her feel vulnerable, although clearly he hadn't disturbed her. She'd slept through whatever noise he might have made, and her little cocoon was tucked as securely as it had been last night. More importantly—she thrust her hand under the pillow, searching until her fingers closed around cool metal—he hadn't retrieved his keys and abandoned her.

Although she would have sworn she'd made no noise and no movement other than opening her eyes and locating the keys, he knew she was awake. Without glancing in her direction, he asked, "Are you planning to lie there all day? 'Cause I'm leaving in half an hour."

Slowly she sat up, keeping the covers around her. "I need to take a shower."

"Then get moving."

Maybe he had zero modesty, but she did—and no robe either. "Couldn't you wait outside?"

Finally he turned his head to look at her. His expression was as dry as the desert in August. "I saw you get into bed last night. Unless your panties shrank during the night, there's not going to be anything new to see this morning."

Scowling at him, she maneuvered the bedspread free of the other covers, then wrapped it around her before awkwardly rising from the bed. It took an effort, but she managed to make it as far as the bathroom door with her suitcase and tote bag before shedding the cover and disappearing inside. She locked the door, scooted her bags up against it, then tossed the car keys on top.

When she came out a short while later, showered, shampooed and shaved, he was sprawled in the same position, with the volume turned up on the television. He gave no sign of noticing her except to say, "You've got nine minutes."

Brush her teeth, dry her hair, fix it, put on makeup and repack in nine minutes? Yeah, right. Even at her quickest, she needed a minimum of fifteen minutes before she would be ready to walk out the door.

She brushed her teeth first, then shoved yesterday's clothes into an outside pocket of the suitcase. She was just finishing her makeup when Logan's reflection appeared in the mirror. He came too close, reached around and patted her pockets to locate his keys in the right one. He was wiggling his fingers into the tight space when she spun around, slapping at his hand. "Hey! Stop that!"

He didn't, of course. "Time's up. I'm outta here."

She used one of her self-defense moves, grabbing his hand, putting pressure on the sensitive spot, bending it back. He didn't let out a squeal like the last guy she'd done it to and he didn't back off—the last guy had dropped to one knee—but he did stop probing in her pocket.

"I'm ready," she said in a warning tone.

His gaze flickered to her hair, still wet and combed straight back from her face. She neither wanted nor needed his confirmation that it wasn't a flattering style, but she could take care of that in the car.

"Just grab my suitcase," she went on in the same voice, "and I'll be right behind you."

"Grab your own suitcase, lady. I'm not your servant." He yanked his hand free, snatched up his duffle and headed for the door.

Gritting her teeth, Bailey shoved everything but a comb into the tote bag, then rummaged inside for an elastic band and some gold clips. Feeling like a pack mule, she hauled her stuff to the car outside and, smiling the phoniest polite smile she could manage, handed him the keys.

"Are we stopping for breakfast?" she asked as they settled in their respective seats.

"I don't eat breakfast."

She did, but she wasn't about to insist on it. If he wanted to be inconsiderate, let him. Eventually they would have to stop for gas, and when they did, she would stock up on munchies to get her through the quirks of his schedule.

The morning air was cool enough that they didn't need the windows down more than a few inches, so she took advantage of the relative calm to French braid her hair. It was a job best done by someone else, in front of a mirror and not in the confines of a small car, but at last she was satisfied with the results, at least from the front. She couldn't see how the back looked and decided it didn't matter.

"You could just cut it," Logan said when she was finally finished.

"Or, gee, you could have given me five minutes to dry it."

He shrugged. "Thirty minutes is plenty of time to shower and make yourself presentable. It's not as if you were ugly to start."

Her gaze narrowed as she looked at him, then she offered a simpering smile. "Why, thank you for that gracious compliment, Mr. Marshall."

Wonder of wonders, he actually shifted uncomfortably and color darkened his face. "I wasn't offering a compliment—just stating the facts."

She dropped the comb in her purse, then tilted her head back. It was a lovely morning. She'd slept well; her store of patience wasn't dribbling away like sand in an hourglass—yet— and she'd made Logan Marshall blush. Things were going so well at the moment that she might even make an effort to be sociable.

Another wonder—the same thought had apparently occurred to Logan, because before she could think of anything to say, he spoke. "How'd you wind up with a name like Bailey?"

"Hey, Bailey is a perfectly respectable name."

"Yeah, generally a perfectly respectable last name or man's name."

"Logan is generally a last name, too." So was Brady, for that matter.

"Logan's a family name."

"So is Bailey…sort of." When he glanced her way, she shrugged. "When my mother got pregnant the first time, she knew exactly what she was going to name her son—Lee Aubrey Madison the third. But she had a daughter, so she named her Neely. I came next and got Bailey. Then there's Hallie and Kylie."

"Good thing she stopped before she got to Holly, Molly and Polly."

"At least if we all had to be *lees,* we got unusual *lees.*" Without pausing, she went right on. "You said Logan's a family name. Whose?"

"It's my paternal grandmother's maiden name."

"And Brady is…your maternal grandmother's maiden name?"

His only response was the tightening of his fingers on the steering wheel. "Where do the other *lees* live?"

"Neely's in Heartbreak, Oklahoma. She's a lawyer and her husband's the county sheriff. Hallie's in Buffalo Plains, about twenty miles away. She's a stay-at-home mom and her husband is—" she caught his warning breath "—not open to discussion. And Kylie lives in Dallas, where she's happily single and breaking hearts every day."

"Why didn't you call her last night?"

"Oh, I don't think that would have been a good idea. She would have asked a lot of questions and she's not nearly as tactful as I am." Besides, Kylie would have wanted to do something, and Bailey never could have relaxed with Logan out of her sight. The rat likely carried an extra set of keys to the car and would have been long gone before she returned.

"You're the tactful one." His words were heavy with doubt.

"No, actually I'm the smart one. People labeled us when we were kids to help keep us straight. Neely's the determined one, Hallie's the popular one, Kylie's the pretty one, and I'm the smart one."

"And the hardheaded one," he muttered.

"Oh, we're all pretty hardheaded," she said easily. "Besides, you've got no room to talk. You're about as stubborn as they come."

He treated her to a dry, sarcastic smile and repeated her earlier words to her. "Thank you for that gracious compliment."

"Hey, I told you I'd pass on any impressions as they came to mind." She kicked off her shoes, propped one foot in the narrow space between window glass and door frame, then pressed the stereo on button. "Let's see if we can agree on good music."

Chapter 3

They couldn't.

She liked country; he liked rock. She could listen to classical; he'd rather have a root canal without anesthesia. She couldn't stand techno; he wasn't about to sit through unending hours of jazz.

The radio went back off and stayed that way.

"God, does this state never end?" she groused. It was mid-afternoon, and the temperature had risen a few degrees past comfortable about sixty miles back. She looked cranky, and Logan felt it.

"Nope, it goes on forever. When I left home, it took me six months to get from Marshall City to Pineville."

That made her look at him—something she'd avoided doing after they'd gone through the entire radio dial, AM and FM, three times without finding anything to agree on. He'd been happy being ignored and he'd done a good job ignoring her in return, though he had stopped for lunch when he heard her stomach growling.

"You were fifteen," she commented. "Where did you go?"

Vaguely he wished he hadn't mentioned that last part. The last time he'd talked in any detail about running away had been to Sam and Ella, right after he'd gotten caught stealing food from their crops.

But he'd opened the subject, and nearly twenty years had gone by, and none of it really mattered anymore. "I hitched rides to Dallas and stayed there a while, until I realized I hadn't gone far enough." He'd been doing okay. He'd hooked up with some other homeless kids, and they had shown him the ins and outs of living on the street. He'd gone hungry a lot, and home had been a ratty mattress in an abandoned building, but it had been a better life than he'd ever known living in the family mansion in Marshall City.

Then one day he and his buddies had been hanging out downtown, picking pockets, looking for trouble, and he'd seen a familiar face. Business trips to Dallas weren't unusual for his father; he'd just never thought he could possibly run into him in a city of that size.

That afternoon he'd headed east, intending to keep moving until he'd reached the Atlantic Ocean. He'd made it only so far as Pineville. A few years later, when he hadn't needed to run, he hadn't stopped at the ocean. Germany, Korea, Afghanistan, Iraq…

"What made you stop in Pineville?" Bailey asked.

"My last ride let me off there. I was headed east, but he'd turned north before I realized it. He let me out at the Jensens' road. I was hungry, so I decided a little alfresco dining would be nice and I got caught." He shrugged as if that was the end of the story.

"Most people who catch someone stealing from them don't invite him into their homes and make him a part of their families."

"No," he agreed quietly. "Most people don't."

"They must have been very special."

They'd never been able to have a family of their own—not that they hadn't tried. Ella had miscarried four times, and the one baby who'd made it to term had died three days after birth.

That was when she'd accepted that God intended her to mother other people's children, and she'd done it with a vengeance. Everyone in town had regarded her as the mother or grand-mother they'd always wanted.

"Is there any doubt that Pete MacGregor killed them?"

"None."

"Is there any proof?"

Logan felt the tension growing inside him. It was always there, and had been for nearly a year, but sometimes it was so strong he could feel it hum. This was one of those times. He gripped the steering wheel tighter, ground his jaws together and answered in carefully controlled words. "I left that morning to go to a doctor's appointment. The only people at the farm were Sam, Ella and Mac. When I got back that afternoon, I found Sam's body in front of the barn and Ella's on the kitchen floor. The farm truck was missing, and so was Mac. Who do *you* think killed them?"

"He could have been a victim, too."

"Right. Someone breaks in, kills an eighty-year-old couple and leaves them where they fall, but they dispose of the body of the young, six-foot-tall, two-hundred-pound man who was staying with them."

"Maybe he was taken hostage."

"Okay. You're a burglar. You break in to a place and you think you might need a hostage to ensure your escape. You have a choice between two frail little eighty-year-olds and a twenty-something, six-foot-tall, two-hundred-pound soldier. Which one are you gonna choose?"

"I'm just considering the possibilities." She laid her hand on his arm, and the muscles clenched even more. A glance at the speedometer showed the needle hovering between ninety and ninety-five. With a deep breath, he eased off on the pedal until the speed dropped back to the legal limit. Then he shrugged off her touch. She didn't look offended or rebuffed or really much of anything but thoughtful.

"Where are we headed?" he asked to break the silence. So

far she'd given him simple directions—get on the interstate and keep going west.

"To the border."

"There's a hell of a lot of border. Where in particular?"

"I'll tell you when to turn."

He didn't like being in the dark. If he'd learned anything in the Army, it was how to lead. He'd held a hell of a lot of responsibility, especially in the war, and he'd lived up to it. It rubbed him the wrong way to now be denied even the most basic of information.

Not that she didn't have a good reason for withholding it.

"You have any reason to believe Mac has anything to do with this brother of his?"

She propped her bare feet on the dash, wiggling her toes for a minute before letting them relax. Her skin was pale gold, her nails were painted crimson and a silver band encircled the second toe on her left foot. A matching chain around her ankle was just visible under the hem of her jeans leg.

There was something…appealing about the sight. Something that made him think of those tiny little panties he'd picked up in her room back in Pineville. That made him wonder if she was that small all over, if she was wearing a similar bit of silk and lace right now, if she wore any other jewelry he couldn't see.

Jeez, they were *feet,* he berated himself. Prettier than most, more decorated than most, but utilitarian just the same. Definitely no reason to be thinking in any way about sex.

Finally she looked his way, but with sunglasses covering half her face, he couldn't read anything in her expression. "Are you looking for an explanation for his lies regarding his family? He didn't know about the brother and therefore he didn't lie when he said he didn't have one?" She gave a shake of her head. "A couple years ago MacGregor got arrested for public drunk in the town where his brother lives. You think that was just coincidence?"

Of course it wasn't. And it stood to reason that, being in trouble with the law again—in *serious* trouble—Mac would turn to his brother for help.

"And how did you find that out?" he asked sourly.

"I have my sources."

"You got a cop friend to run a criminal history, didn't you?" He didn't need more of an answer than the pink staining her cheeks. "That's illegal, you know."

"Charlie's Rule. The ends justify the means."

"Who's Charlie?"

"A guy I work with." She said it so casually that Logan knew immediately there was more to the relationship than that. A guy she was adversarial with, was jealous of or was intimate with? A guy who'd seen those same tiny panties, only with her in them?

It didn't matter to him. He'd never cared about anyone's sex life but his own, which had been pretty much nonexistent in recent years. She could be sleeping with half the men in Memphis and he wouldn't give a damn. Not as long as she kept her end of the bargain and helped him find Mac.

"What else did you find out about this brother?" He was scowling, he realized. Probably because the sun was low enough in the western sky to blind a man. So what if the visor blocked the worst of the glare and his sunglasses took care of the rest? It was still there, and he knew it.

"Señor Escobar is a rancher. He's married and has two children."

"And you're going to help with him how?"

This time when she looked at him, she was smiling. "Despite his married status, Señor Escobar considers himself a ladies' man. I consider myself a lady. We should have a great deal in common."

Logan's chest tightened until the only breaths he could take were shallow. Escobar might be a hundred and eighty degrees opposite from his brother…or he might be just as dangerous, maybe even more so. And she was planning to toy with him? "This is your great plan—flirt with the guy in the hopes that he'll spill his brother's whereabouts in the heat of passion?"

"I don't intend to sleep with him," she said haughtily. "Look, we can't decide on any course of action until we get to town and see what's what. Who knows? Escobar may not have anything to do with MacGregor. He may have zero interest in protecting a brother he may not be close to."

That was logical. How much would *he* risk for Brady? Nowhere near as much as Brady had once risked for him.

"What about the law in this town? Are they honest, corrupt, incompetent or just inefficient?"

"I don't know. But they did arrest MacGregor."

"Public drunk isn't a big deal," he pointed out. Escobar might not have cared that his brother was inconvenienced and out a few hundred dollars for the fine, especially if Mac was guilty. But something bigger like desertion or murder, something that carried a bigger punishment than a night in jail and a fine, *that* he very well might care about.

"What does it matter if the cops *are* corrupt?" Bailey asked. "You can turn MacGregor over to the state cops or the state bureau of investigation or the Army or someone."

She was right about his options. There were any number of agencies who would be more than happy to make an arrest on a double homicide. But the question mattered because he didn't want to kill any cops, not even dirty ones, along with MacGregor.

"You *are* intending to turn him over," she said tentatively when he offered no response.

He scowled at her. "I told you, I'm no murderer." He had killed a lot of people, but not one who hadn't been trying to kill him at the same time. If he needed the rationalization, he had no doubt Mac would try to kill him, too. But he wasn't intending to rationalize his actions. His plan was simple: Mac was going to die.

One way or another—self-defense or cold-blooded murder—Logan was going to kill him.

The sun had long since set when they finally stopped for the night. Bailey, so tired she could hardly keep her eyes open, roused when Logan pulled up to the entrance of a motel a few hundred yards off the interstate in El Paso. As he went inside, she straightened in her seat, then looked around.

Light spilled from everywhere—street lamps, neon signs, headlights—to dispel the night's darkness. The area was typical for its location—fast-food restaurants, motels ranging from good to beyond seedy, bars, gas stations and convenience stores. This particular motel—not good, but not seedy—shared its parking lot with a two-pump station and a convenience store and its roof with an establishment identified in pink neon as Pepe's Cantina. The vehicles on the motel side of the lot were mostly big rigs, on the cantina side, mostly pickups and nondescript sedans. Logan's GTX stood out, while her car would have blended right in.

Logan returned with a key, hardly noticing that she was alert, and drove to the side lot away from Pepe's. She'd passed the last two hundred miles in an exhaustion-induced fog, wanting desperately to stretch out somewhere and sleep. He'd shown no such interest, though, and damned if she was going to whine or plead for a break.

He parked in front of Room 17, hefted his duffel out of the trunk, then left her to retrieve her own bags and close the trunk. By the time she did so and made it to the sidewalk, he was already inside the room, turning on lights and lowering the temperature on the air conditioner.

The room was about as clean as she expected—she wouldn't walk barefooted on the carpet, but crawling under the covers wouldn't give her the willies. She dropped her bags on the bed farther from the door. Only the need for the bathroom and a slathering of moisturizer on her wind-burned skin kept her from joining them.

Feeling marginally better when she came out of the bathroom, Bailey grabbed her tote off the bed, set it on the counter next to the sink, then spun back around. Her suitcase was where she'd left it, Logan's duffel was where he'd left it and the door was closed…but there was no sign of Logan. She reached the door in three strides and jerked it open. The GTX was still parked outside, but its owner was nowhere to be seen. Damnation! Where had he gone, what was he doing and why had she let him out of her sight?

Walking back into the room, she closed the door hard. The rush of air sent a piece of paper fluttering from the foot of the first bed onto the stained carpet. *Gone to Pepe's for a beer,* it read in sharp, bold letters.

Great. Instead of crawling into bed and getting the sleep she craved, she was going to spend the next however long in a smoky, noisy bar drinking a beer she didn't want just so she could keep an eye on the partner who didn't want *her.* Wonderful.

"Lexy, I hope you appreciate this," she muttered as she grabbed her purse and headed out the door.

Pepe's Cantina didn't disappoint. As bars went, she'd been in worse—Thelma's immediately came to mind—but she'd seen plenty better. The lighting was too dim by half, the music too loud by half, the air too polluted to breathe. Before she'd gone ten feet inside the door, a niggling pain started in her forehead with the intention of becoming a full-blown headache.

After giving her eyes time to adjust to the low light, she scanned the crowd. There were a lot of men wearing cowboy hats, a lot of women with big hair. Everyone's jeans were tight, their smiles bright, their moods cheery. They'd come out tonight with the goal of having a good time and, by God, they weren't going to fail.

Except for the lone man standing at the bar. He leaned his elbows against the scarred wood, dangled a bottle in one hand and gazed at the couples on the dance floor with a nine-mile stare.

She made her way across the room, slid onto the stool next to him and ordered a beer before swiveling to face him and smiling brightly. "If you'd mentioned you wanted a beer, I would have walked over with you."

"If I'd wanted you to come with me, I would have mentioned it." He tilted the bottle to his mouth and took a healthy swallow. "I figured you'd be snoring away by now."

"I don't snore."

"Of course you don't. That was just a funny little rattle the car developed a hundred miles ago."

She would have said she hadn't slept in the car—tried to, wanted to, even drifted into a state of semiconsciousness, but never actually slept. But she didn't argue the point with him. "Aren't you tired?"

"Why would I be?"

"Because you drove over six hundred miles today."

He glanced at her for a moment before twisting farther around to catch the bartender's attention and order another beer. "Six hundred miles is nothing," he said, then added, "However, six hundred miles with you…"

The bartender delivered both beers at once. Bailey took a sip of hers, cold and sour, and thought longingly about the bed awaiting her. If she offered a respite from her company in exchange for his car keys, would he agree? Maybe. Definitely, if he had a spare set of keys somewhere.

Turning the stool, she faced the dance floor, as Logan was doing, and took another small sip of beer. Without a doubt, he was the best-looking guy in the place, as well as the least approachable. Though the women gave him admiring looks, not one hit on him, asked him to dance or even did more than smile hesitantly on the way past.

She wasn't so lucky. She'd managed to down maybe a third of her beer when a bear of a man walked right up to her, stopping a little too close and greeting her with a grin. "Hey, darlin', wanna dance?"

He was very big, broad-shouldered and muscular. His beard was neatly trimmed, his long hair pulled into a ponytail. He wasn't scary or even unattractive. He just roused zero interest in her. She smiled politely and said, "No, thank you."

"Oh, come on. I'm good on the dance floor."

"I'm not."

He gave her a long look that started at her face and drifted its way down to her toes, and the grin widened. "Now I don't believe that, sugar. Come on, let me show you how good you can be."

"I appreciate the invitation, but—" He caught hold of her hand and was pulling, making her scramble to her feet to avoid falling into his arms. She caught her balance a short distance from Logan, then moved a few steps closer to him as she tugged to free her hand. "Really, my boyfriend doesn't like for me to dance with other guys."

The man's gaze shifted from her to Logan, apparently sizing him up and finding him no threat—clear evidence that he'd had far too much to drink. "Aw, you don't mind, do you, buddy?"

Logan's smile was thin and amused. "No, not at all. Go on, sweetheart. You'll enjoy it."

Bailey shot him a killing look. "I wouldn't think of leaving you here all alone, honey."

"Nah, I don't mind. Go ahead and take a spin around the dance floor. I'll wait for you over there." With his bottle, he gestured toward an empty booth along the far wall, then pushed away from the bar.

Wishing looks *could* kill, she watched him go, then turned her attention back to her admirer when he pulled on her hand. "What's your name?"

Taking the question as a sign of surrender, the big guy smiled ear to ear. "Billy."

"Well, Billy…" Stepping closer, she straightened his collar with her free hand, then brushed nonexistent lint from his shoulder. "If you don't let go of me right now, I'm going to have to hurt you. Now, I don't *mind* hurting you, but it's just going to embarrass you in front of all your friends, and then you're going to get pissed off with me and we'll both go away thinking badly of each other. You don't want that, do you?"

He gave her another of those long looks and finished it even more tickled by her words than when he'd started it. Ducking his head the necessary distance to bring his mouth close to her ear, he asked, "And just how do you think you're gonna hurt me, sweet pea? You gonna do some kind of karate chop? Or maybe you got a nasty left hook? No, I know—you've got some kind of secret powers."

Bailey sighed regretfully. "You really want to do this?"

"More than you can guess."

Billy's amusement grew with each moment that she considered her options. He had likely reached the conclusion that she'd merely been bluffing when she stomped her boot heel into his instep, kneed him in the groin, then kicked him across the backs of the knees, sending him crumpling to the floor in a groaning heap.

Crouching beside him, she bent to look into his face. "Satisfied, Billy?" she asked sarcastically before giving his shoulder a vigorous pat. "Don't hold a grudge, will you?"

She ignored the curious looks as she straightened and crossed the dance floor to Logan's booth. "Stand up," she commanded, and to her surprise, he did. Taking a cue from his action that morning, she wriggled her fingers into the right front pocket of his jeans, searching for his keys, and he grabbed her wrist.

"What the hell are you doing?" he demanded, applying just enough pressure to keep her hand still. "You want it that bad, sweetheart, just ask."

"Give me your keys. And your wallet."

"And why would I do that?"

"Because I'm tired and disappointed in you and I want to go to bed."

"Go to bed. I'm not stopping you."

"I want your keys and your money and your weapons to make sure you'll be here in the morning." She was standing closer to him than she'd ever been, close enough to feel the heat and the tension coming off his body. Close enough to hear the hitch in his breathing. Close enough to see the faint surprise in his eyes as the denim of his jeans tightened across her hand.

She glanced down automatically, unable to see any sign of his arousal in the dim light but feeling it just the same. Heat warmed her face as she jerked her gaze up again. Her throat had suddenly gone dry, making it impossible for her to swallow, but she tried anyway. "L-let go, and I'll pull m-my hand out."

"Maybe in a minute," he replied, his voice silky, steadier than hers had been. But he did let go, let her slide her fingers free and take a step back. A moment later he picked up her hand, laid his keys in her palm, then added the battered wallet from his hip pocket.

"Now go away," he said quietly. *Warned* quietly. "Leave me alone."

She was happy to comply.

I'm disappointed in you.

Logan hadn't needed to ask what she'd meant by that. He'd spent fifteen years of his life with Brady, who always did the right thing, the hero thing. Brady never would have walked away and left her with the gorilla. He would have taken care of the guy for her, and she would have been grateful for the rescue. Everyone Brady rescued was supposed to be grateful.

Well, Logan wasn't into the hero thing and never had been. She was a grown woman; if she wanted to go into a bar, she should be prepared for whatever happened. Besides, she hadn't needed his help. The gorilla had been eight inches taller and a hundred pounds heavier, but *she'd* walked out the door while he'd lain on the floor, whimpering and holding his balls. It was only in the past few minutes that his buddies had finally gotten him to his feet and out of the bar.

Not that it mattered whether she thought less of him for not intervening. Once he'd taken care of Mac, he would never see her again. She was nothing more than a necessary nuisance…

…who had given him the first hint of a hard-on in months. It didn't have anything to do with her, of course. Any woman who shoved her hand in his jeans pocket and started groping like that would have brought the same response. That was what happened when he went so damn long without. While it was nice to know that part of him was still alive, he had neither the time nor the desire for anything beyond justice. Vengeance. Once he'd gotten that, then he could think about sex.

He finished his third beer and debated a fourth, but, suddenly feeling the exhaustion of the day, decided against it. His eyes were gritty and wanted nothing more than to close and stay that way for six or eight hours, and he couldn't take a deep breath to save himself. In his two years in Afghanistan and Iraq, he'd learned his physical limits and he knew he'd reached them.

Sliding out of the booth, he headed for the door. When he stepped out, the chill night air served to rouse him a little. Hunching his shoulders, he shoved his hands into his jeans pockets…and found the room key among the change in his left pocket. Had Bailey gone to the office and talked the clerk out of another key? Was she waiting outside the room or had she headed back to the bar to find him…and run into the gorilla and his friends on the way?

Refusing to acknowledge the sudden chill as anything close to panic, he lengthened his strides and turned the far corner of the motel. The sidewalk in front of Room 17 was empty. Of course it was, because she was inside the room, tucked in her bed in that T-shirt and those ridiculously tiny panties.

He unlocked the door and swung it open, only to find the room empty. The bathroom door was open, the light off, and there was no sound but the hum of the air conditioner.

He was about to head back to the motel office when a look at the Plymouth stopped him. She had the keys to his car. If she couldn't get into the room and didn't want to brave the bar again, what better place to wait?

Sure enough, she was curled up in the backseat, her head pillowed on her purse, his jean jacket tucked around her. It was proof of her exhaustion that she'd managed to doze off in the cramped space, because she damn sure couldn't be comfortable all twisted up like that.

Logan leaned against the rear quarter panel, hands resting on the cool metal. Maybe the gorilla wasn't the type to take public humiliation personally…but he could just as easily have wanted retribution. A lone woman against one man might not be a problem, but against three? He should have walked her to the room, not so much for her own safety but for the safety of the information she hadn't yet given him. He wasn't into the hero thing, but he did believe in protecting what was his.

He rubbed his hands over his eyes, then turned and rapped sharply on the window. The first three taps brought no response at all. After the second three, she finally shifted and damn near slid into the floorboard before catching herself.

"Come on, Madison, let's go to bed," he called through the closed window.

Innocent words to conjure up not-so-innocent images. It was her fault, for looking softer and sweeter when she was only half-awake, for the braid that had come loose and the tendrils of pale brown hair that framed her hazy expression.

It took her a moment to reach the door handle, to push the passenger seat forward and to maneuver through the narrow space. She swayed and would have stumbled out of the car if he hadn't caught her, hands on her shoulders, deliberately keeping her at a distance. As soon as she seemed steady, he let go and locked the car door while she headed blindly for the bed visible through the open room door. She didn't move her suitcase, didn't bother to undress, but took a header onto the bed, pulled the denim jacket around her again and lost consciousness again.

Sleeping in her clothes wouldn't hurt her—he'd done it for months at a time in the war. Neither would sharing half her bed with a suitcase. She'd just proven she could sleep damn near anywhere. And if she got cold, well, she'd wake up long enough to pull the covers over her.

Still, after locking the door and securing the chain, he moved the suitcase to the floor, then unzipped the clunky black boots and set them next to the bag. He pulled her purse strap from around her neck and over her shoulder—just so she wouldn't risk choking herself in the night—and set it on the nightstand, then pulled the loose half of the bedspread up to cover her.

He wasn't being considerate but, rather, selfish, he told himself as he stripped to his boxers and crawled into bed. She wasn't the best of traveling companions under good circumstances; she was likely to be even worse without a good night's sleep. He was just looking out for himself.

As he'd done since he was fifteen.

As he would always do. Just himself, and nobody else.

Logan had always been a light sleeper. Rita Marshall hadn't liked it when her sons slept through the alarm, and the punishment for disrupting her morning routine had been severe. She'd also had a fondness for hauling them out of bed at odd hours of the night, using their disorientation at the abrupt awakening against them, so he'd learned over the years to awaken quickly and to come instantly alert.

The room's quiet was broken only by the distant sound of traffic. Light filtered in through a crack in the drapes above his bed and sent a wedge of illumination across the floor and onto the opposite bed. That bed was empty at the moment; it must have been Bailey's movement that roused him. He lay motionless on his left side as his gaze searched the dark room for the source of the noise. He located the shadowy form an instant before it disappeared into the bathroom. After the door closed, the bathroom light came on, seeping underneath the door to illuminate a patch of dirty brown carpet.

The bedside clock showed that it was three forty-seven. If he wanted to be a real bastard, he could be up when she returned and insist that they go ahead and hit the road. He didn't move, though. He was still tired. She hadn't deigned to share with him how much farther they had to go, but hands down, it was better to do it well rested. Who knew? He could drive into the town where Señor Escobar lived and see Mac right off the bat…or Mac could see him. Best to be sharp.

The bathroom light went off an instant before the door opened. When she approached the bed, the light through the curtains showed her feet, narrow and pale, with that silver chain wrapped around one ankle. It also showed a length of bare leg—she'd removed her jeans while she'd been up and had traded her shirt for a doll-sized tank top. It clung everywhere and ended well above the panties that hugged her hips. If he was interested in sex or in her, it would be torture to lie there in his bed the rest of the night while she lay in hers wearing so little.

But he wasn't interested in sex or in her, he thought as he adjusted his erection to a more comfortable position. All he cared about was finding Mac and seeing that he paid for Sam's and Ella's murders.

Bailey slid into bed and tugged the covers high around her neck, gave a soft sigh and closed her eyes. He debated saying something—to let her know he wasn't asleep, that he'd seen her—but decided against it. It would just embarrass her.

And then he wouldn't get to see her like that again. His current lack of interest in sex aside, that would be cause for regret.

It was nearly noon when they stopped for lunch in a dusty New Mexico town. Esperanza was exactly how Bailey had imagined a small desert town to look—mostly shades of brown, not too prosperous, not too hospitable. The only green was on the occasional building or sign, and the only hint of friendliness was in…well, her. Neither the waitress nor the other customers in the diner showed any sign of welcome—or curiosity, for that matter.

"Esperanza," she said thoughtfully as she removed the lettuce from her BLT and laid it aside. "That means 'hope' in Spanish, doesn't it? Wonder how you say '*lost* hope'?"

"Why do you order a BLT if you don't like lettuce?" Logan asked.

"Because if I asked for a BT, no one would know what I wanted. Do you speak Spanish?"

"Some."

Which probably translated to *fluently,* she thought as she chewed a bite of crispy bacon and vine-ripened tomato.

"Do you?"

She shrugged. "I know the important phrases, like *Where's the bathroom?* and *I need chocolate.* What other languages do you speak?"

"A little German, a little Korean, some Farsi."

"What did you do in the Army?"

This time he shrugged. "How much farther?"

"Maybe twenty miles."

"Twenty miles? Then why the hell did we stop here?"

"Because I thought we needed to discuss your plan."

He squirted jalapeño ketchup over his burger, replaced the top half of the bun, then took a hungry bite. While he chewed, he looked everywhere except at her.

"You do have a plan, don't you?"

He chased the food with a gulp of pop, then scowled at her. "My plan is to find out if Mac is in the area."

"Which you can't do by just showing up in town. This guy knows you. He'd disappear into the woodwork if he saw you snooping around where he's hiding out."

"*If* he's hiding there."

"Right. *If.* But we'll never know if you go waltzing into town."

His scowl deepened, but he didn't admit that he hadn't thought that far ahead. For months, Bailey knew, his search had been fruitless, going places Mac had been, talking to people Mac had seen, but long after the fact. Covertness hadn't been an issue. Now it was. "So what do you suggest?" he asked grudgingly.

She smiled. "Simple. *I'll* waltz into town."

"And…?"

"Ask questions. Gather information. Find out whatever I can."

"And you'll be successful because…?"

"Mac doesn't know me. I do this sort of thing for a living." Just a little lie, she told herself. She did help locate missing people; she'd just never been out in the field before. "And I'm a woman."

"And that gives you an edge?"

She filched a couple of his fries from his plate, dipped them in the spicy ketchup and enjoyed them before replying. "Men still have a lot of old-fashioned notions about women. They see them as weaker, more delicate, in need of their protection. They think we're not as smart, not as capable, and they want to take care of us. I'm talking about *most* men, mind you. There are a few exceptions."

Color rose into his cheeks, shading them dark bronze, but she thought it was from annoyance rather than embarrassment. "You didn't need my help last night."

"No, I didn't," she agreed. She'd handled the situation all by herself. On the one hand, it had been something of a triumph seeing all those self-defense classes pay off. On the other…maybe it was the wrong attitude for an independent career woman to have, but it would have been nice if Logan had cared enough to step in. Brady would have. Her other brother-in-law, Reese, definitely would have. Practically every man she knew would have considered it his duty to rescue her from Billy's unwelcome attentions. But not Logan. He wouldn't have cared if the jerk had thrown her over his shoulder and carried her out of the bar.

It made her think a little less of him.

"If you had needed help, I would have been there."

That was an easy statement to make when the situation was over and done with. Maybe it was true, maybe not. Either way, it was good to know that he'd placed definite limits on their partnership. If she got into trouble with Mac or his brother, she wouldn't make the mistake of counting on Logan to help her out.

Dismissing the subject, she turned to business. "The town we're going to is Nomas. Legend says that a group of travelers were crossing the area a hundred and fifty years ago in the hottest July anyone could ever recall. After days of blistering heat, sand and wind, one of the travelers insisted he would go *no más*—no more—and it stuck, though somewhere along the way it became one word and the accent transferred to the first syllable. It's about a half mile north of the border and has all the conveniences—motels, restaurants and bars. Mac's brother has a ranch about five miles east of town that backs right up to the border. Whether he actually does any ranching is anyone's guess."

"Have you been there?"

"No. I checked it out on the Internet. Great little resource when you need information." Of course, he didn't look like a computer-friendly person. Come to think of it, he didn't seem much of *anything*-friendly. He loved his car, but that was the only thing he showed any fondness for.

And Sam and Ella Jensen. He'd loved them, and blamed himself for their deaths. If nothing else, she could cut him some slack for that.

"Unless I find out that Mac's *not* there, you'll have to keep a low profile. That means staying out of sight at the motel. It also means—" she let her gaze drift out the plate glass window to the GTX parked out front before turning a big grin on him "—letting me drive your car."

"When hell freezes over," he muttered before taking the last bite of his burger. "Nobody drives that car but me."

"I know." And that would make it even sweeter when she slid behind the wheel. All that power…and all the satisfaction of knowing it was killing him…*too* sweet.

He stood and tossed a couple ones on the table, then picked up the check. "What's going to be your excuse for asking questions about Mac? He's not the sort of person who will take kindly to some nosy broad poking around."

She stood, too, and studied her reflection in the window. "I haven't decided yet." Grabbing a handful of her shirt in back, she pulled it tight, then slid her free hand over her stomach. "Maybe I'll be searching for the father of my baby."

That brought a scowl that made the others look like mild grimaces, and he murmured something as he stalked off to the cash register near the door. Catching the words *stupid* and *idiot,* she decided not to ask him to repeat the rest.

It was hot and sunny, with a dry breeze out of the west.

Bailey would have appreciated just a drop or two of humidity, even if it did make the heat more uncomfortable. Too much time in this environment, and she feared she might shrivel up and blow away in that wind.

"Seriously," Logan said after putting a few miles between them and the diner. "You need a reason for asking about Mac. What is it going to be?"

"Seriously I don't intend to ask about Mac to start. I intend to look around, meet some people and go from there. Who knows?" she added as she kicked off her sandals, then propped one bare foot out the window. "Maybe I'll romance the information out of Hector."

She expected some sort of response from Logan—*Pete MacGregor's brother's name is Hector Escobar?*—but he remained silent so long that she finally looked his way. His jaw was clenched tighter than usual, and he had the steering wheel in a grip better suited, she imagined, to her throat.

He shifted his gaze to her for only an instant before turning back to the road. "This isn't a game," he said, grinding out the words. "If you can't get that through your head, you need to get the hell back to Memphis where you belong. Pete MacGregor is a cold-blooded killer, and I doubt his brother is much better."

"I don't know," she said more carelessly than she felt. "You and Brady are brothers, but you're nothing alike. Mac and Hector are only half brothers, and they didn't grow up together. For all we know, Hector could be a God-fearing, churchgoing, law-abiding man."

"Providing refuge for his fugitive brother? I doubt it."

She didn't have to doubt it—she had proof otherwise. Hector Escobar had an arrest record going back to his teen years and had spent time in prison on drug and assault convictions. In the pictures she'd seen of him—booking photos and prison shots—he was one scary-looking man. Big, tattooed, with wild hair, a wild beard and wild-eyed. But he hadn't been arrested even once in five years. Maybe he'd grown up and gotten his temper under control. Or maybe he'd just gotten better at what he was doing.

But Logan didn't need to know any of that. He might actually show concern for her safety, though he'd be more likely to use it as an excuse. He would ditch her, take care of Mac on his own, then disappear again without a thought for his promise to meet Lexy. Because she didn't trust him as far as she could throw him, she was sticking to him until the day she delivered him to his family in Buffalo Plains.

"It's not a game," he repeated, still looking and sounding as if he might grind his molars down.

"I know that. You know, I've dealt with people like Hector before." Another lie, unless via the computer counted as *dealing with*. "Don't worry about it. I can take care of myself. Remember?"

As expected, he let the matter drop. In fact, he spent the rest of the drive to Nomas in cold silence, radiating enough hostility that she should have withered under the intensity. But she was stronger than that. She *could* take care of herself.

After miles of nothing but mountainous desert on either side of the highway, the town appeared, wavering under the hot sun like a mirage. The first business they approached was one of the two motels. "This is where we'll be staying," she announced, half expecting him to slow and turn in. Of course, he didn't.

Nomas was larger than Esperanza by a thousand people or so and had a compact district in the center of town that boasted shops, restaurants and the usual businesses. The courthouse was a small two-story adobe set down by itself in the middle of the centralmost block and flanked on three sides by churches. Like most small towns she knew, the number of churches about equaled the number of bars, but where the churches were prominently located, the bars were banished to the fringes of town.

After a slow drive through town, Logan turned onto the main east/west thoroughfare. Businesses soon gave way to gas stations and bars, then to scattered houses, then desert scrub as they left Nomas behind. The road narrowed and grew bumpy as the maintained portions came fewer and farther between.

"Do you think we're going to find a sign that says Hector Escobar Lives Here?"

Logan ignored her.

"I have his address on my laptop."

He ignored that, too.

"I also have directions to his ranch."

That made him look at her. Even through his dark glasses, she could feel his scorn. He pulled off the road, shut off the engine and offered his keys. "Get it."

Shoving her feet back into her shoes, she climbed out and stretched before circling to the trunk. After retrieving her laptop case, she returned to the passenger seat and booted up the computer, grateful she'd created multiple files for this case. No sense letting him stumble across anything he didn't need to see, such as Hector's criminal history. "I downloaded these off the Internet, so there's a good chance they're not entirely accurate, but this is as good a time as any to find out."

They had to return to the edge of town to clock the mileage. Two miles east, they turned north and followed a dirt road that meandered in every direction, including up and down. When the odometer reached the correct mileage, there was no sign of a house or any life whatsoever. Logan looked at her, one brow quirked above his shades.

"I told you they might not be accurate. Keep driving."

Sure enough, a half mile later they topped a hill and saw a ranch spread out in the valley below. The road dead-ended just past the driveway, where a mailbox listed to one side.

Logan backed up until the buildings were hidden once again, then climbed out and took a pair of binoculars from the trunk. He walked back up the hill, Bailey on his heels, and sighted on the mailbox. "E-s-c-o…the rest is too faded."

"So that's it."

"Probably." He turned the binoculars to the ranch buildings, and she looked that way, too. The house was two stories and sprawled across the barren land. Out back stood a barn and several other outbuildings, and parked in between were half a dozen vehicles, mostly pickup trucks and SUVs. The one thing missing that a person would expect to see on a ranch was livestock. There wasn't a four-legged critter around as far as she could see. Granted, just as the mountains had hidden the ranch from them until they were right above it, they could also be hiding the stock, though she doubted it.

Abruptly Logan lowered the binoculars and headed back to the car with a long-legged stride. "Let's get back to town. We've got things to do."

Chapter 4

The motel Bailey had picked appeared to be the better of the two, though that wasn't saying much. Logan pulled up to the side of the office where he wasn't visible through the windows, then waited restlessly while she went to check in. The place looked like something out of the forties, with individual cabins instead of the usual connected rooms. Each cabin had a tiny stoop that held a lawn chair of about the same age, and air-conditioning units balanced in two windows per cabin. The landscaping was desert-style—a lot of dirt, rocks and cactus, with a pot of fake flowers beside each door.

"Isn't this quaint?" Bailey asked as she plopped back into the seat beside him.

"It's something, all right."

"We're in Cabin 7, back there next to the end. Each cabin has a kitchenette and satellite TV, so you'll have something to do while I'm out looking for Mac. There's no swimming pool, though the owners' kids keep begging them to put one in, but with most people just spending the night, then moving on, what's the point? An argument I'm sure the kids don't agree with."

Logan gave her a sour look as he parked next to number seven. "You ever meet a stranger?"

Though he'd meant the question as an insult and was pretty sure she knew it, she answered seriously. "Hey, people talk to me. I think it's because I'm nice. You should try it sometime."

He'd been *nice* to Mac and invited him home to recuperate since the guy had had no place else to go, and look how that had ended. It wasn't a mistake he would make again.

The sun had leached all the color from the carnations outside their door, leaving them a lifeless shade of nothing, and the desert heat had wilted the plastic-and-wire stems, making them droop pitifully. He didn't have much hope for the inside looking any better as Bailey slid the key into the lock, then swung the door open, but he was surprised.

They walked into a living room/dining room/kitchenette, the walls painted bright white, the floor easy-to-clean vinyl. The furniture was mismatched but serviceable, and the air conditioner came on with a blast of cold air the instant he turned the knob. The bedroom was through the only door, with one double bed and a dresser bolted to the wall, and the bathroom— toilet, sink and shower—was clean. All the comforts of—

His gaze jerked back to the bedroom. One double bed. Aw, jeez, that was just what he needed to guarantee he wouldn't sleep for however many nights they were there. Maybe she *could* romance Hector Escobar and leave this bed to him…though he was scowling before he completed the thought. No way she was getting involved like that with anyone close to Mac, even if it meant he never got to sleep again. He had enough on his conscience already. He didn't need her there, too.

She either hadn't noticed or didn't care about the bed. "This is cute. And it doesn't even smell musty. That's because Faith— she's the owner, with her husband—makes her own potpourri and uses it in all the rooms. By the way, I told her that I won't need maid service while I'm here, so you won't have to worry about someone walking in on you during the day." She grinned slyly. "I told her I'm compulsively neat. That'll give you something else to do during the day."

He returned to the living room, stopping in the middle of the room, and said, "I don't like this."

She followed, taking a look around. "Oh, come on, it's not bad. I'm assuming you slept on the ground a time or two in the war, and at least here there's no one shooting at you."

Yet. "I'm not talking about the room. I don't like hiding here while you go out looking for Mac. This is my job, my responsibility."

She shrugged carelessly, making the clingy knit of her shirt ripple before it settled against her skin again. "Yeah, well, even you can't do everything alone. Just remember that I'm not doing this because I like you. Once Mac is in custody, *you're* going to Oklahoma to make your niece's dream come true."

He was nobody's dream. Lexy, her sister and their father would all be better off not seeing him, and *he* for damn sure didn't want to see them. He'd held a grudge against Brady for so long that it had become a part of him. He ate, worked, slept and cursed his brother anytime he thought of him. He didn't know how to let go of it. More importantly, he didn't *want* to let go. If he didn't hate his parents, if he didn't resent his brother, then what *would* he do?

"So what's your plan for today?" he asked grudgingly.

"I'm going to look around, then pick up some groceries. Is there anything in particular you want or don't want?"

He shook his head grudgingly.

"Good." She stuck her hand out and he stared at it. Her fingers were long and slender, her palm smooth and uncallused. She knew how to shoot and presumably knew something about fighting, but her pink-polished nails and soft skin didn't look as if she did anything more physical than blow-dry her hair or apply her makeup.

When she cleared her throat, it startled him out of his thoughts. He looked up to find her watching him with a challenge in her eyes, her brows delicately arched. "Keys?"

He didn't want to give them to her. That car was his baby, the one thing he'd kept as he'd transferred from base to base, the one thing he'd truly missed while in Afghanistan and Iraq. He hadn't been kidding when he'd told her that no one drove it but him, not in the twelve years he'd owned it.

But what choice did he have? It would take time they didn't have to backtrack to the nearest city with a car-rental agency, and he couldn't ask her to walk all over town. Nomas was small, but not that small.

Reluctantly he pulled the keys from his pocket and handed them over. "Don't hot-rod it. And don't park next to anybody. And be sure you lock it when you get out. And—"

"Hey, I know how to take care of a car. I'll see you in a few hours." With a triumphant grin, she walked out the door.

He locked it, then watched through the window as she started the car, backed out and followed the narrow lane to the highway. There was no squealing of tires, no fishtailing in the soft dirt—not that that made him feel any better about letting her take the car.

Maybe he could call a rental agency and offer someone enough money to deliver a car to them. He could afford it—he had the money he'd inherited from Sam and Ella, along with the sizable trust fund his grandmother had set up for him when he was a kid.

Or maybe he could forget about the car and keep his mind on what was important here. Finding Mac—killing Mac— would be worth seeing the GTX reduced to a pile of bolts. After all, it *was* just a car. It could be replaced.

Sam and Ella couldn't.

And neither could Bailey, a traitorous voice whispered.

It was easy to talk tough and act experienced when you were totally safe from danger, Bailey acknowledged as she drove down the main street of Nomas, but not so easy now that she was out roaming around Mac's territory—or, at least, his brother's—on her own. Granted, she had her cell phone, with the motel's number programmed in, and her weapons. But still, there was something incredibly reassuring about Logan, even if he wasn't inclined to be helpful all the time.

"Just remember Lexy," she murmured as she turned the corner, then pulled into a parking space. Her niece had had a tough life before going to live with Brady and Hallie—a new stepfather every time she turned around, a mother who cared more for her own comfort than she did for her daughter, no one who really wanted her. Family was important to her, and if she wanted to meet her only uncle, then there was nothing Bailey wouldn't do to make it happen.

She rolled up her window, then leaned across hot leather to crank up the passenger window. She hadn't been at all surprised when Logan had handed over the keys, though she'd thought he'd been. He might be hostile and rude and unchivalrous to the max, but he was reasonable enough to understand that she was right and he had to stay out of sight until she confirmed that Mac was in the area.

After locking the doors, she walked the few yards back to the main drag and turned left, window-shopping her way along several blocks. She smiled and greeted the few people she passed, pretended interest in the businesses and stores, looked in the windows and watched the passing cars, searching for familiar faces. She'd spent a great deal of time studying the photos of both Mac and his brother. Hairstyles and colors could change, beards could be grown or shaved off and eye color could be changed, as well, but things like bone structure and the shape of the eyes stayed the same. She felt relatively certain that if she saw either man, no matter what superficial differences there were, she would recognize him.

And probably freak out.

After covering the downtown area on foot, she wandered into the drugstore on the corner opposite from where she'd parked. An old-fashioned soda fountain lined one wall, with bar stools along the counter and two booths, their vinyl seats well patched with duct tape. She chose a stool, studying the menu on the wall while she waited for an employee to come. The food side of the menu was sparse—pimento cheese and grilled cheese sandwiches, each served with chips and a pickle—but the fountain side more than made up for it with cones, malts, milk shakes, sundaes, banana splits and root beer floats. She'd decided to limit herself to a diet limeade, but when a woman finally showed up behind the counter, a request for a root beer float somehow slipped out.

"You passing through?" the woman asked as she scooped vanilla ice cream into a tall frosted glass. She was probably in her late twenties, her hair red, her skin freckled and pale. The name tag on her shirt identified her as Marisa.

"More or less," Bailey replied. When Marisa gave her a quizzical look, she shrugged. "I don't really know where I'm headed or how long I'm staying. I'm just going."

"Looking for a new place to settle."

The way she said the words made Bailey wonder if she'd entertained ideas of leaving Nomas for someplace new. The town certainly didn't seem to offer a lot for young people. The shopping was adequate but didn't hold a candle to any big-city mall; there were no bookstores, movie theaters, trendy restaurants, flashy clubs or sporting events besides high school football and the occasional rodeo. Even if it was home, Bailey could easily imagine wanting to leave.

"Yeah," she replied as Marisa stuck a long straw in the glass, then slid it across the counter to her. "Nothing left for me at home."

"Is that your car?" Marisa gestured to the Plymouth, visible through the plate glass window. "I used to date a guy who had one like that. If he'd treated me half as well as he did it, we'd still be together."

It must be a guy thing, Bailey acknowledged as she took a long drink from her float. She liked her car well enough. It provided economic, reliable transportation, but it was nothing to get passionate about. "I'd sell it in a heartbeat for something with air-conditioning."

"Oh, man, I know. It got to the point where we'd take separate cars when we went out, because I didn't see any point to dressing up, fixing my hair and putting on makeup, just to get in that thing and be all windblown and wilted by the time we got where we were going." With another glance at the car, Marisa grinned. "But I bet it's got a hell of a stereo."

"Oh, yeah. They could hear it in the next county."

The amusement turned to speculation. "But it's not a real typical woman's car. I'd guess that the car has something to do with why you're looking for someplace new to settle. Does it involve an ex-boyfriend or ex-husband?"

Bailey shrugged as she took another deep drink, leaving it to the woman to interpret it however she wanted.

"Hey, you've gotta admire a woman who leaves a man but takes his car."

"You heard that old joke? A guy says, 'My wife left me and took the dog. Boy, I sure miss that dog.' I'm sure he's missing the car way more than me." Not that she and Logan had any kind of personal relationship. Not that she was even remotely interested in one. She liked being single and answering to no one but herself. Men were great for sex, companionship and fun, but she wasn't looking to fall in love, get married and do the kid thing. Maybe a few years down the line. Or maybe never. After all, when she got the occasional maternal feeling, a visit to her nieces fixed her right up.

Even if she *was* looking for a relationship, Logan Marshall would *not* be in the running. He was too hostile. Focused. Intense. She liked guys who were easy to get along with, and there was nothing faintly *easy* about him.

However, for a purely fantasy one-night stand…

Pushing him out of her thoughts, she fixed a pleasant smile on Marisa. "What's the job situation around here?"

"What can you do?"

"I've waited tables before, I'm a pretty good cook and I know a bit about computers." Quite a bit, which was one of the reasons her boss had stuck her in an office for so long—that, and he didn't think she had what it took to work in the field. After this case, maybe he would change his mind. Or maybe she'd lure Charlie into leaving the agency and setting up their own business together. She would even let him have his name on the door, as long as she got to do some of the real work.

Marisa picked up a dishcloth and began wiping the counter. "I don't know of anything offhand, but someone's always looking for help. Pay's not much, but then, the cost of living isn't bad here either. The newspaper comes out on Wednesdays. You can check the ads then. Or if you go by the paper office before then, Belle—she's the owner, editor and chief reporter—will tell you what she's got."

"I'll do that if I decide to stay a while." Bailey took another long drink of root beer and melting ice cream before asking, "What's the available-male situation?"

"We've got our share of single guys…if you're not too picky," Marisa replied with a grin. "Nobody *I'd* want to settle down with, but they're okay for fun. We've got local guys who've lived here all their lives and the hands on a few ranches outside town and, of course, the border-patrol guys."

"Ranches." Bailey strived for a carelessly disinterested tone. "I can't imagine how you could possibly raise anything out here."

"They manage. One of 'em does quite well at it. But you got me as to how. I can't even keep the marigolds on my porch alive, and my cat freaks out if he thinks he might have to go outside in the heat to pee."

"This one who does quite well…give me his name and point me in his direction." Bailey hoped she sounded as teasing as she was trying for. "I could do with a guy who doesn't rely on me to support him."

Marisa turned a shade less friendly. She walked to the end of the fountain to hang the towel on the bar there, then came back, leaned against the work counter and folded her arms over her chest. "I don't think you'd be real interested in Hector. He falls in that category of 'if you're not too picky.'"

Was Marisa interested in him herself? Or was there bad blood between them? As much as she'd love to know, Bailey didn't ask but instead made a production of slurping up the last of her float. With a great satisfied sigh, she pushed the glass away. "That was wonderful." She slid to her feet and opened her purse. "How much do I owe you?"

"One-oh-five. Come back tomorrow and I'll fix you the best banana split you ever had."

"I'll be here." With a wave, she left the drugstore, crossed the street and gingerly settled into the inferno the car had become while she was gone. A root beer float and the best banana split ever…ah, the sacrifices she made for work.

When Bailey returned to the cabin, Logan was waiting just inside the door. He accepted the grocery bags she shoved into his arms without glancing at her but looked outside instead. The car appeared none the worse for wear. Except for a heavier coating of dust, it was in the same excellent condition as before—at least, the part of it he could see. After sunset, he would have to make a closer inspection.

Looking damp and flushed, she brought in four more bags, shoved the door with her foot and dumped everything on the kitchen counter. Her shirt was damp and clung to her spine, and the loose tendrils of hair around her face were also wet. "You know, even old cars can be retrofitted with air-conditioning."

"That car wasn't meant to have air-conditioning."

She hastily transferred sweating groceries to the refrigerator and freezer before going to stand directly in front of the window unit. "Yeah, well, *I* wasn't meant to *not* have it."

He watched as she lifted the tail of her braid off her neck, then tugged her shirt away from her body. When she released the fabric, it drifted back down to mold against her every curve. He pretended not to notice as he fixed his gaze somewhere to the left of her face. "What did you find out?"

"That wearing jeans in this heat is suicide. I've got to get out of these clothes." With a burst of energy, she crossed the room into the bedroom, hefted her suitcase onto the bed, then stilled. "Hey, there's only one bed in here."

"Can't hide anything from the hotshot private detective," he murmured, taking the place she'd vacated in front of the air conditioner. The cold air lowered the temperature of his skin a few degrees, but he still felt restless and hot inside. Even cold storage wouldn't help that.

But Bailey could.

She pushed the door shut, for all the good it did. He had an excellent imagination and could see in his mind's eye as she peeled the damp top over her head and slid the tight jeans down those long legs. She would stand in front of the bedroom AC in her bra and those ridiculous panties, raising goose bumps on her arms and legs, across her breasts and down her stomach, before finally pulling on shorts and a clean top, probably a soft cotton T-shirt that fitted as if made for her and—

Muttering a curse, he stalked to the kitchen table and began unloading the rest of the groceries. She'd bought chips and cookies, fruits and vegetables and dressing to go with the salad mix in the refrigerator. He left the produce on the counter and crammed the snacks and canned goods into the one cabinet that didn't hold dishes, then grabbed a beer from the six-pack before putting it in the refrigerator.

He'd downed half of it when the bedroom door opened and she came out again, in shorts and a soft cotton T-shirt. It didn't hug her the way it should but hung loosely, as if made for someone six inches taller and fifty pounds heavier. A boyfriend?

Her sandals flip-flopped on the vinyl as she crossed to the couch, plopped down and gave a sigh. "That feels better."

He went to sit in the sole chair, a glider that was comfortably worn in all the right places. "Well?"

"I didn't see either Mac or Hector, but—"

"How do you know what Hector looks like?"

Looking annoyed by his interruption, she frowned at him. "I'm a private investigator, remember? I found a photo of him."

"Let me see it."

In an instant, her gaze flickered away, then back again. She certainly was prickly about being in charge. No wonder she was spending so much time working for a kid. She probably had problems with adult clients who wanted some input…or vice versa. "I'll find it later. Now—"

"What do you mean, 'find it'? Tell me you don't have a neat little file somewhere labeled Photographs."

Her hazel eyes narrowed suspiciously. "I'm *trying* to tell you what I found out in town today. We can discuss my files later…unless you take some sort of perverse pleasure in being difficult and obstructive."

He was supposed to take offense at the insult, but he'd suffered much worse. Instead he slowly smiled. "Only with you, Madison. Okay, so what did you find out?"

"I met a woman named Marisa who thinks I'm considering relocating to Nomas."

"And she thinks that because?"

Bailey tilted her head to one side and quirked one brow. "Because I told her so. She also thinks, and *not* because I told her so, that I left my rat-bastard boyfriend—gee, that would be you—and took his car to get back at him."

"Like that would ever happen," he said with a snort.

She turned to sit sideways on the sofa, the padded arm at her back, and stretched her legs out in front of her before crossing them at the ankle. That little silver chain managed to find some light to reflect as she waggled her foot from side to side. "Which part are you objecting to? That you're a rat bastard? That I'd get away with taking your car? Or that you'd be my boyfriend?"

Boyfriend, girlfriend. Old-fashioned words for an old-fashioned notion. In his experience, relationships with women were about sex, good times and little else…not that his relationships were likely to be typical. Nothing about his life ever had been, not when his earliest and most enduring memories were of being beaten by his parents. But he couldn't imagine himself ever being part of an honest-to-God, boyfriend-girlfriend thing. He was too old, for starters—he hadn't been a boy since he was about six—and too cynical. He didn't believe in emotional intimacy, didn't believe in friendship.

"Would I have sex with you? Sure. Would I do it more than once? No. Would I be friends with you? No way. Would you ever get the chance to steal my car? Not while I'm still breathing. And if you ever managed to succeed, I would hunt you down and make you damned sorry."

She stopped jiggling that foot, and the chain settled. Her skin was golden, a nice contrast to the silver that circled her ankle, the ring on her second toe and the crimson of her toenails. He wondered if she was that shade all over, wondered if she wore jewelry in any other less common places.

As if she didn't notice that he'd fixated on her ankle, she casually responded, "I'd be insulted if I hadn't already decided that you're one-night-standworthy but nothing more. Anyway—"

For an instant he zoned out. *One-night-standworthy.* For years that was all he'd ever aspired to. He didn't have anything more to give, didn't want to take anything more. He'd learned young to count on no one, to need no one. Oh, sure, he'd depended on his squad in the war, had known they would be there watching his back when the fighting started, and they'd known the same of him, but that was different. That was part of being a soldier. It had nothing to do with *him.*

Even so, he was torn between affront that she'd deemed him worth one night of her time, nothing more, and interest that she'd deemed him worth one night of her time and nothing more. One night of hot sex—that was all he would want, all he'd ever wanted from a woman, and all she would want. Intriguing possibilities.

"When we were talking about available men, Marisa mentioned a rancher here who does quite well for himself by the name of Hector. I tried to learn a little more about him, but she reacted kind of strangely. I don't know if she's interested in him herself and doesn't want any competition or if she's got something against him, but I plan to find out. She asked me to come by again tomorrow. I'll get her talking again—we can swap more stories about Neanderthal men who value their cars more than their women—and see if I can get anymore out of her. Other than that…Nomas is a nice little town, slow-paced, offers all the necessities but few of the extras that make life worthwhile. The people seem friendly enough. No one acted suspicious or even overly curious about me. It doesn't seem the sort of place a murderer would hide—which, of course, makes it ideal."

There were murderers everywhere. People just didn't recognize them until it was too late. He'd thought he was a better judge of character than most people. He'd been through combat with Mac, had fought side by side with him when their convoy had been ambushed, had provided cover fire when Mac had rescued one of their fallen comrades and done the rescuing while Mac covered him. He'd trusted his life, and the lives of his squad, to Mac, and vice versa.

And Mac had killed the only people who'd ever meant a damn to Logan.

Slowly he became aware that Bailey was watching him with an expectant air, as if she'd asked some question that he should be answering. About the same time, he realized his right fingers had curled into a fist, clenched so tightly that white spots appeared on his knuckles. He forced the muscles to relax, the fingers to lie flat against the glider's wooden arm, then sullenly asked, "What?"

"I asked why he did it. Why did he kill Mr. and Mrs. Jensen? Was he that desperate to avoid returning to Iraq?"

Logan's fingers itched to clench again, but he held them flat. "He was a mean son of a bitch."

"There has to be more to it than that."

"Why? Because it'll make you feel better if you can come up with some reason to explain what he did? Because people who do terrible things for a reason aren't as bad as people who do terrible things because they want to?" He shook his head vehemently. "Mac could have stolen Sam's truck and Ella's money without hurting either of them. Hell, he could have *asked* for them, and they would have handed them over. He didn't have to kill them. He wanted to."

"But—"

"'But' nothing. Like I told you, Madison, this is *not* a game. Mac is one sick bastard. You can't reason with him. You can't make excuses for him. You piss him off, he's likely to kill you, too. Get that through your thick head or get the hell out of here."

He was right, of course, Bailey thought later as she rinsed the last of the dinner dishes. It was easier to believe that people who committed horrible crimes did so because they'd suffered horribly themselves. Physical and sexual abuse and emotional torment could leave a person so warped that all the therapy and medication in the world couldn't make them right again. But at least there was a chance they could be identified and helped before they reached that point. But someone who killed because he liked it, someone who was just plain mean…how did you identify him before he started killing?

You couldn't. She'd seen photos of Mac—smiling, benign, round-faced, glasses. If he'd approached her in a club, she would have responded with friendliness. It might not have gone beyond that, but who knew? It might have. He looked like someone you'd trust, someone you might take into your life and your home, someone who might charm your feet out from under you…before he left you gasping for air in a pool of your own blood.

A chink of porcelain against porcelain startled her out of her thoughts as Logan put the last plate into the cabinet. He hung the dish towel over the drainer to dry, then walked to the front window, lifted the curtain and stared out.

The sun had set and taken the day's heat with it. The night was fairly quiet—no traffic rumbling by on the highway, no loud noises from any of the other cabins. When she finished wiping the counters and turned away from the kitchenette, everything was still. Especially Logan.

"Do you engage in such mundane activities as watching television?" she asked as she rubbed a dollop of lotion into her hands.

"Go ahead if you want." He let the curtain fall and started toward the bedroom. "I'm going out."

She darted after him, reaching the room in time to see him strip off his T-shirt. The scars that crisscrossed his back made her stiffen, though she managed not to gasp this time. He seemed relatively comfortable with them—he made no effort to hide them as so many people would. Maybe that came from being in the Army, with its inherent lack of privacy. More likely it was his don't-give-a-damn attitude. *Take me as I am or screw you.*

His comfort aside, the scars made her wince inside. She couldn't imagine the level of pain associated with injuries so extensive. Nobody deserved that.

Except possibly Mac.

"Where do you think you're going?" she asked as he rooted in his duffel, then came up with a black T-shirt.

"Out."

"Where?"

After pulling the shirt over his head, he turned to scowl at her as he tugged it down. "I'm going to do a little reconnaissance."

"I'll go with you."

"I don't need you to go with me."

"You may not *want* me to go, but you can't possibly know that you don't *need* me, since you can't know what might happen."

He reached into the bag again, this time withdrawing a holster and a .45-caliber pistol. The opening in the barrel was bigger around than her little finger. It was a serious weapon for serious shooting.

For serious killing.

She couldn't afford the time to change from shorts back to jeans, but she grabbed his jean jacket from the bed, kicked off her sandals and shoved her feet into a pair of running shoes as he headed for the door. Halfway there, he remembered she still had his car keys and turned back, hand extended. She smiled. "I'm going with you."

"I don't want you."

"Gee, haven't you learned by now that we can't always get what we want?" Her shoelaces flopping, she picked up her purse from the back of a dining chair, then waited for him at the door.

Grimacing, he led the way out, waited while she locked up, then followed her to the car. Once they were both settled inside, she handed the keys to him.

"What do you think I'm going to do?" he grumbled. "Leave you here and rent the cabin next door? Get a room at the other motel? Try to maneuver around this wide spot in the road without running into you at every step?"

"Maybe find Mac, turn him over to the authorities and disappear before I have a chance to deliver you to Lexy?" She propped one foot on the dash and tied the laces, then repeated the process with the other foot. She hated wearing shoes without socks almost as much as she hated the idea of tramping around the desert…at night…in shorts. Back at the agency they had Charlie's Rule; maybe she could come up with Bailey's Rule. *Always be prepared for anything.*

Even if it did sound like a wordier rip-off of the Boy Scout motto.

Logan took side streets to the east end of town, past houses that ranged from mobile homes to sturdy, unimaginative structures. There were lights on in almost every one, people sometimes visible through the windows. The lush green yards she was accustomed to were lacking, but a few houses had lush, brightly blooming flower beds. Presumably none of them was Marisa's, with dying marigolds on the porch.

It was fully dark by the time they turned off the highway at the two-mile point. Bailey rummaged in her purse, dumping items onto her lap—the .9-millimeter pistol, a palm-sized notebook with an equally small ink pen and a mini flashlight. She slid the notebook and pen into her shorts pocket, hooked one finger through the ring on the flashlight, then cradled the pistol between her thighs.

"You know how to use that thing?" Logan's voice came out of the darkness, quiet and husky. When she glanced his way, even with the faint illumination from the dashboard lights, she could read nothing on his face.

"I shoot a two-inch grouping."

"Shooting at a paper target and shooting at a person are totally different things."

"Gee, I didn't realize that. Thank you for pointing it out."

He chose to ignore her sarcasm. "You ever shoot at a person?"

"Not yet."

He made a derisive sound but didn't pursue the subject.

She did. "Had you ever shot at a person before the war?"

He slowed to guide the GTX over a particularly bumpy passage, then the corner of his mouth turned down. "No."

"But when someone was shooting at you, trying to kill you, it wasn't so hard to shoot back, was it?" It would be the same for her. She'd learned to shoot for one reason: self-preservation. When the only choices were kill or be killed, she would kill. If there was emotional fallout, she would deal with it later.

Because he couldn't argue the point with her, he remained silent. After a time, he slowed to little more than a crawl, his gaze scanning the road on either side. "There," she said quietly, gesturing ahead. A narrow lane angled off the road, disappearing behind the outcropping that sprang up from the earth. He turned onto the lane, followed it to its end less than fifty feet in and shut off the headlights, but not before she saw the trash pile ahead. She hadn't considered that anyone besides Hector might live in the area, but logic suggested that someone else did.

Logan shut off the engine and looked at her in the darkness. "I don't suppose you'll wait in the car."

She glanced around again, at the misshapen rocks, the shadows that were garbage heaps and discarded appliances, the other shadows that were God knew what. The place could give her the creeps if she thought about it. What better place for a cold-blooded killer to dispose of a nosy victim than a garbage dump? "You got that right," she said a little too vehemently.

Without another word, he got out, closing his door without making any noise. She did the same, then joined him at the trunk, where he took out the binoculars and another object. He put both into a black backpack, slid the straps over his shoulders, then closed the trunk and started back toward the road.

She shoved her pistol into her shorts pocket long enough to shrug into the jean jacket and button it against the night chill. It had the added benefit of offering extra concealment by covering her yellow T-shirt. Wishing for a holster for the pistol, she freed it from her pocket, tugged her shorts back up to her waist and followed in his tracks.

They didn't walk along the road but a few yards off to the side. With little ambient light to guide them and too wary to use the flashlight, Bailey stumbled, sent rocks skittering across the desert floor and just generally navigated poorly, while Logan made very little, if any, noise. Imagining the scorn he was sending her way, she was wishing he would fall flat on his face and wipe away that smug look he was no doubt wearing, when suddenly she realized he was no longer in front of her. Panic just under the surface, she darted a quick look around just in time to see him disappear behind a boulder to her left. Relief washed over her as she hastily followed.

When she caught up, he was kneeling on the ground, the backpack in front of him. She was about to sit on a chunk of rock nearby when he said, "Watch out for snakes."

Her knees automatically straightened, stopping her downward movement. Who needed to sit? She wasn't tired, after all. She was in good shape. Besides, it was too cool tonight for snakes…wasn't it?

While he fiddled with the pack, she walked a few yards ahead, up a rise that grew steadily steeper. By the time she reached the top, she was face-to-face with bare rock blasted by the wind into gently rounded shapes. A touch confirmed that it still held the day's heat—something snakes likely sought out when the temperatures dropped.

Taking a step back and another to the side, she found an unrestricted view of the valley below, with Hector's ranch prominently situated. Light spilled yellow from windows on both floors, unhampered by curtains or blinds, but no one was visible through the windows.

For someone who did "quite well" for himself, Hector didn't appear to spend much on his house. It was adobe, or plastered to resemble it, and a simple rectangle. The porch that ran the length of the front was just deep enough for a couple of rockers, with simple poles providing support for its roof.

The vehicle parked nearest the house, however…someone had spent some bucks on that. It was a pickup, extended cab, and sat high off the ground. She couldn't tell the color—she was betting on wine or deep purple—but it gleamed in the thin light that came from a nearby flood lamp. Bearing less dust than Bailey had accumulated on their short walk, it likely had every extra the manufacturer offered.

"Scoot."

She startled, but caught herself and moved to one side to make room for Logan. He knelt where she'd been standing and raised the binoculars to his eyes. She wondered how much he could see and received an answer when he curtly said, "Write this down."

He read off license tag numbers and descriptions of vehicles, and she dutifully copied them with the aid of her mini flashlight. By the time he finished, she had seven sets of information of New Mexico registrations. "Sam's truck was never found, was it?" she asked curiously.

"No."

Surely if Mac had left it in any city or town or traded it for another stolen car, it would have been located before long. Even if he'd abandoned it on a rural road, on some logging trail or isolated camp trail, someone would have discovered it by now. But if it was hidden in one of Hector's outbuildings or on some corner of the ranch…

She tapped the ink pen against the pad. How difficult would it be to check out the buildings? They would have to gain access to the property, of course, and walking up the driveway wasn't going to cut it. They would have to sneak in across the desert, as they'd done tonight, and hope there weren't perimeter alarms, motion detectors or anything of that nature around. And even if they found Sam's truck, all it would prove was that Mac had been there. It wouldn't tell them a thing about when, or where he was now.

"You have a friend who can run those?" Logan asked.

She gazed at him blankly until he nodded to the notebook. "Oh, the tag numbers. Sure. Not a problem."

"Oh, yeah. I forgot. Your brother-in-law's a sheriff."

His snide tone rolled off her like water. "My other brother-in-law's the undersheriff."

For an instant, surprise reflected on his face as he realized she was referring to Brady. What had he expected his brother to become? A businessman like their father? A rancher or oilman like their grandfathers? Brady was less suited to business than anyone she knew, with the possible exception of Logan. He'd worked a variety of jobs after leaving Texas, but when he'd gotten into law enforcement, he'd found his niche. He liked his job and did it well. She couldn't imagine him doing anything else.

The surprise disappeared behind studied indifference. "Run 'em, and we'll find out which one belongs to Hector. My money's on the big burgundy extended cab."

"Then what?"

He lifted one brow.

"We'll know what kind of vehicle Hector drives. Then what?" While she waited for an answer, she looked around carefully, then sat down. There was no hint of thoughts racing through Logan's mind—primarily, she suspected, because he had none. He was a smart, capable man; an outstanding soldier; tough and no doubt resourceful; but he wasn't a cop or private investigator. And though she *was* a private investigator, she wasn't sure her ideas were any better than his. After all, this *was* her first real case. So far she'd succeeded brilliantly—she'd found Logan—but that still left Mac.

"We wait. We watch," Logan said at last.

"How about you wait and watch while I make an effort to meet Hector?"

"No." He said the word quickly, biting it off as if he didn't trust himself to say more at the moment. She would like to think it was concern for her safety, but she knew better. After a sharp breath, he went on, "If Mac is there, a stranger coming around might scare him off."

"If Mac is there, we could wait and watch for months from a distance and never know it." She drew her knees up, rested her elbows on them, then settled her chin in her palms. The position generated a degree or two of warmth to combat the night chill. "I can tell Hector that someone in town told me he might be looking for help—a cook, a housekeeper. It'll get me in the door, where I can take a look around. And if he hires me—"

"You're not the smart one. You're insane."

She couldn't argue that with him. After all, she knew things about Hector that he didn't. "It's our best shot. We can't wait forever. For all we know, Mac could be anywhere in the country—anywhere in the world. How much time do we waste hanging around Nomas if he's not here?"

Logan stared past her into the night, his jaw clenched.

She gave an exaggerated shrug. "Do you want to find Mac or do you want to sit around and accomplish nothing? It's up to you. *But,* whatever you decide, you owe me a trip to Buffalo Plains. Don't forget that."

Chapter 5

When had he lost control? Logan wondered.

Easy answers: the day he'd gone home and found Sam and Ella dead. And the day Bailey Madison had come into his life. Two totally separate incidents, yet integrally entwined. If he wanted justice for Sam and Ella, he had to get it through Bailey.

What she was proposing was dangerous. Granted, he knew nothing about Hector Escobar to suggest that he was anything like Mac, but he got a sick feeling in his gut at the thought of her walking into Hector's territory as if he was just another job opportunity. His instincts insisted the man was a threat, and his instincts had saved his life on numerous occasions. He trusted them.

More than he trusted Bailey.

"What do you know about Escobar's background?" he asked as he turned to study the ranch house again.

From the corner of his eye, he saw her shrug. "I've told you most of it."

"What have you not told me?"

She remained silent so long that he lowered the binoculars

and studied her. Was that guilt that tugged at the corners of her mouth, that made it impossible for her to look him in the eye? Had she lied to him about Hector?

"You ran a criminal history on Mac." He waited a moment, and she nodded. "And you also ran one on Hector. What did you find out?"

She straightened, looked away at the valley, then back at him. "He had some problems when he was younger. Drugs. Assault. Typical teenage stuff."

"I never got arrested for drugs or assault when I was a teenager and I bet you never did either."

A thin smile curved her mouth. "I bet you were never the typical teenager either."

He acknowledged that with a nod. "What about since then?"

"He's a respected member of the community. Hasn't been arrested in years."

That didn't mean he'd given up breaking the law—just that he might have gotten better at it or that the local law didn't care.

Or it could mean he really was a respected member of the community. Kids did stupid things and then they grew up. Though Logan *had* avoided arrest, he had done some damn stupid things himself when he was younger. It was, as she'd said, pretty typical.

But he'd given up stupid behavior when he'd grown up, and letting Bailey approach Escobar on her own struck him—and his instincts—as incredibly stupid.

He was saved from having to discuss it further when movement in the valley caught his attention. Holding the binoculars with one hand, he reached back, grabbed her by a handful of jacket and yanked her to the ground beside him. Wisely she bit back the surprised sound that tried to escape.

"Here," he whispered, handing her the binoculars, then taking the night-vision scope from the backpack. It had the same magnification as the binoculars; if there hadn't been enough light to read the tag numbers with the binos, he'd intended to use the scope.

He scanned the five men now standing on the porch, searching each face for familiar features. A knot of disappointment formed in his gut when he acknowledged that Mac wasn't among them. "Which one is Escobar?"

She studied the men, then said, "The big one."

"They're *all* big." The smallest of the bunch had forty pounds on *him,* and the biggest was probably twice that. "Which one?"

"Second from the right."

He *was* the biggest, standing close to six foot six and tipping the scales somewhere around two-eighty. He had long black hair, parted down the center and tied at his neck with a piece of leather, and a neat beard covering much of his pockmarked face. Like everything else about him, the grin he wore was big, and so was the pistol holstered on his belt.

If Hector Escobar was a God-fearing, law-abiding man, why did he feel the need to wear a pistol in his own home? Because he truly was a rancher living in an isolated valley and had to deal with desert predators, both two- and four-legged? Maybe he had a real dislike for sidewinders and wanted to be ready if he ran into one. Or maybe the snakes he dealt with were only the two-legged, criminally inclined variety.

The men talked for a few minutes. Their voices were inaudible, but their laughter wasn't. Escobar slapped one man on the shoulder, nearly knocking him off the porch, helped him catch his balance, then hugged him tightly.

"There's someone still inside," Bailey murmured. "See?"

Logan refocused the scope on the open door, where part of a figure was visible. It was impossible to tell whether it was a man or a woman or what it was doing. After a moment, it moved completely out of view.

Escobar finished saying good-night to his guests, and they trooped off the porch to their vehicles. He watched them drive away, two heading past the rear of the house, the other two following the driveway to the road. Then he returned inside and closed the door.

"Could that have been Mac inside?" Though the men were gone, Bailey was still whispering. It seemed the right thing to do.

"It could have been anyone." All they'd really seen was someone's midsection—jeans and untucked shirt. It could have been a little green man from Mars for all they knew.

After a moment the first two of the trucks came into view to the north, one following the other along a bumpy road. Logan scanned ahead with the scope and located their destination, a structure a half mile from the main house. It was a house—small, square, steps leading to the door but no porch. Built of stone, it looked as if it had been a part of the landscape forever. Maybe it had been the original ranch house, from when the ranch really had been a ranch. He didn't know what it was now, but a legitimate livestock operation didn't rank high on his list of possibilities.

The pickups stopped in front of the stone house and their headlights went out. A moment later a light came on inside.

"Where do you think he keeps his cattle?"

Logan didn't glance at Bailey, still stretched out on the ground beside him. "A better question would be *does* he keep any cattle?"

"Marisa says he's a rancher."

"That doesn't make it true. You just got a good look at him. Is he the sort of person you'd want to tell a stranger runs drugs, smuggles illegal aliens or dabbles in the slave trade?" Finally he did lower the scope and looked at her. He'd pulled her to the ground, had known exactly where she was lying, but somehow he hadn't realized exactly how close that was. Instinctively he scooted away, opening a few inches between them. "Is he the sort of person you want to piss off?"

"Of course not."

"Then you'll forget this stupid idea of hooking up with him."

She glared at him. "We were talking about Marisa and why she would say he's a rancher when he might not be. She's got to live in the same town with him. I don't. I get to play by a whole other set of rules."

"I didn't know insane people played by rules."

She studied him a moment before turning back to the valley. "You know, Logan, I'm not the sort of person you want to piss off either. I could take your car tomorrow to meet Marisa and not come back. Or I could call Lexy tonight and tell her exactly where you are. She and Brady would be here first thing in the morning, and without a car, you'd have no way to avoid them. I'd be out working on finding Mac while you'd be stuck entertaining your family."

He glowered at her, but she was too engrossed with the binoculars to notice. "Why do you bother? She's not even really your niece."

Though she didn't look at him, her voice became heated. "She most certainly is, as much as Brynn is. Hallie's the only real mother Lexy has ever known, and my sisters and I are the only aunts she's ever known. We're *family*."

Obviously the concept of family held vastly different meanings for them. Logan hadn't seen any of his family in nineteen years and would be happy if he never saw them again. Bailey loved her family so much she extended that love to non-blood relatives like Brady's daughter.

He considered whether that meant anything to him: *his niece.* He couldn't honestly say it did. It sounded too foreign, *felt* too foreign.

The guys he'd served with had talked about family easily— *my mom, my dad, my brother, sister, aunt, granddad.* Whenever the conversation had gone in that direction, he'd usually wound up discussing something else with Mac, since they were both without family. Obviously, he thought, Escobar's image flashing through his mind, Mac had lied.

But so had Logan.

"Just a word of warning." Bailey turned her head to glare at him. "When you meet Lexy—and you will—you won't do one thing to hurt or disillusion her or you'll answer to me."

"Oh, now I'm scared," he mocked, though at the same time he wondered if Lexy knew how much her non-aunt cared about her. Since leaving Marshall City all those years ago, he'd met very few people he couldn't intimidate with nothing more than a look. Not only was Bailey unintimidated, but she had the nerve to threaten *him*. Considering what a pain she'd been the few days he'd known her, he had no doubt she *could* make him damned sorry.

One way or another.

After a leisurely breakfast the next morning, Bailey called Reese at the sheriff's department in Buffalo Plains and cajoled him into running the tag numbers for her. Sitting at the dining table, she read off each number, then brushed off his questions about what she was doing, where and why.

"I thought you only worked in the office," he said when she'd sidestepped him yet again. "On the computer. Where you don't run into anything more dangerous than a virus."

"What makes you think I'm not in the office?"

"Because you have your own contacts in Memphis law enforcement. And because caller ID on this call comes back to a motel in freakin' New Mexico."

Aware of Logan listening even as he did the dishes, she smiled. "Don't be such a pain. You're my brother-in-law, not my brother. That limits your rights of interference. If you can run those tags for me…"

"I can run them. Soon as you tell me why."

"You know, Reese, I do have a contact in the Memphis Police Department. He'll run them, and all it'll cost me is a date. No interrogation, no big-brother acts." It was partly true. She'd dated a robbery detective with the Memphis PD who was still willing to provide her with information from time to time—and still interested in getting back together. It really did just cost her a dinner date…plus fending off unwanted attention when the evening was over. He never pushed too far, though. They shared the same martial-arts instructor, and he knew she was the better student.

"How's my sister?" she asked before Reese could demonstrate the stubbornness he was known for.

"Which one?" he asked grudgingly.

"Either. Both."

"They're fine. Keeping busy. Wondering why you haven't called and when you're going to visit again."

"Tell them I'll make it up there before too long. How about Brady and the kids?"

"They're fine, too…more or less. Lexy's got a crush on one of my deputies, and it's about to kill Brady."

Bailey snorted. "Lexy's had a crush on Mitch since she met him last summer, when those guys tried to kidnap her, and Brady's just figuring it out?"

"He's a father. Fathers don't want to know those things about their teenage daughters. I told him Mitch hardly knows she exists. She's just a kid to him, after all—and the boss's kid, no less."

"Give her a few years," Bailey teased. "That'll change. Hey, give my love to everyone. I'll call you back later today for that info, okay?"

Hanging up, she drained the last of her coffee, then took the mug to the sink, sliding it into the soapy water where Logan's hands were immersed. He looked as if he wanted to ask questions but wasn't sure where to start. She doubted he was the least bit interested in her relationship with Detective Cadore back home, and if he'd picked up on it, she'd rather not discuss why Reese worried about her being out of the office. Since she was expecting him to put his faith in her training, she preferred not to admit that this was the first case she'd handled from beginning to end all on her own.

She chose the one bit of conversation she did want to discuss and gave him an opening. "Hard to imagine your brother being the father of a teenager, isn't it?"

"It's hard to imagine anything about him when you never give him a first thought, much less a second."

Ignoring his sullen answer, she leaned against the cabinet, arms crossed over her middle, and watched him work. "I told you Lexy's nearly sixteen, didn't I? She has a thing for one of

Reese's deputies. Mitch isn't really so much older than her, and you know teenage girls today—they look so grown up and sexy. It's driving Brady insane, even though said deputy hasn't yet forgotten that he works for her dad."

He pulled the plug and let the soapy water drain, then began rinsing the dishes stacked high in the second sink. She figured he was going to pretend she wasn't there until she finally gave up and went away for real, but after a while, he reluctantly asked, "What was that about a kidnapping?"

Through sheer will, she kept the triumph off her face and out of her voice. "Attempted kidnapping, at least that time. Last summer Lexy ran away from home in Marshall City and went looking for the father she'd never known. When she left, she unwittingly took with her some records documenting her stepfather's illegal activities. He wanted them back, so he sent some goons after them. Eventually all the bad guys wound up in jail, Brady asked Lexy to live with him and Hallie persuaded her mother to let her go."

"Persuaded how?" He still sounded and looked utterly disinterested, as if the conversation was only slightly better than silence, but she didn't believe the act for a minute.

"She gave Sandra fifty thousand reasons to finally do the right thing for her daughter."

"Sandra… From Marshall City?"

Bailey nodded.

"Sandra Whitfield? Pretty? Brown curls? Hot body? Greedy little bitch?"

"I don't know about the rest of it, but 'greedy bitch' sounds right."

He made a sound that was part derision, part laughter. "She must have chewed Brady up and spit him out. She was hell and gone out of his league. And he was stupid enough to marry her. I bet she got a hell of a lot more than fifty grand out of that."

Annoyed by his amusement, she pushed away from the counter and crossed to the sofa. When bedtime had come the night before, he'd worn a wary look, as if he'd expected her to claim half the bed. She'd been tempted, just to see if she could turn wariness to alarm, but good sense had stopped her. The bed was only a double, and she was a snuggler. The instant she hit REM sleep, she would have plastered herself against him and not let go until he pried himself free.

Instead, just as naturally as if it had been discussed and agreed upon, she'd taken extra linens from the bedroom closet and made up the sofa. She'd spent a few minutes in the bathroom, removing her makeup, combing out her braid, then come out, tank top in hand, said a cheery good-night and left the room. He'd still been standing beside the bed when she'd shut off the living room lights.

Now she picked up the linens she'd already folded and returned them to the closet. She took a notebook from her laptop case and shoved it into her handbag, then returned to the living room. "I'm outta here," she called.

She managed to get the lock undone, but opened the door only a few inches when a darkly tanned hand shoved it shut again. She followed the arm attached to the hand up to a broad shoulder, a strong neck and a perfect scowl.

"Going where?"

"I've got things to do and people to see," she said flippantly.

"What things? What people?"

With a sigh, she retreated a few steps from the door. "I thought I'd check out the local library and see if I can learn anything about the Escobar family. I also plan to stop by the newspaper office and see if I can charm anything out of Belle—the owner, editor and chief reporter. Later I'll stop in and talk to Marisa again, as I told her yesterday I would." She didn't mention possibly driving out to the Escobar ranch. He wouldn't approve and couldn't go along, so why bother telling him?

"And that's all?" Suspicion darkened his voice and his features. It was a comfortable look for him, speaking clearly of how little trust he had to give.

"As far as I know." His gaze narrowed, and she hastily went on. "I could meet someone else who's worth talking to, or someone could invite me to lunch. You have to be flexible in this game, you know—and I know, I know, it's not a game. I was just using it as a figure of speech."

She waited a moment for him to say something, but he didn't. He did lift his hand from the door, though, wrapping his fingers around the knob and opening it for her.

"I'll see you later," she said as she stepped outside onto the stoop. She was pulling the door shut when his response came, so quiet that she barely heard it.

"Be careful."

Would wonders never cease, she thought as she turned the key in the lock. There might be a decent human being underneath all that arrogance and hostility, after all.

Though the morning breeze was cool, the day promised to be another hot one, and she'd dressed accordingly, in neatly tailored shorts, a crisp sleeveless top and sandals that offered good support and protection from the hot pavement. She'd secured her hair on top of her head and left her makeup at a minimum, figuring much of it would melt off anyway before the morning was over.

She had seen the library the day before, located a half block off the highway in an aged adobe building. There was only one car in the parking lot when she arrived and only one person inside—the librarian. The woman was about a hundred years old, practically short enough to hide behind the counter and apparently deaf as a post. Though the bell over the door rang when Bailey walked through and she called a cheery hello, when the librarian happened upon her in the reference section a few minutes later, she gave a start of surprise.

"Why, I thought I was all alone in here," she said loudly. "Is there something I can help you with?"

"Thanks, but not right now," Bailey replied, then, seeing no comprehension on the woman's face, she repeated it at twice the volume.

"You're new in town."

Stick with the same lie, Bailey counseled herself. "I'm thinking about settling down here."

"Oh, you don't want to do that. A girl your age, you should be off in the city where there's plenty to do and plenty of handsome young men around to do it with. Nomas is in woefully short supply of both interesting things and interesting men."

"Have you lived here long?"

"All my life—seventy-seven and three-quarters years. Taught school most of that time, but when they took away my paddle, I gave them my resignation. If you can't discipline the miscreants, you can't teach. But they said I was too old to be paddling teenagers. Hmph! My boys are in their fifties now and they're still scared enough of me and my paddle to do what I say the first time I say it." She slid into the chair opposite and stuck out one fragile hand. "I'm Celia."

"Bailey."

"Hmm. I had a dog named Bailey once. Little bugger had the sharpest teeth you ever saw. So…" Celia peered through thick glasses at the book Bailey had opened—*A History of Nomas*. "Dry, dull stuff. You want to know something about the town or the people who live here, ask me. I know it all."

"Okay." Bailey scanned the open page, picking out a name from the text. "Eladio Estevez."

"Used to be the mayor. His son was, too, and so was his grandson. They're all dead now, but there are still Estevezes around, just not bearing that name. After that grandson, they turned out generation after generation of girls. But you'll find Estevez blood in the Watkins family, the Gomezes, the Parkers, the LaBeaus and so on."

Bailey pretended to look again, then casually said, "The Escobars."

Celia's expression turned distant. "A proud family…once. They donated the courthouse a hundred years ago—built this building, as well, and paid for the books that first filled it. But somewhere along the way, things went wrong. Me, I blame that Henley girl. She went to school with my boys and was nothing but trouble—cute, flirty and selfish as the day was long. All the boys were fascinated by her, even my own, but the only one offering what she wanted was Alfonso Escobar. If she married him, he promised, they would shake the dust of this one-horse town from their heels and move away to Albuquerque, El Paso or maybe even Dallas." As an afterthought, she added an insulted "Hmph," as if forgetting that she'd just advised Bailey not to settle in a place like Nomas.

"Did she marry him?" Bailey asked, though she knew, of course.

"Yes, ma'am. So quick everyone's head was spinning."

"Did they move away?" She already knew that answer, as well. Ellen Henley Escobar had gone to the big city by herself, leaving both husband and son behind.

"No," Celia replied. "Alfonso never had any intention of leaving Nomas, not even for a girl as pretty as that one. Everybody knew that except Ellen. He kept promising her next week, next month, next year, and she kept counting the days. But at the same time, he was working his ranch, investing what little money he had and all his energy in it. Once Hector was born, there was no question that Alfonso was staying put. That land had belonged to his father and grandfather before him, and he intended to pass it on to his son."

"So Ellen left without him."

Celia nodded. "About broke his heart. But she left the boy here. If she'd taken Hector, it would have killed Alfonso." Removing her glasses, she wiped them on a handkerchief from her pocket before grimly finishing. "Hector took care of that a few years ago."

For an instant Bailey's breath caught in her chest, then she exhaled sharply. Surely the old lady meant Hector's actions had contributed to his father's death and not that he'd been directly responsible. If he'd been a suspect in a murder, Bailey certainly would have found at least a mention of it somewhere. "What happened?"

Celia replaced her glasses with a sigh. "Hector got married…oh, ten years back, and a few years later, he and Shelley had twins, a boy and a girl. One day she loaded them up into the car to run to the grocery store, and they were never seen again. A few days later, the police up in Deming arrested a man driving her car. Claimed he found it on the side of the road with the keys still in it. Her purse was on the floorboard with the shopping list in it, and the babies' seats were in the back, but there was no sign whatsoever of her and the babies. Alfonso had never been the same after Ellen left him, at least until those grandkids came along. Losing them finished the job Ellen had started. They said it was a heart attack, but you'll never convince me he didn't die of a broken heart."

"Do you think Hector killed his wife and kids?" Merely voicing the question sent a shiver of alarm down Bailey's spine. She would do just about anything for Lexy, but get close to a man capable of killing his own children? Could anyone ask that of her?

"No, not at all," Celia replied with such confidence that relief rushed through Bailey. "I think he made life so miserable for her that she had no choice but to run off, only she didn't leave her kids behind like Ellen did. Mind you, I have nothing to base that on, but it's what I believe. Hector was so enraged when they disappeared. He ranted and raved and offered rewards for their return. He knew she'd left him and he genuinely wanted them back."

"You don't think he was putting on an act?"

Celia snorted. "I had him in my drama class. Trust me, he's not that good an actor." Abruptly she squinted at the large round clock above the door, then got to her feet. "I'd best get back to work. I've bored you long enough."

"I'm not bored at all. It's better than watching a soap opera."

"Hmph. Wouldn't know about that. Never seen one. Stay long as you like…though be warned—stay long enough and I'll be back for another chat." With a grin, Celia disappeared into the stacks.

Bailey put away the history book and moved to the microfilm reader and the rolls containing old issues of the local paper. Hector's marriage had taken place ten years ago, the children's births a few years later. That gave her roughly eight years' worth of newspapers to go through for information on Shelley Escobar's disappearance. Luckily, with only one issue a week—and a short one, at that—it didn't take her long to find a story related to the disappearance. She scanned back until she located the original story, nearly six years earlier, headlined "Local Woman and Children Missing."

She read the articles, one a week for nearly two months, in order, and learned little more than Celia had already told her. The authorities had taken dogs to the location where the thief claimed he'd found the car, picking up a trail that led only twenty feet, presumably to another car. Whether she and the children had gone into the other car willingly was only one of the unknowns in the case. There had been no problems in the marriage, a Deming lawyer had said on Hector's behalf. Rumors of abuse were untrue. Shelley and Hector were happy and in love. Mr. Escobar was *devastated.*

There were no comments from Shelley's family—no mention of a family at all. Had she been alone? Or was Hector the only one who mattered here?

Bailey's eyes were gritty, leading her to return all the spools to their cases, then shut off the machine. She was on her way toward the door when a bookcase of high school yearbooks caught her attention. Laying her purse on a nearby table, she calculated when Shelley Matthews Escobar would have graduated. That annual was missing from its spot, so she chose the one for the year before. Flipping through to the juniors' section, she located Shelley's photo and her gaze widened. Red hair, pale, freckled skin…she looked so much like Marisa at the drugstore that it was eerie.

So it was safe to assume that Marisa wasn't interested in snaring Hector for herself. Which made it also safe to assume that, if it became necessary, Bailey could trust her with at least part of the truth.

She was about to close the book when a name a row above caught her eye. Fair, blond hair with a hint of red; blue eyes;

glasses; a friendly smile…Peter Alan MacGregor hadn't exactly quit school in the eleventh grade, as her information had suggested. He'd completed at least a part of it here in Nomas.

After photocopying the page, she put the book back, shouted a goodbye to Celia, then went outside. The bright sun raised a sheen of perspiration on her cool skin and made her fumble in her bag for sunglasses as she crossed the sidewalk to the car. Instead of heading for the newspaper office or the drugstore, she turned back toward the motel. She was halfway there when a truck pulled off a side street directly into her path.

Her foot jammed the brake to the floor as she steered away from the big extended cab, all the while praying, "Oh, please, oh, please, oh, please." Logan would kill her if she brought his precious car back with so much as a scratch on it, and that monster truck looked as if it could do a whole lot more damage than a mere scratch.

The car was still shuddering from the abrupt stop when a man ducked to peer in through the passenger window. "Sorry about that, man. I just wasn't paying attention. Are you okay?"

Bailey forced her fingers to unclench from the steering wheel, took her first breath in what seemed like hours, then faced the man and lost all that air again.

It was Hector Escobar.

"You okay?" he repeated.

"Y-yeah. Just thinking what would happen if I banged up this car."

His worried expression transformed into a broad grin. "Aw, if I'd done the banging, I would've paid to have it fixed so no one could tell the difference." He stuck his right hand inside the car. "I'm Hector."

"B-Bailey." She shook hands with him, his oversize hand swallowing hers. It would be so easy for those hands to squeeze the life out of a woman—out of his own babies? So easy for him to drag her across the seat, out the window and into his own vehicle. No one would ever know what had happened to her—at least, no one who didn't have to live in the same town as Hector.

Then he released her hand, and the panic receded. "If you have a free hour or two tonight, stop in at Pat's Place. I'll buy you a beer to make up for this."

"Thanks."

With a grin and a salute, he returned to his truck—it was burgundy, as Logan had guessed—and drove off. She was slower to guide the car back into her own lane and drive the remaining hundred yards to the motel entrance.

She thought she was pretty much back to normal by the time she let herself into the cabin, but Logan's first words suggested otherwise. "What's wrong?"

She hung her purse on the back of a dining chair, then headed for the air conditioner. "Nothing," she remarked.

Leaving the glider, he came to stand a few feet in front of her. "Yeah, right. You look like you just saw a ghost."

"My ghost," she murmured, turning to face the vents. "When you found out what I did to your precious baby."

Gaze widening, he pushed past her to lift the curtain. Apparently seeing no damage to the front end or the driver's side of the GTX, he let it fall again and faced her accusingly. "Did you back into something?"

"Of course not. I've been driving for more than half my life. I don't back up without looking first."

"Did someone back into you?"

"No. No one actually did anything." Rolling her gaze heavenward, she explained. "I was on my way back here when someone turned in front of me. I swerved and hit the brakes and just barely missed him. And, gee, thank you for asking if I'm okay."

He gave a careless shrug that made her want to hit him. "If no one actually did anything, why wouldn't you be okay?"

"Because all I could think was you would kill me and it wasn't even my fault." She watched him walk away, pull open the refrigerator door and remove a cold beer. He twisted off the cap and took a drink, then pulled out a package of sliced ham and closed the door with his hip.

"It was Hector Escobar," she said flatly.

Logan's jaw tightened, but he gave no other response.

"He invited me to meet him at Pat's Place tonight so he can buy me a beer to apologize."

That made him stiffen all over. He set the ham on the counter, then paced toward her, gesturing with the bottle. "You're not going."

She snatched the beer from him and took a long drink, forgetting she didn't like the taste until it hit her throat and sent a shudder of revulsion through her. Shaking it off, she took another swig before handing it back. Vile though it tasted, the alcohol warmed her a badly needed bit. "Do I look like an idiot?"

"No, but looks can be deceiving."

She smiled sweetly. "I know. *You* look like a rational human being."

Surprisingly her remark brought a smile from him. "I'm hungry. I'm never rational when I'm hungry."

"What are you planning to eat?"

He returned to the counter and picked up the ham.

"That and nothing else?"

"You didn't buy any bread for sandwiches."

Relieved for something more normal to think about it, she crossed to the refrigerator and started unloading ingredients into his arms. "Of course not. No one eats sandwiches on bread anymore. How did you ever survive in the Army?"

"Honey, turn me loose in the desert, mountains, jungle or ocean, and I can find something to eat."

Honey. She stilled for a moment. It meant nothing—a careless endearment that he no doubt used often to avoid having to remember names. But it was the first time she could remember that he'd called her anything besides her last name. That was the only reason she'd locked in on it.

Pushing it aside, she asked, "But the kitchen stumps you?" As soon as he'd dumped everything on the counter, she went to work, methodically putting together two tortilla wraps with ham, turkey, cheese and the works. After pouring ranch dressing liberally over both, she rolled them tightly, cut them in half, then shook a serving of chips onto each plate. After presenting one plate to him with a flourish, she carried her own to the table and sat down.

"Gee, and here I was wondering why you aren't married," he said drily as he sat across from her.

"I don't have to wonder why *you're* not married. Not exactly a prize, are you?"

He feigned offense. "What do you mean by that?"

"Well…" She washed down a bite with a drink of pop. "You're bossy, arrogant, obnoxious, critical and difficult."

"Maybe that has something to do with the company I'm keeping."

"And did I mention rude and insulting?"

"While you're—what?—just brutally honest?"

She considered that while she chewed another bite. "No, I can be rude and insulting, too. But tell the truth—you're not interested in getting married, are you?"

"Not in the least."

"Me neither." At the moment, that was entirely true. The only partnership she intended to pursue was in her career. She doubted her current boss would ever consider her even junior-partner material, but someday, when she had more fieldwork under her belt, she fully intended to be a partner in *somebody's* agency.

But it would be nice at some point to have someone in her life—someone to come home to, to snuggle with, to care what happened in her day. Not a husband, necessarily. Just *someone.*

Then she glanced at Logan and amended that. Someone not quite so intense. Not quite so difficult. Not quite so…*so.*

But wasn't intense better than boring? And wasn't difficult more worthwhile than easy, at least to a point?

She rolled her gaze again. She shouldn't have drunk that beer. She'd never been able to handle her liquor well, and in the middle of the day when she was already feeling a bit shaky from her near miss with Hector…

This was no time to be thinking of a man in her future or the lack thereof. She had a case to solve, a reputation to bolster and a niece to make happy. Business as usual—that was her focus.

It had to be.

Chapter 6

It was Friday night, and Logan was sitting in the glider, absently gazing at the television. Before the war, Friday nights had always been a time to unwind and celebrate the end of another week. He'd done his share of drinking, partying and picking up women with his buddies, had awakened to his share of hangovers and strange women naked in bed beside him. Some part of him missed those days—not for the activities but for the attitude. Things had been easier then. There had been a balance to his life.

Then one of those buddies had killed his surrogate parents, and everything had been out of balance since. Sometimes he thought if he ever got his feet squarely back on the ground again, he wouldn't know what to do. The only interest he'd ever had was the Army, and he'd given that up to track down Mac. Once he found him, what would he do? Who would he be?

He didn't have a clue.

Maybe he should say *if* he found Mac. He had to believe that someday it would happen. God or fate or karma couldn't let him get away with what he'd done. And it wasn't as if Logan had anything else to do. He would camp out here in Nomas for the rest of his life if that was what it took. He for damn sure didn't have any other leads to follow at the moment.

Rising from the couch, Bailey stretched her arms above her head. Her shirt rode up and her shorts slipped lower, revealing a twinkle in the middle. He'd wondered the other day about other bits of jewelry—there it was, a small stud in her navel.

He'd always been a sucker for hot bodies with pierced navels. Knowing that she had both wasn't going to make his confinement any easier.

Without so much as a glance at him, she went into the bedroom. A moment later the bathroom door closed.

He forced his gaze back to the television, but he hadn't followed any of the show so far. He wasn't likely to pick up on the rest of it.

A segment of the show and two commercial breaks had passed before the bathroom door opened again. Bailey came out wearing jeans that rode low on her hips and a lace-edged shirt that fit snugly. The neck dipped low over her breasts, exposing golden skin and tantalizing curves, and the stretchy fabric clung to her middle before ending an inch or two above the jeans. Her hair was down, brushing her shoulders and pulled back from her face and held by a silver clasp in back. She'd touched up her makeup, added earrings and a pendant that rested at the top of her cleavage—as if a man needed any more inducement to look that way—and switched from sandals into boots.

His mouth dry, Logan got to his feet. She stopped in the bedroom doorway, a small purse in her hands and a look of uncertainty on her face. Surely she wasn't doubting whether men would look at her; that was an absolute given. So she must be wondering if he was going to give her a hard time about going to meet Hector.

Damn straight he was.

His first impulse was to order her back into the bedroom and out of those clothes, but while he was accustomed to giving orders, she wasn't accustomed to following them. If he pissed her off, she would go just to spite him, and if anything happened…

He stared at her so long that she shifted uneasily. There wasn't a scant inch of fabric in that white top to conceal or sway with the movement.

"How do I look?" she asked at last.

The answer came out without thought. "Hot."

Smiling weakly, she swept her hair off her neck for a moment, then let it fall. "Yeah, well, you try getting dressed and putting on makeup in an unair-conditioned bathroom."

"No. I mean…*damn.*"

The smile strengthened as she strode across the room to the table. She wasn't trying to be sexy; it was just the way she always walked. But there *was* something damned sexy about it—the long legs, the sway of her hips, the slighter sway of her breasts. She picked up her purse and returned to the couch, where she transferred a few things to the smaller bag. When she was done, she stood again, but this time he was blocking her way.

"What happened to 'Do I look like an idiot?'"

"I thought it over. It's the most popular bar in town. There will be a lot of people there. Nothing's going to happen."

"Right. Because I'm going with you."

She shook her head.

"I'll wait in the car while you go in, check the place out and make sure Mac's not there. If I don't hear from you in ten minutes, I'll know it's okay to go in."

"I don't think—"

"You can't go alone."

"Marisa says it's not a bad place."

After calling her brother-in-law again, she'd gone back into town that afternoon to have a banana split with Marisa. It turned out Escobar's missing wife was her older sister, and she had no clue where Shelley and the kids were or if they were even alive, so there was no love lost for her brother-in-law.

"If Escobar goes there, it's not a great place either. Humor me on this, Madison. If something goes wrong, you'll need backup."

A look crossed her face, there and gone. Doubt? Distrust? Was he going to have to pay forever for not rescuing her from that drunk in El Paso when it had been so damn easy for her to rescue herself?

"I have backup," she said with a brittle smile as she held up the .22 Beretta she'd switched from one bag to the other.

"Either I'm going or you're not." Even if it meant he had to tie her to the sofa.

Though her expression appeared on the verge of surrender, she still argued. "It's a risk, I know, but a calculated one—"

"No. Taking me along makes it calculated. Going by yourself is just plain lunacy." He waited, expecting more from her, but after a moment she sighed.

"You know, considering that I don't work for you, you sure do boss me around a lot."

"Someone has to save you from yourself. Let me get my weapon." It took him about a minute to claim the .45 and to grab a leather jacket along the way. When he returned, she was waiting restlessly near the door.

Outside he climbed into the backseat and wedged himself into the same space where she'd slept a few nights ago. It was a much tighter fit for him, made more uncomfortable by the scent of her perfume that permeated the leather. The fragrance was light, not too sweet and reminded him of a spring day after a rain—fresh, clean, sunny. Not sexy at all.

Sure.

Instead of talking on the short drive to the bar, she turned on the radio and tuned it to a country station. "Oh, please," he mumbled. It wasn't enough that every breath he took had to smell like her, but he had to listen to her music, too?

"She who controls the car controls the radio," she replied. He could hear the damn smile in her voice.

After a couple of twangy somebody-done-somebody-wrong

songs, she lowered the volume. "Here we are. And, gee, there's Hector's truck, along with one…two…three of the tags we copied down. I'm going to park on the west side. There aren't as many cars there."

The car bumped across the gravel lot, then eased to a stop and the engine went quiet. A dim light came on in the interior as she made a show of checking her lipstick in the mirror. "Give me ten minutes to make sure Mac's not there, then come on in."

"Right." He checked his watch as she got out, then settled in to wait for ten minutes that were going to last at least an hour. Time was relative, Einstein said, and the old man had damn sure been right.

The engine clicked as it cooled. Other cars came and left, their headlights arcing across the side of the building. Voices passed by on their way to the entrance, and faintly through the wall came the sound of music. Country music. Damn.

Finally the second hand counted off the tenth minute. He eased into a sitting position, scanning the parking lot to make certain no one was around before opening the passenger door.

His boots crunched on the gravel as he headed for the front door, then stopped just inside. Pat's Place could have just as accurately been called Pat's Dive. The building was cinder block, the door metal, without so much as one window. If cleaned of their layers of cigarette smoke, the lights would have been twice as bright, though the customers might not appreciate that. A fair number of them reminded him of nocturnal creatures—pale, squinty-eyed, furtive in their mannerisms.

He spotted Bailey right away, like a beacon in all that gloom. She was standing at the bar, a drink in hand, gazing around the room. She didn't pause for even an instant when she saw him but continued to scan the area. That was okay. She could ignore him, since everyone else was, and he could look at her, since everyone else was.

Finally he moved away from the door to a table in the darkest corner, sat with his back to the wall and watched. Escobar and company occupied a table at the edge of the dance floor, the top littered with empties and overflowing ashtrays. Besides three of the men from the night before, there were two other men and two women at the table, and everyone appeared to be having a good time.

Logan caught a waitress's eye and ordered a beer before Bailey set down her drink and purposefully pushed away from the bar. His gut tightened as he watched her approach Escobar, stopping beside him, resting her hand on the back of his chair. The light overhead gleamed off her hair and made the white of her shirt seem whiter while casting him in shadow. Bright and dark. Sunshine and shadow. Good and evil.

Evil. Logan had little doubt that Escobar was dirty. Whether he ran drugs, guns, cattle or people, whether he'd killed his wife and kids or had just terrorized her until she had no choice but to leave, whether he'd provided refuge for his fugitive brother, he was dirty and dangerous, and Logan wanted Bailey hell and gone from him. *Now.*

He remained in his seat, though, fingers gripping the beer bottle tightly enough to go numb. They were in the middle of the bar, surrounded by people, doing nothing more than talking. She was capable of taking care of herself. If she needed him, he was only ten yards away.

"I can provide an introduction if you'd like."

The voice coming from his right startled him. He'd been so focused on Bailey and Escobar that he hadn't noticed anyone taking the next table. Though he'd never seen the woman before, one glance confirmed who it was. Bailey had been right. Marisa Matthews did bear an eerie resemblance to her older sister. She toyed with her beer mug, looking put out.

"Is she intruding on your territory?"

She snorted. "The only way I'd get that close to Hector is if he was dead, so I could spit on him."

"Who is he?"

"A no-good lowlife." Her gaze widened, revealing a less-than-sober glint to her eyes. "Oh, sorry, that's what we all privately think. Publicly we're supposed to say he's a rancher, though it's an odd thing—he's got plenty of ranch hands but no livestock. Don't you think that's odd?"

Logan returned his gaze to Bailey. One of the men had pulled up a chair so she could join them. She was leaning forward, one arm propped on her knees, chin propped on that hand. So she wouldn't have to sit back, where Escobar's arm draped the wood back?

"Is she a friend of yours?"

Marisa shrugged. "Just met her. Thought she seemed smarter than to fall for him. She'll live to regret it…if she lives." Abruptly she put on a smile, goofy and out of focus. "I'm sorry. I shouldn't be talking about family like that, should I? Did I say that I'm Marisa? I am. Marisa Matthews. Welcome to Nomas. Pleased to meet you."

She swayed unsteadily toward him and he took her hand to steady her. "Nice to meet you, Marisa. Why don't you join me?" It didn't seem wise to give anyone a chance to overhear the sort of conversation she'd engaged in so far. Escobar would be pissed if he heard about it, and Logan suspected bad things happened to people who pissed him off.

With another of those goofy smiles, she brought her drink and moved unsteadily to the empty chair on his left, where she had a clear view of the center table.

"You said he was family," he prompted. "Really?"

"Really. Sort of. He's my brother—" a hiccup "—brother-in-law. We're not a close family."

There were several ways he could pursue that subject. He chose the one that led directly in the direction he wanted to go. "You're married to his brother?"

A wide-eyed look of horror crossed her face. "Good God, no. Have you ever met his brother? Of course you haven't. You're just passing through. M-Mac is—" another hiccup "—a-a toad. A cold-blooded snake. A-a low-down cur. A—"

"I get the picture." So Mac *had* been in Nomas and had either royally offended Marisa, or she was much more perceptive sober than Logan was. He gestured toward the table. "Which one is Mac?"

She squinted as if confused, then relaxed. "No, no, Mac isn't here. He just comes by from time to time. He's a pig. Looks as different from Hector as night from day, but they've got the same black heart."

"When was the last time Mac was here?"

Marisa lifted her glass, realized it was empty and signaled the waitress. She was opening her mouth when a new song started on the jukebox, and her face screwed up in a disgusted grimace. "Oh, jeez, now he's gonna ask her to dance. He is *so* predictable."

Sure enough, less than ten seconds into the song, Escobar stood up and offered his hand to Bailey. Her smile remained fixed in place as she took it and let him lead her onto the dance floor. It was a slow song, mournful, an excuse to hold her close. Logan watched her move and his mouth went dry, watched Escobar's beefy hand slide a few inches below her waist and every muscle tightened.

The waitress's arrival with Marisa's refill gave Logan the push he needed to force his attention away from Bailey. "You were telling me the last time Hector's brother was here."

Marisa took a sizable enough gulp of her drink to make *his* throat burn, then set the glass down with a thunk. "Hector's brother…oh, a couple months ago, maybe. He'll be back soon. Trouble always comes back, you know."

As the song on the jukebox dragged on, Logan hoped that was true.

Because this time he intended to be waiting.

Though her body remained relaxed and her expression was locked into some semblance of *pleasant,* all Bailey could think about was a hot, stinging shower with the strongest antiseptic her skin could stand. Just being close to Hector made her feel dirty; letting him actually touch her…

"How long are you gonna be in town?" he murmured loud enough for her to hear over the music.

"I don't know. I might stay."

"Anything I could do to help sway you that way?"

Not in this lifetime. She smiled the best she could. "I don't know. I'd have to think about that." Before he could narrow his offer down to specifics, she shifted the conversation to him. "Have you always lived here?"

"All my life."

"What do you do?"

"I have a ranch a few miles from here." He grinned, and despite everything, she recognized a certain charm to it. "Want to see it?"

"Not tonight. But maybe some other time." Sometime when she wanted to make Logan freak out, when she wanted to wonder about her own sanity. "Are you married?"

"Would I be here dancing with you if I had a wife?"

She gave him a chastising look that made him laugh.

"Okay. Yeah, I guess I am, but my wife took off about six years ago and I haven't seen or heard from her since."

"I'm sorry…or were you happy to see her go?"

His fingers tightened where they pressed against her, and his eyes turned nearly black. "She could be dead for all I care, except that she took my kids. I haven't seen them since either."

"I'm sorry." This time she more or less meant it. According to Marisa, most folks in town believed Shelley and the twins were dead, likely at Hector's hand, or that he had made her so miserable that she'd had no choice but to disappear with the kids. But there was a third option, she admitted now: he could be innocent of both murder and abuse. Shelley might not have been the victim she was painted as. She might have disappeared with the kids to punish him. It wasn't at all uncommon in divorces for noncustodial parents to take off with their kids not out of concern and love for the children but to strike back at their exes.

Personally, though, Bailey still liked the victim-with-no-choice theory. *She* would certainly be eager to escape Hector and she'd spent less than thirty minutes with him.

"Do you have family here? Parents, brothers, sisters?"

"My parents are dead. No sisters. I've got plenty of aunts, uncles and cousins, mostly across the border."

"And a brother?" At his raised brow, she said, "I asked about parents, brothers and sisters. You answered about parents and sisters."

He drew her a little closer, despite her best effort to maintain the distance between them. "I've got a brother. He comes and goes. Why the interest?"

She shrugged, said a silent prayer for forgiveness, then lied. "I don't have a family, so I'm always curious about people who do. I always thought it would be great to have a sister. We would be best friends and do everything together. Are you and your brother close?"

"Close enough. Stick around Nomas and you'll meet him before long. Though I'll warn you—his charm doesn't begin to compare to mine."

She could believe that, she thought as she stifled a shudder. After all, she only suspected Hector was capable of murder. She *knew* Mac was.

When the song finally came to an end, she pulled away when he would have held on. "I'm going to find the ladies' room."

"It's right back there." He pointed toward the corner where Logan sat. "Don't be long. I still haven't bought you that beer."

As if she would drink anything he set before her. But hiding the thought behind a smile, she nodded, then made her way around tables toward the corridor where a dim bulb illuminated the Restrooms sign. She was only a half dozen feet from the hallway when she could finally identify Logan at the dark corner table—and sitting beside him, Marisa. She looked done in, her eyes unfocused, her body limp, her head titled to one side.

"Marisa?" When she didn't respond, Bailey looked at Logan. "Is she all right?"

"She's drunk."

That made Marisa rouse. "Not so really," she said, her voice insubstantial. "How was your dance with the toad?"

"I'm glad it's over. You need to go home and get some rest."

"I know. I'm going." Instead of getting up, though, Marisa raised her glass to her mouth, turned it completely upside down, then squinted as if surprised to find it empty. Before she could return it to the tabletop, it slid from her limp grip and Logan caught it. Her mouth turned down in a frown. "No more drink." Then, after a big exhalation, she smiled. "I can order another. Yeah. Drinks all around. Lori Anne, hey, Lori—"

Bailey caught the hand she was waving to get the waitress's attention and lowered it to the table. "Marisa, you don't need another drink."

"Hey, you don't need a banana split, but do I tell you that when you order one? I just want one more…one last taste…one for the road…."

As Marisa tilted precariously in her chair, Logan caught her with one hand. "Are you through getting cheek to cheek with Hector?"

"Yes." She had no intention of joining him again tonight. Like anything dangerous, she figured it was best to strengthen her immunity to him by increasing her exposure gradually.

"I'll take her home. Follow me."

His offer to get Marisa home safely was exactly what some part of her expected…and took another part of her completely by surprise. He'd spent mere moments with Marisa, but was volunteering to look out for her just because she was drunk, while he'd left Bailey at the mercy of a drunk. But Bailey could take care of herself, he'd said, and Marisa looked fragile and vulnerable, two qualities sure to appeal to any macho man.

"I'll see you outside." She retraced her steps to the center table and bent close to Hector. "I'm not feeling really great. Loud music and smoke always get me. I'm going home."

"I'd be happy to give you a ride." Then he grinned suggestively. "I'd be happier to take you someplace quiet and not smoky."

"Thanks, but no. I don't want to put you out. I'll see you around."

"I'm sure you will, darlin'."

She reached the door in time to hold it open for Logan, half carrying Marisa. "Her car's over by mine," he muttered. She didn't respond but walked ahead to the car, buckled in, started the engine and watched as he easily lifted Marisa into the passenger seat of a dusty red Mustang. She backed out of her parking space, waited until he pulled out of his, then stayed a few car lengths behind him until they reached a neat little house in the center of a block only one street over from the drugstore where Marisa worked.

Logan pulled the Mustang into the driveway while Bailey waited at the curb. She didn't get out to help him get Marisa inside. If he wanted to play the hero tonight, he could do it on his own. Besides, Marisa was a skinny thing who could apparently eat all the banana splits she wanted without suffering the consequences. He didn't need any help from Bailey.

He was inside the house less than five minutes. He left a light burning in the living room, pulled the door shut behind him and jogged across the barren yard to the GTX. They were halfway to the motel when he broke the silence. "Did you learn anything?"

"Mac comes and goes. If I stick around Nomas, I'll meet him before long, but he's not nearly as charming as Hector."

"Marisa said the same thing—except for the charming part. She called him a cold-blooded snake, black-hearted and a low-down cur."

"You think maybe she doesn't like him?" She glanced at him but her sarcasm didn't so much as make his mouth twitch. Slumped in the passenger seat—halfhearted camouflage, since she was supposed to be in town alone, or legitimate fatigue?— he was staring blankly out the window.

"He offered to show me his ranch." Another glance showed no response to that either. "I told him some other time."

Another few blocks passed in silence before he finally spoke. "How long can you afford to be away from work?"

"As long as the agency's fee is getting paid. As long as it takes."

"And who's paying the agency's fee?"

This time it was she who chose not to respond. Lexy had offered to sign her check over to Bailey every payday—she worked part-time as a clerk in an antique store—but Bailey had turned her down with the assurance that she couldn't charge family. She'd paid the necessary expenses instead. A few hours' research here or there, a few phone calls—so far it hadn't amounted to much. Even now, she was using vacation time. But once that was gone, her boss fully expected her to pay the going rate, less an employee discount. She could afford it...for a while.

Naturally her silence didn't fool him at all. "You're doing the work for this niece *and* paying the costs? Just how big a chump are you, Madison?"

The question made her bristle as she turned into the motel lot, then followed the lane to their cabin. There she shut off the engine and the lights, then faced him. "You know what? The more time I spend with you, the more I understand why Brady hasn't tried to find you himself. After all, he *knows* you."

She got out, slammed the door, jerked it open again and shoved the lock button down, then slammed it even harder. She made it up the steps before Logan got out and was a few feet inside before he reached the stoop. A few feet was all she made, though. He caught her arm and swung her around to face him.

"Brady doesn't know shit about me," he said hotly, his voice sharp-edged and cold enough to send a chill through her. "And neither do you."

When they'd left for the bar, they had turned off the lights except for a dim bulb in the kitchen, and she hadn't turned them on when she'd burst inside. Now she stared at him in the near darkness, unable to identify anything but anger in his expression. "I know you feel responsible for Sam's and Ella's deaths and betrayed by Mac. He suckered you, and you resent it like hell. And I know you resent Brady for not going through what you did with your parents and Lexy for expecting you to behave like family and you *really* resent having to rely on me for anything."

He leaned a few inches closer, enough to invade her space, enough that she could smell him in every breath, could feel his heat, and he lowered his voice to a silky, soft tone that would have been sexy as hell if it wasn't so damn menacing. "Like I said, Madison, you don't know shit."

As he'd done once before, he shoved his hand in her jeans pocket, groped and came out with the car keys. He released her so abruptly that she staggered a step back, that a chill rushed over her in the absence of his heat, and he stalked toward the open door. Hugging herself, she muttered after him, "Some kind of hero you are."

He didn't slow his steps, didn't look back, didn't even close the door behind him. A moment later the car started with a roar, and a moment after that all was silent again.

Bailey stood where she was a long time. If she had any sense, she would pack her bags, get a ride to the nearest city and find her way home. She would tell Lexy she'd been unable to find her uncle or maybe even trust her niece with the truth that Logan wanted nothing to do with her. The kid was tough; she'd endured worse rejections in her fifteen years.

But there was no reason for her to endure *this* rejection. And Bailey had given her word that she would help Logan find Mac. His promises might mean nothing to him, but hers meant the world to her.

With a sigh, she closed the door and locked it, turned on the overhead light, then flipped on a lamp in the bedroom. She stripped out of her clothes, kicking everything into a smoky-scented heap in the corner, and gathered all the necessities for a shower.

All she really needed tonight was to feel clean again. She could deal with the rest in the morning.

Chapter 7

Some kind of hero.

According to the United States Army, Logan *was* a hero, with commendations, medals and scars to show for it. But that didn't matter much in the real world. Anyone could be heroic under fire; everyone's instinct for self-preservation was strong.

But in the real world he'd never wanted to be anyone's hero, including Bailey's. Especially hers. He didn't give a damn what she thought of him. Whether she respected him. Whether she despised him. All he cared about was getting Mac. Punishing Mac. And then…

Saying goodbye to Bailey? Making some sort of life for himself? Finding something he could do, someone he could be?

He was thirty-four years old. He should have some sort of future ahead of him. He should have plans…but his only plans would be fulfilled the day Mac died. Then there would be nothing left for him.

When he'd left the motel, he'd turned north, away from the town, and opened up the GTX, flying over the empty road at speeds in excess of a hundred miles per hour. If he could, he would drive all night and into the next day. He would drive until he ran out of road and then he just might make his own and drive on to the end of the earth.

But Bailey was at the motel alone, and if Hector didn't already know where she was staying, it would be easy enough to find out. She wasn't safe, and he wasn't sure she was smart enough to realize that. So after only fifteen miles of freedom he made a tight U-turn and headed south again, this time keeping it well within the speed limits. By the time he reached the motel again, he was calmer, though not by much. There was still a knot in his gut, still a tension that made his muscles ache and kept his senses on alert. Dread? Apprehension? Foreboding?

Lights shone in the cabin windows. Everything was quiet, with no vehicles that didn't belong, no people who didn't belong. He parked in the usual space, steeled himself to face her as soon as he walked in the door, then walked in…to an empty room. The air conditioner was turned to Low and the television was off. From the bedroom doorway he saw his bed, still made, and a pile of clothes on the floor.

The clothes Bailey had been wearing when he'd left.

He realized the shower was running an instant before it shut off. Since she was alone, she hadn't bothered to close the bathroom door; the scrape of metal curtain rings on a metal shower rod seemed to echo through the small space and into the bedroom. She was getting out…naked…and he couldn't move from the bedroom doorway, couldn't force his gaze from the bathroom doorway, to save his life.

The mirror was fogged over, reflecting nothing—a mercy, or maybe torture. The first thing he saw was the flip of a towel, then an expanse of long leg propped on the counter as slender hands rubbed the towel briskly. That leg disappeared, and the opposite one appeared for a moment before also dropping out of sight. There was some rustling and rubbing, a spray of deodorant, a dusting of baby-scented powder, then she stepped into the doorway wearing that tiny tank top that hugged her body and a pair of pale blue panties that revealed far more than they concealed. Her hair, towel-dried, swayed damply around her shoulders as she stopped abruptly.

He wished she was naked and thanked God she wasn't. Already he was so hard that it hurt. He couldn't swallow, couldn't think or move or speak. Could only want.

She didn't move or speak either but just watched him warily. Some kind of hero, she'd called him in that scornful, disappointed tone. Neither his absence nor her shower had improved her opinion of him, if that look was anything to judge by.

But he could change it—if he touched her, if he kissed her, if he tried. He could make her forget he wasn't the man she wanted him to be, at least for a few hours, but then she would go back to being disappointed and he…he would be tempted to try to be that man. That hero.

God help him, he couldn't.

Moving—and not toward her—was the hardest thing he'd done. Everything in him wanted to cross the room, slide his hands into her hair, fill her mouth, fill *her,* fill himself. He wanted to take her, to crawl inside her and never come out, to lose himself in her warmth and trust and peace.

But warmth turned cold, trust died and peace was nothing but an illusion.

His movements wooden and stiff, he walked to the bed, keeping his back to her, and pulled back the covers, then kicked off his shoes. "Close the door when you go out, would you?" His voice sounded hollow, as if it was coming from someplace other than him.

The door closed with a solid thunk, and he breathed a sigh of relief. If she was the least bit spiteful, she would have known how easily she could torment him by dallying, but she wasn't. He pulled his shirt over his head, unbuckled his belt and laid the pistol on the nightstand, then unzipped his jeans. Something alerted him an instant too late that he wasn't alone, then her long, cool fingers touched his back. His scars.

"Why did they beat you?" she murmured softly as her fingertips moved across his skin, so light he barely felt them, gliding from one scar to another.

"Because they were mean bastards who enjoyed inflicting pain." Again his voice was different—harsh, guttural, as if coming from someone else. He wasn't bitter about his parents. They were dead to him, and had been for years.

Her touch was more substantial now, rubbing rather than brushing, leaving the scars for the taut muscles in his neck. "Why did they choose you?"

His eyes drifted shut as his head automatically tilted to one side, giving her better access to the cramped muscles. "What do you mean?"

"Why did they beat you and not Brady?"

The mention of his brother was like a shower of ice water. He opened his eyes, shrugged away from her touch and turned to face her. "Let's get one thing straight, Madison. You want to stay in this room, we won't be talking about Brady. In fact, if you want to stay in this room, you'd better be prepared to ditch those clothes, get in that bed and put your mouth to far better use than talking. Understand?"

Her gaze flickered down to his erection straining toward her beneath tight denim, then shifted back to his face. Even without makeup, with her hair wet and clinging, she was quite possibly the most beautiful woman he'd ever seen. Her features were fine, her skin delicate gold, her mouth too kissable and her eyes...

Her eyes were the last thing he saw as she leaned forward, glided her fingers into his hair, then fitted her mouth over his. She slid her tongue inside, probing, tasting, and just like that his body went hot, his blood sizzling. He staggered a step or two, until the wall was against his back, then he slid his hands to her bottom, callused palms against bare skin, and lifted her against him, rubbing, pressing, wanting....

Then she was gone.

It took several tries to get his eyes open, to focus them on her, standing a few feet away, looking hot and wanton, looking like exactly what he needed. Her eyes were glazed, her lips soft and parted, her nipples swollen beneath the thin cotton of her top. Arousal surged through him, until he thought he might explode or burst into flames or both if he didn't touch her, kiss her, spend the next hundred days and nights inside her.

She blinked, drew a breath, then said, "No."

"No?" he repeated dumbly.

"I don't sleep with men too afraid to deal with their pasts."

I don't sleep with men... She was turning him down. Looking the way she looked, kissing him the way she'd kissed him, and she was refusing his invitation. He was about to combust, thanks to her, and she didn't give a damn. Anger surged through him, forcing him to remain where he was, to keep his hands at his sides and away from her throat. "The past is over and done with," he said, grinding out the words, the tightness in his chest and the lump in his throat translating into raw hoarseness. "There's nothing to deal with. Even if there was, it wouldn't be any of your damn business."

"It's not over and done with. You can't even talk about your brother."

"Because he means nothing to me. Like his daughter. Like you."

His barb hit its target, making her flinch, but so slightly he would have missed it if he hadn't been watching. It gave him some measure of satisfaction...and something that felt oddly like shame.

"Obviously he means something or you wouldn't be so hostile nineteen years after last seeing him."

"You don't know when to give up, do you, Madison? Let me make it real clear for you. I'm going to start counting, and if you're not out of here by the time I reach five, you're not getting out, not tonight. I haven't had sex in one hell of a long time and I'd be more than happy to let you be the first."

Something passed through her eyes—desire?—as she hesitantly moistened her lips with the tip of her tongue. "You wouldn't force me."

"I wouldn't have to force you." As proof, he freed one hand from its grip, laid his palm against her cheek, rubbed his thumb over her lips. Her lashes fluttered to half-mast, then closed completely as he slid his fingertips down her throat, across soft skin, over the swell of her breast, then cupped the weight in his hand, gently teasing her nipple between his thumb and forefinger. Her skin flushed and grew warm, her nipple hardened even more and a soft, pleasured sigh escaped her before he let go. He gave her a moment to recover, to realize he'd stopped, then harshly said, "Get in bed or get out."

Her eyes opened, and the dazed look was gone, replaced with mocking. "Such a romantic invitation. How can I possibly refuse?" Her smile was mean-spirited, no less than he deserved. "But I must be stronger than I realized, because I am refusing. Good night, Logan."

She turned and walked away, and a groan choked him. He vaguely remembered rubbing her against his erection and feeling nothing across her bottom but soft, warm skin, and now he saw why—she wore a thong, a little scrap of lace and fabric in front, next to nothing in back. It was an amazingly erotic sight and it was going to keep him aroused for the next month.

She crossed into the living room, started to close the door, then peeked around with it with a knowing smile. "Sweet dreams."

As she made up her bed on the sofa, Bailey was rewarded with a hoarsely muttered, "Damn you, Madison. I hope you burn tonight."

He probably meant in hell, she thought with a grim smile, but her body had its own ideas about the sort of fire it wanted. She was hot, achy and throbbing all over and felt cheated that she got the torment without the payoff. She could take care of herself—the familiar phrase made her send a scowl Logan's way—but that wouldn't begin to satisfy her. Multiple nights—and multiple days—with Logan would.

Except they'd each agreed the other was worthy of one night

and no more. Maybe they could reassess that decision…. Sure. And while she was it, she could also call up Hector and say, *I've changed my mind about seeing your ranch. Let me throw on a pair of shoes and I'll be right there.*

After all, she admitted as she shut off the lights, then slid between the sheets, she couldn't honestly say one man was more dangerous to her than the other.

Once her body temperature had cooled, once the slightest brush of the covers against her breasts had stopped sending tingles all the way through her, Bailey had slept surprisingly well. When she awakened Saturday morning, the sun was doing its best to pierce the curtains over the east-facing windows, sending sharp, bright angles of light through each gap, and the smell of coffee was drifting in from the kitchen. She turned onto her side as Logan came around the corner, mug in one hand, the other filled with dry cereal to munch.

His hair was damp from a recent shower, his jaw stubbled with beard that gave him a faintly disreputable—and overwhelmingly sexy—look. He wore jeans that slid low over lean hips, but no shirt. His chest was smooth brown, all muscle and bone and perfection. What a shame that the back view was nothing but scars. His parents would certainly be damned to eternal hell for the pain they'd caused him, but she hoped they'd suffered here on earth, as well, hoped they missed their sons and their grandchildren and were miserably unhappy each and every day they lived.

Adding a sofa pillow to the bed pillow beneath her head, she settled comfortably, then said, "Good morning."

His glance her way was brief—too brief even to see that she was covered from neck to toe. There was discomfort in his expression, his manner. Was he regretting that she hadn't slept with him last night? More likely he regretted that he'd even wanted her to. After all, she meant nothing to him.

But that was okay. She didn't *want* to mean anything to him. She just wanted to keep her promise to Lexy and her promise to Logan, and most of all she wanted to keep her promises to herself—that she would get the experience needed to get out of the office and into the field. That she would prove her abilities. That she would be established in her career before getting seriously involved with a man. That when she did fall for a man, he would be her perfect type—easygoing, easily managed, easily loved and, if necessary, easily forgotten.

It didn't take a brilliant P.I. to know that Logan was none of the above.

"How did you sleep?" she asked, perversely cheerful as she slid into a sitting position, letting the covers fall to her waist.

"I didn't," he muttered, still standing near the kitchenette, still holding the coffee and cereal as if he'd forgotten what they were for.

"Too bad. I slept like a rock. Want to go somewhere today?"

Finally he looked at her—really looked. Rather, really scowled. "Where?"

"I don't know. Deming. Las Cruces. Someplace that isn't here."

"What about Mac?"

"We know he's not in town at the moment. If he shows up while we're gone, well, hell, we'll be back tonight. He'll still be here."

He looked as if he wanted to refuse but couldn't quite force the words out. Maybe he wanted to see something other than the motel room for a while. Maybe he felt the same need for a break that she did. Or maybe he just couldn't think of a good reason to refuse.

Whatever, he responded with a shrug that made all that smooth brown skin ripple and left her throat parched. She managed to swallow as she pushed the covers back. "J-just let me get dressed and—" Modesty struck about a half instant after he abruptly turned away. It had been one thing to sashay her mostly naked butt across the bedroom last night; he'd been such a jerk that he'd deserved it. But in the cold light of morning, with Marisa's comment about the banana split still on her mind, wrapping up like a mummy in her covers seemed by far the best choice.

She tripped her way into the bedroom, closed the door and tossed the covers on the bed, then hastily dressed in a short white denim skirt and a sleeveless chambray shirt with tails that tied just above the waist. After a quick French braid and a go-round with the cosmetics that filled her bag, she put on a pair of high-heeled sandals that made her legs look a mile longer, spritzed on perfume, then returned to the living room. "I'm ready."

He turned to look at her, and a pained expression crossed his face. Rummaging through the larger of her two handbags, he pulled out the .45, crossed to her and pressed it into her hand. "Go ahead and shoot me now, would you?"

She looked at the gun, then back at him. He looked so hard, so tough and unyielding…but he wasn't. Shifting the pistol to the other hand, she smiled nicely. "If you'd rather stay here and talk…"

Oh, he'd rather stay, all right, but just like last night, *talk* didn't make the list of things he wanted to do. Looking even more pained, he shook his head, mumbled something about dressing, then went into the bedroom. While she waited, she returned the pistol to her bag, sipped the coffee he'd left on the table, then munched on a handful of cereal. When he came back, he wore a gray T-shirt that read ARMY across the chest in faded black letters, had added running shoes and combed his hair into some sort of style.

Since he had the keys, Bailey left him to lock up while she took the steps two at a time. She was halfway to the car when a cheery voice called, "Good morning. I haven't seen you around much…."

Looking up, she saw Faith, the motel owner, coming from the cabin next door. Her words had trailed off because she'd just noticed Logan, standing motionless at the top of the steps. Well, this was awkward…and careless and incredibly stupid. It could have just as easily been Marisa or Hector standing outside—or, with her luck, Hector and Mac. Her cheeks warming, Bailey took a few steps toward the woman. "Good morning. I, uh, I've been around. Looking around town, talking to some people."

"Getting to know some better than others," Faith murmured with a pointed look at Logan.

"I, uh, was just giving him a ride back to his car." Her blush was heating into a full-fledged fire, and even Logan's cheeks were turning bronze under Faith's measuring look.

"In exchange for the ride he gave you?" Faith smiled. "Don't look so shocked. I was single once myself…a long time ago. I'd say have a good time, but you look like you already have. By the way—" she came nearer, then lowered her voice conspiratorially "—where did you find him? I might go looking myself next time my husband's out of town."

"Uh, we met at P-Pat's Place."

"Hmm. You are some kind of lucky. A man like that comes into Pat's only once in a blue moon. Usually the best they get is Hector Escobar and his crew, and that ain't no competition." With a glance at her watch, Faith's teasing disappeared. "Sheesh, I'd better get to work so I can get the kids to their karate class on time. See you." Then she turned a sly smile and a wink on Logan. "Hope to see you again."

Bailey returned her smile and wave, then gave a sigh of relief as the woman passed their cabin and went into the next one.

"Jeez." That was all Logan said as he settled in the car behind the wheel. It was enough.

They drove mile after mile without conversation. The windows were down, the sun was shining and the temperature was still quite pleasant. It was almost like a normal Saturday…except that she was hundreds of miles from home, and instead of running usual Saturday morning errands, she was going out for the day with a man who wanted her but didn't much like her, and instead of her usual lazy Saturday evening at home, she would probably be heading back to Pat's Place for another cheek-to-cheek with Hector. Just the thought of it was enough to make her skin crawl.

Yep, just a normal Saturday…not.

She had no idea how far they'd gone when Logan abruptly slowed, then turned onto a narrow mountain road that snaked its way around sharp curves and bumped over dry streambeds as it climbed, dipped, then climbed some more. They passed an occasional house, usually shabby, more often than not with rusted vehicles decorating the yard. After a time they reached the crest of that particular mountain. Though the road continued, Logan pulled off to the side, shut off the engine and got out of the car. Curiously Bailey followed him.

The place had expansive views to the southeast and northwest—mile after mile of desert and mountain. There was a stark beauty to it—the subdued shades, the sparse growth, the absence of towns—but she found herself wishing for an oasis of lush green grass, of oaks, maples and elms and shockingly colored flowers. She wanted to see not just survival but abundant, bounteous, thriving life.

Like the desert, Logan was just surviving. He needed a reason to live, something more than avenging the Jensens' deaths. Maybe Brady and Lexy could help him with that. Maybe when he got to know the family he'd denied, he would find that reason.

She would be lying if she didn't admit that some tiny foolish place inside her would like to be part of that reason. After all, what woman *wouldn't* like being part of an incredibly sexy, handsome, dangerous man's reason for living? To be that important to someone, that special…a woman could put her career aspirations on the back burner for something like that.

But the odds of her being Logan's someone were somewhere between slim and none. He didn't even like her. She wasn't looking. They might have great sex, but anything else between them was unlikely.

He stared out over the valley a long time before moving to lean against the front fender. "How long have you known Brady?"

She caught her breath. Was that the first time he'd brought his brother into the conversation? The first time he'd willingly discussed him? "We met at Neely's wedding a little more than a year ago."

"So you don't know him well."

She hated to agree with him. She loved Brady for being a good father, and for treating Hallie the way she deserved to be treated. She loved him for being good and decent when he'd been raised by people who were anything but. But the truth was, Logan was right. She didn't know Brady as well as she would like. "I live in Tennessee. They're in Oklahoma. I don't see them as often as I wish I could."

Circling the car, she stopped a few yards in front of him. "If you're going to tell me something ugly about him, I'll tell you right now, I won't believe it of the man I know."

Logan gazed someplace beyond her—nineteen years into the past? "I don't know anything ugly about him. He was damn near perfect. A goddamn hero."

She couldn't think of anything to say to that. It wasn't the words that left her so blank but the emotion on his face, in his voice. Bitterness, anger, hatred and guilt…so much guilt. Whatever had happened between him and his brother to create such guilt in him, she'd seen no sign of it in Brady. He missed his brother and had—despite her angry words the night before—made several efforts to locate him. He didn't blame Logan for anything that she could tell.

"You asked last night why our parents beat me and not Brady… They did. Longer. Harder. He's probably got scars that make mine look like nothing but scratches."

Bailey had known Brady was estranged from his parents; even Lexy, who'd known the Marshalls in the years she'd lived with Sandra, refused to talk about them. She also recalled that during several visits to Buffalo Plains, they'd had family cookouts around the Marshall family pool, where everyone had gone in except Brady. She'd just assumed he didn't like the water, but maybe he was more self-conscious of his scars than Logan was.

"So…if he wasn't the favorite son, why do you resent him?"

"One day I broke one of the rules. I didn't go straight home after school and I lied about it. I did it on purpose. I was so damn tired of everything. I knew they'd punish me and I didn't care. But Brady told them he did it. I denied it, but they didn't believe me. They beat him damn near to death…because of me. I left that night and I never went back."

"And you've never forgiven yourself."

He pushed away from the car and walked to the far edge of the road, his back to her. "Damn straight I haven't. He had no right—" Abruptly he turned back to her. "Myself? I've never forgiven *him*. It was none of his damn business. I didn't ask him to interfere or to lie and take the blame. I didn't need his protection."

"But he needed to give it."

"That's his problem, not mine."

"I beg to differ. He took *your* beating and damn near died for it, and you feel guilty as hell for it. You can't forgive yourself, so you blame him instead. That makes it your problem."

It also explained his unwillingness to step in at the bar Wednesday night. He'd hated being rescued himself so much that he wasn't going to rescue someone else unless there was absolutely no choice. She'd never been in any real danger at the bar; if she had, he would have intervened, just as he'd said he would the next day.

She aimed for a conciliatory tone. "Look, I understand guilt and shame—"

Heat flared in his eyes. "I never said I felt guilty or ashamed."

"Yes, you did. Not in so many words, but it's in your eyes, in your face, in your voice."

Muttering an obscenity, he forced his features into a cold, dark scowl. "I have nothing to feel guilty for."

"I agree. Brady knew what he was doing. He knew the consequences and he suffered them. For you. And that's kept you running all these years."

"I'm not running. I'm living my own life away from people I don't give a damn about."

"If you didn't give a damn about your brother, we wouldn't be having this conversation." She really believed he cared less than nothing about his parents. He'd left their home, their town and *them* nearly twenty years ago and he'd never looked back. Never regretted it. He talked about them as dispassionately as if they were total strangers…but not Brady.

He crossed his arms over his chest and said belligerently, "You're wrong."

"I guess we'll find out soon enough, when I take you to Buffalo Plains for a visit."

A look flickered through his eyes, gone in the time it took him to open, then close his mouth. He still intended to break his word and disappear once Mac had been taken into custody. He couldn't have made it any plainer if he'd gone through with saying so aloud. And she still intended to hold him to it, even if it meant locking him in the Plymouth's trunk for the long drive.

"You know," he said snidely, "you can go home now, and I'll give you a call when I'm on my way to Oklahoma."

"There's a call that'll never come," she murmured with a roll of her eyes, then patiently said, "I can't go home. You need my help."

"Not anymore. Not now that I've met Marisa. I bet she'd be more than happy to let me know when Mac shows up. She would even let me move in with her if I asked."

Bailey wondered if Marisa had said or done something the previous night to make him so sure of himself. It would be typical of her luck that while *she* was enduring Hector's all-too-close company, Logan was getting hit on by a reasonably attractive woman who he had no reason to dislike.

But he'd still gone back to the cabin with *her,* a petty voice whispered. He'd still come on to *her.*

"Marisa's already lost her sister, niece and nephew because of Hector. You can't ask her to risk her life just because you have a vendetta against his brother."

"But it's okay to ask *you* to risk your life."

Would it matter to him if something happened to her? Sure, but only because of that guilt he insisted he didn't have. He would feel responsible because she was helping him, but that was all. There wouldn't be any personal aspect to it—no regret or missing her or mourning what might have been.

"I'm a professional," she said quietly. "I carry a gun. I'm an expert at self-defense. I don't have a personal investment in this case. I'm strong." Marisa couldn't hold her own against a gust of wind, and she'd suffered so much emotionally with her family's disappearance. Bailey, on the other hand, could hold her own against anyone.

Logan came a few steps closer. "You didn't answer the question. Is it okay to ask you to risk your life to carry out my vendetta against Mac?"

Did he want a positive answer to assuage his guilt? Or a negative one, to strengthen it? She settled for the truth as she saw it. "I'm not risking my life. I'm doing the job I trained for. I can take care of myself, and if all else fails, I've got you. And just so we're really clear on this, I'm not doing this for you, Logan, so if anything does go wrong, you won't have to feel responsible. I'm here because of Lexy. No other reason."

He stared at her a long time, his expression utterly blank. Finally he moved toward the car, jerked open the door and said testily, "Let's go."

She walked around to the passenger door, said a silent prayer for patience, then climbed in.

This was promising to be *such* a fun day.

Okay, Logan admitted to himself. So he felt guilty. He'd been looking to piss off his parents all those years ago, had deliberately provoked them, but he hadn't meant for Brady to suffer for it. Hell, over time he'd done his share of turning Jim and Rita's wrath from Brady onto himself. They weren't as hard on him as they were on Brady, and it meant less to him than it did to Brady. His brother had still felt some stupid connection to Jim and Rita—after all, they were *family*. Logan figured *he'd* lost all faith in that concept sometime before he was five.

But his feeling guilty didn't absolve Brady. He should have kept his damn mouth shut. He shouldn't have interfered. Logan hadn't cared about the impending beating. What was one more in a lifetime of them?

But it hadn't been just *one more*. When they were finished with him, Brady had been in and out of consciousness. Logan had half carried, half dragged him to bed, where he'd done his best to stop the bleeding and doctor the injuries. It hadn't been easy when every touch had made Brady moan, when tears had blurred his vision. When Brady had passed out, for one hellish moment Logan had thought he was dead and he'd decided then that it had to end. Either he would leave or he would kill his parents.

Since Brady wasn't dead, Logan had opted for leaving. He'd packed what he could carry and he'd walked away without a single regret.

Except that he'd been responsible for Brady's worst beating ever.

Except that he was leaving his brother behind to be the sole target for Jim's and Rita's rage.

Except that his brother had damn near died because of him, and this was the thanks he got.

But, damn Bailey Madison to hell, he didn't feel guilty for it!

They were on the outskirts of Las Cruces before he realized it. They crossed the Rio Grande, then he exited the interstate and drove a few aimless miles before finally looking Bailey's way. She hadn't spoken since they'd gotten back in the car, since she'd made their situation *really* clear. *I'm not doing this for you.*

He knew that, damn it, and he didn't care. The only thing that mattered to him was getting Mac. *Nothing* about Bailey was important.

Yeah, right.

Though her spine was straight, her chin lifted, she looked comfortable and not at all as if she was pouting. Her legs were crossed, exposing more long, tanned skin than he needed to see, and she was gazing out the window as if the scenery actually interested her. Dark glasses hid her eyes, but her mouth was curved up slightly, as though she was already halfway to a smile and just waiting for a reason to let it form. She looked…

Giving a grim shake of his head, he refused to finish the thought and distracted himself instead. "Where do you want to go?"

That was the reason. She looked at him and the smile damn near blossomed. "I don't know. Are you hungry?"

He thought about it a moment. "Yeah, I am."

She turned back to the view. "Then pick a place and stop. I'm easy to please."

"Sure you are," he muttered.

That earned him another quick look and a brighter smile.

After driving past several fast-food places, he turned into the parking lot of a shabby diner that had definitely seen better days. The plate glass windows were covered with hand-painted signs advertising their breakfast specials, the parking lot was practically full and the air was redolent with the smells of bacon, onions and grease when they walked in the door. He half expected Bailey to turn up her nose at the place, though he wondered why. She hadn't done any real complaining yet—not when he'd dragged her out of bed hours before she was ready, refused to stop to eat or kept her going long after a reasonable person would stop. All in all, she'd been as flexible and agreeable a partner as he could have hoped for.

They claimed the only empty booth and she picked up the plastic-encased menu but didn't look at it. "When I was a kid, my parents used to take us to a place like this every Saturday morning for breakfast. Mom and Dad sat in a booth, and my sisters and I got stools at the counter. The four of us always ordered the same thing—a pecan waffle, hash browns and a slice of ham—and then we'd trade around. Neely and Kylie ate all the waffles, Hallie took the ham and I ate everyone's hash browns."

"And you can still eat banana splits," he said drily. He'd caught the narrowing of her eyes when Marisa had made the insult the night before. Whether it was the booze, jealousy or just spite talking, the woman couldn't have been more wrong. There was absolutely nothing wrong with Bailey's body…and he'd seen enough of it to know that for a painful, sleep-robbing fact.

Before she could respond, he changed the subject. "That's the first time you've mentioned parents, besides explaining how you got your names."

"Did you think we came from a test tube somewhere?" She turned her attention away from him long enough to order—the usual—then waited until the waitress had left to resume the conversation. "Of course we had parents."

"Had? No longer have?" Not that he cared. But as long as he kept the conversation centered around her, she couldn't turn it back to him.

"Our mother lives in Illinois. Our father was murdered years ago, when I was a kid."

That startled him. Most people had no personal experience with murder. When they told him how sorry they were about Sam and Ella, that they knew just how he felt, he'd known it wasn't true. Unless they'd been through it themselves, the best they could do was guess. But Bailey *knew.* "What happened?" he asked quietly.

She pulled off the paper band that secured her napkin around the silverware, then toyed with it, rolling it around her finger, folding it, wrapping it into a narrow tube. "He was framed for murdering his boss. After seven years in prison, his name was cleared, but not before another inmate killed him."

"I'm sorry." Such useless words. He'd hated hearing them from others, but maybe his *knowing* gave them some meaning.

She smiled faintly. "I know." She watched the waitress approach with an armful of plates, which she set between them before hurrying off to take another order. Bailey sorted through them, sliding his heart-attack special across the table to him—two eggs over easy, bacon, sausage, hash browns, pancakes, biscuit and gravy—and claiming her own three dishes.

"That's why Neely became a lawyer," she went on as she sprinkled salt over her potatoes. "Because Dad got a really lousy deal. We couldn't afford a lawyer, and his public defender was neither competent nor interested. That's why I decided to be a lawyer, too, though it was no surprise to anyone that it didn't work out."

"Why?"

"After Dad went to jail, our mother kind of fell apart. That left Neely to be the manager, the caretaker, the negotiator, the arbitrator, and she did it very well. She could talk anybody into anything. I, on the other hand, tended to do my persuading with my fists, and I also did it very well. I got into more fights…"

It was hard to imagine Bailey of the short skirts, tight blouses, thongs, lacy bras and pierced belly as a rough-and-tumble tomboy defending the family honor. She was so damn womanly. But hadn't he been telling her as well as himself that she could take care of herself?

"So you were a tough kid."

"Who grew into a tough woman—and don't you forget it."

Though she feigned a fierce look, *tough* was the farthest thing from his mind when he looked at her. Soft, maybe. Definitely desirable. Beautiful, without a doubt. *I'm strong,* she'd said that morning on the mountaintop, and he believed her, now more than ever.

It was a good thing, too, because he was feeling pretty damn weak. He was feeling tempted to try to be the man she wanted him to be, just so he could be the man she *wanted.*

It was just sex, he reminded himself. He'd gone without for months at a time—a year while he was in Afghanistan, another year in Iraq. He'd never been tempted to compromise who and what he was in order to get it. It was too easy to find, with women too easy to forget.

But it wasn't some forgettable woman who'd brought his libido back to life or who'd kept him tossing and turning all last night or who'd disturbed what little sleep he did get with erotic dreams.

And the very last word he would associate with Bailey Madison was *easy.*

Seeking control, he forced his attention back to the subject of the Madison sisters. "So Neely's a lawyer, and you're a private investigator. What do the others do?"

"Hallie's currently a wife and mom, and Kylie...I don't know exactly what it is Kylie does—something involving finance and corporations. Neither math nor business being my strong suits, I always zone out when she starts talking."

"What did Hallie do before she married..." It was stupid, but saying his brother's name out loud didn't come easy, not when he'd avoided it for more than half his life. Part of it, he suspected, was the fear that if he got used to saying the name, before long he would get used to the idea of seeing him, of having him in his life again—which was exactly what Bailey intended.

"Before she married Brady?" she finished for him.

"Before she married his bucks."

For a time she stared at him, her expression part offense—presumably at the suggestion that her sister would marry for money—and part amusement. The amusement won out, evidenced by an ear-to-ear grin. "You think your brother's money mattered to Hallie? Oh, please. My sister made a fine art out of marrying well and divorcing better. Her last marriage left her with more money than she and Brady could spend in a lifetime."

"Just how many times has she been married?"

Her grin disappeared, and she concentrated intently on cutting the perfect square of waffle, with just the right amounts of butter and maple syrup. "Brady's...number..." Her mumble became almost unintelligible as she chewed the bite.

"Number four? Is that what you said? Holy sh—" at her sharp look, he substituted "—cow. First he marries Sandra the conniving bitch and then a three-time loser? Just how big an idiot is he?"

Bailey swallowed, very carefully set her fork down, very carefully patted her mouth with her napkin, then fixed a glare on him. He imagined it was the same look she'd worn back when she was a kid and about to defend the family name, though this time she would use words rather than her fists. "My sister is *not* a loser," she said stiffly. "She went into every marriage with the hopes and dreams and intentions of making it last, and every time these men who promised to love her forever screwed her royally. But she loves Brady more than anything, and he loves her, and this time it really will be forever. You'll see that when you meet them…if you're even capable of recognizing true love and commitment."

"I don't even believe in it," he muttered as he returned to his breakfast.

"Bull. Did Sam love Ella? Was she committed to him?"

The questions sent a pain straight through him. Sam and Ella had been like two halves of the same person. He'd finished her sentences; she'd anticipated his every need. They'd shared so many years, so many memories, that when one of them had said, "Remember that time…?" the other had known immediately *which* time, out of the thousands they had in common.

She didn't make him answer because she knew the answers and knew he did, too. "That's how Hallie and Brady are. You'll see."

No, he wouldn't. He didn't know what his future held, but he did know it wouldn't be the past. Getting reacquainted with Brady didn't rank much higher than going back to Marshall City and dropping in on Jim and Rita. It would be pointless. Painful.

And he'd had enough pain for ten lifetimes.

And enough guilt for twenty.

"Enough about your family," he said, sliding his plate of hash browns across the table to her, then spearing a piece of her ham. "What are your plans for Hector?"

Chapter 8

Unfortunately never seeing Hector again wasn't an option, Bailey groused as she studied her reflection in the bathroom mirror that evening. Unless she wanted to truly take up residence in Nomas, she needed to not just see him but talk to him, draw him out, find out anything he was willing to share about his brother. He'd already told her Mac wasn't in town; now if he would just tell her where he was….

As satisfied as she was going to get, she left the bathroom and went into the living room, where Logan was waiting at the front window, peering out through a gap in the curtains. He wore his usual jeans and dark T-shirt, with a black leather jacket to cover the pistol holstered on his belt, and he looked quiet and sexy and dangerous—and that was from the back. Heat was kindling in her belly, waiting for that instant when he turned and she would see his beard-stubbled jaw, hard, sensuous mouth, intense dark eyes.

"I'm ready," she announced. Ready to go, ready to face him. "How do I look?"

He turned, his gaze sliding over her, and the intensity ratcheted up a few notches. "Do you have to wear that shirt?"

She glanced down. The shirt was red, sleeveless, cotton with a bit of stretch to it so it clung snugly but wore comfortably. It more than modestly covered her breasts and was suitable for anything from a date to shopping to church. It had the added benefit of covering the stud in her navel. Something told her Hector would *really* like that stud. "I considered going without it, but I figured that was probably a bad idea."

Not even the faintest hint of a grin twitched his lips. "What's wrong with that T-shirt you were wearing the other day?"

She shrugged into his jean jacket, then slung her small purse over her head and one shoulder. "Tell me, Logan—when I was wearing that T-shirt, did it stop you from noticing my breasts or any other part of my body?"

"No," he grudgingly admitted.

"So why would it stop Hector? And why are we even discussing this? It's not as if you care." She figured he would send her into the bar wearing nothing but the tiniest and laciest of her bras and a matching thong if it would get him Mac's current location…but it would be nice to think he'd be jealous when he did it.

It would be nice to think he cared. Just a little.

When he offered no argument to her last statement, she swallowed a little sigh. "Is it clear outside?"

"Yeah."

"Then let's head out." Leaving a light burning in the kitchen, she followed him outside and locked up. He moved through the darkness so stealthily that she could have missed him herself if she hadn't known he was there, easing into the backseat, not closing the passenger door until the same moment she closed her door.

After their late breakfast in Las Cruces, they'd hit the mall for a lot of window-shopping with very little buying, then joined a crowd for a Saturday-afternoon movie. They'd had another late meal before making a leisurely drive back to Nomas, bypassing the interstate in favor of narrow, lesser-used roads. It had been an…interesting day, she decided. They'd been almost like friends…if friends could ever have so much distance between them.

But now it was business as usual. He would spend another portion of the evening sitting in a dark corner, going unnoticed, while she would be on stage, so to speak. Front and center with Hector Escobar, the best Nomas had to offer, according to Faith at the motel. What a sad commentary on the town.

When she pulled into the parking lot at Pat's, she murmured, "Hector's already here. So are his partners in crime. And, gee, there's Marisa's Mustang. Don't get so involved with her that you forget your reason for being here."

"She's not my type," he muttered.

"Huh. I thought your type was anyone living, breathing and willing to settle for nothing." She pulled the visor down and brushed her hair back from her face. "Wait five minutes. If I don't come back, it's safe to come in."

"Yeah. Be careful."

"Hey, I got you this far. I'm not going to blow it."

The impatience in his voice sounded clear and strong in the darkness. "That's not what I meant. Just…be careful."

"Yeah." She gave her reflection a subdued smile. "You, too."

She strolled into the bar as if there weren't ten thousand other places she'd rather be, smiling at the waitress who greeted her, giving a nod in response to Hector's wave, then stopping at the bar to order a beer. As the bartender delivered it, Marisa slipped onto the stool next to her. "Hi."

"Hey." Bailey turned to look at her, finding her none the worse for last night's binge. "How do you feel?"

"I'm fine. Just had a little too much last night."

"That's an understatement. You do that often?"

Marisa shrugged, then smiled halfheartedly. "It wasn't all bad. A gorgeous stranger took me home. Couldn't get him to stay, though. Just my luck." A dramatic sigh punctuated the words.

So she *had* said or done something to give Logan the impression he would be welcome at her house. Bailey had the urge to pour the beer she hadn't yet tasted over Marisa's head or shove her off the stool and onto the floor, but instead she smiled tightly. "Who knows? Maybe you'll get a second chance." That would be just *her* luck.

Marisa sat silently for a moment before glancing at her. "I saw you with Hector last night."

Bailey's answer was airy, careless. "Yeah. He offered to buy me a beer and asked me to dance."

"He's not worth it."

"Not worth what?"

"Risking your life. He can be charming, I guess—Shelley always thought so—but charm doesn't do much for a black eye or cracked ribs."

Bailey eased onto the stool she'd leaned against, then swiveled around to face her. "Hey, I'm not going to marry the guy or even go to bed with him. It was just a beer and a dance. Tonight it'll just be conversation."

"Tonight you should keep your distance," Marisa insisted. "If you really want a guy, try…" She turned to scan the bar, passing over Hector and his boys, pausing on a man alone in a booth, then stopping at the door. "*Him.* The gorgeous stranger who took me home last night."

Gorgeous was right, Bailey admitted as she looked at Logan. Tall, dark, lethal…he was enough to make any woman swoon.

Deliberately she turned back to the bar and her drink. "I don't think so. I'm not his type."

"I watched him watching you last night. You were the only woman in the place who *was* his type. He looked like he wanted nothing more than to carry you off and never come up for air."

The image made Bailey's throat go dry, and a sip of beer didn't help. She swallowed hard instead, then dredged up another careless smile. "You were drunk. Seeing things. Besides, he's not *my* type." *Liar.* "Go on. Here's your second chance. Move in on him before someone else does."

Though if she had any success, Bailey would have to hurt both of them. Badly.

"That's okay," Marisa said. "He's not staying and I'm not leaving. Not until my sister comes home. No use starting something that doesn't have a future."

Of course there was, Bailey thought. Most likely Logan would be the most incredible one-night stand either of them would ever have. Even with no future, no commitment, he would be worth experiencing.

So why hadn't she experienced him last night? He'd wanted her, and God knew, she'd wanted him, too. Yet she'd walked out of the bedroom and closed the door between them. Why?

Because she didn't want to get hurt.

Because he was more dangerous to her heart than Hector and Mac could ever be to her life.

Because he made her want things....

She was thinking about those things, hot and flushed and wishing for a gust of cool night air, when a hand settled on her shoulder. Half expecting Logan, she glanced up with a ready smile...into Hector Escobar's dark eyes.

"I was hoping you'd be back tonight."

Only sheer will kept the smile in place. "How could I stay away? My friend tells me that Pat's Place is the *only* place to spend a Saturday evening in Nomas."

His gaze shifted to Marisa and turned hostile. "What a surprise. Not seeing you here, of course, but seeing you sober."

"And what a shame, seeing you alive," Marisa responded. Picking up her drink, she slid to the floor. "Sorry for abandoning you, Bailey, but I just can't stand the stench. I'll see you later."

Hector leaned one arm on the bar. "If you're looking for friends around here, you can do a hell of a lot better than her."

"Is that any way to talk about your sister-in-law?"

The hostility deepened. "Her sister ran off and took my kids, and *she* blames me. I didn't make the bitch leave. I damn sure didn't tell her to disappear with my kids."

The surprise wasn't that Shelley had left, Bailey thought, but that she'd stuck around long enough—and gotten close enough—to have those kids. She could imagine what life with Hector must have been like, but imagining was as far as she wanted to go.

Apparently putting unpleasant memories out of his mind, Hector straightened and took her arm. "Come sit with us."

She glanced at the central table where his buddies were seated, once again surrounded by empties and overflowing ashtrays. "I don't think so. Why don't we find a quiet table?"

He grinned. "Oh, honey, you want quiet, why don't we go to my house?"

Hopefully her smile didn't look as phony as it felt. "I don't think so." Sliding to her feet, she took her beer and headed for a table near the door. It wasn't as well lit as the center tables, nor as dark as the corner Logan now shared with Marisa; there was nothing to obstruct one's view of the other and there wasn't a risk of getting cornered on a bench by Hector. She didn't look back to see if he followed. Sooner or later, she figured, he would.

She chose the chair nearest the wall, pulling it out as Hector did the same to her left. Once seated, he started to scoot his chair closer, but she stopped him with a direct look. "Don't."

He looked surprised. Had no woman ever set limits on his behavior before? "What do you mean, 'don't'?"

"Don't invade my space."

"Your space?" His expression answered her question regarding limits. "You're not being real friendly."

"I don't get close to people I don't know."

"So if I want to get close to you…"

"I've got to get to know you." She smiled coolly. "That's the way it's generally done in the real world."

"I don't live in the real world," he replied smugly. "I live in Hector's world, also known as Nomas."

His own little kingdom, where he did what he wanted, when and how he wanted, and answered to no one. "Well, I *don't* live in Nomas, and I won't if people piss me off."

"You talk tough for a girl."

"This girl could kick your ass." That was pure boasting, and his grin showed he knew it. But if an ass-kicking became necessary, she could just save herself the effort and shoot him. He wouldn't be so amused by that.

"Man, you've got me shakin'," he teased, but he settled back comfortably in his chair, apparently content to keep his distance. "So what does this getting-to-know-me involve?"

"I ask questions and you answer them. And if you want to ask me questions, I'll answer them, too."

"What kind of questions?"

She shrugged. "About family, friends, work, your marriage. What you like and don't like. Things like that."

"I'll make it easy for you. I don't like answering questions."

"Too bad." Bailey folded one arm across her middle, rested her other elbow on that hand and lifted the beer to her mouth as she gazed toward Logan's corner. He and Marisa sat in shadow, talking quietly, though he seemed to be gazing steadily at Bailey. Did Marisa realize that his attention was elsewhere? Did she wonder why? Did she care?

There was a good crowd for not even nine o'clock on a Saturday evening. At the clubs she frequented in Memphis few people showed up before eleven and a place wouldn't get really crowded before one in the morning. But there were a lot of Saturday-night alternatives in Memphis that Nomas was lacking—restaurants, movies, shows, concerts. Nomas was pretty much closed for the night by eight o'clock, except for the bars, so there wasn't anyplace else to go.

"Okay, already."

Bailey glanced at Hector, looking put out at being ignored. "Okay what?" she asked innocently.

"We'll 'get to know' each other. Ask your damn questions."

She offered him a broad smile, only slightly tinged with triumph. She'd never known a man besides Logan who could stand being ignored for long. Hector's ego tolerated it even less than most. "All right. How long have you been married?"

"Ten years," he answered grudgingly, then asked, "You ever been married?"

"No. Why do you stay in Nomas?"

For a moment he looked baffled by the question, as if he had never considered living elsewhere, then he shrugged. "It's home. Always has been. Why haven't you been married?"

"Never wanted to be." And hadn't been asked, she silently added. She'd never stuck with a relationship long enough to let it get to that point. Career first, family second, fun third. Love and marriage came way down the list. "What was it like growing up with a brother?"

He swigged his beer. "I don't know. Me and Mac didn't grow up together. We didn't even meet until I was out of school."

"Really? How'd that happen?"

"My mother left Nomas and my dad and me, and went off to Chicago and got married again. I didn't even know I had a brother until he came here one day looking for me. He stayed a while, went to school, raised some hell, then took off again."

"So you were grown before you met, but you still became close."

He shrugged. "We're two of a kind."

Now that was a truly scary thought. Bailey tried to ignore the shivers dancing down her spine as she took another sip of beer, hoping for a bit of reassuring warmth. "Does he live around here?"

"I told you, he comes and goes."

"Yes, you did, but that's not what I asked."

Looking exasperated, Hector said, "He doesn't live anywhere. He just travels around. When he likes a place, he stays a while. When he gets tired of it, he moves on. He got that from our mother. She was restless, too."

Deciding that was enough interest in Mac—possibly verging on too much—Bailey shifted the focus. "What do you do for fun, besides hang out here with your buddies?"

The charm was back with a wicked grin and a wink. "Darlin', this ain't fun. This just passes the time. Come home with me and I'll show you *fun*."

"Not tonight, cowboy." *Not ever.*

One of Hector's buddies ambled past on the way to the jukebox, subjecting her to a suspicious stare all the way by. At the last instant his gaze shifted to Hector and he nodded once. Simple acknowledgment? Approval?

Or signaling silent agreement to a prearranged plan? she added a moment later when the same song they'd danced to the night before came on the machine.

"They're playing our song," Hector said, sliding his chair back and offering his hand. "Let's dance."

"No, thank you."

"Aw, come on. I've been good. I've answered your questions. Don't I deserve one spin around the dance floor?"

"We don't always get what we deserve, do we?" If they did, Hector would have been struck dead a long time ago, and so would Mac. Then she never would have had leverage to use with Logan—probably never would have even found him, since it was only his preoccupation with Mac that had allowed her to track him down.

Never having known him would be her loss, though she doubted he could say the same about her.

"One dance," Hector cajoled, wrapping his fingers around her wrist, pulling at her as he stood.

She didn't bother being polite but yanked her wrist free and scowled hard at him. "Which part of 'No, thank you' did you not understand? Trying to force me into doing something I've already refused is *not* the way to get on my good side, Hector."

"From where I sit, there ain't no bad side," he said slyly, then raised both hands palms out as he sank back into his chair. "Okay, okay. You know, you're lucky you're so damn hot, or I wouldn't be so accommodating."

And you're lucky your brother's a killer, or I wouldn't get within fifty yards of you. "You're such a charmer," she said drily.

"Women tell me that all the time." He finished his beer and ordered another before settling his gaze on her. "Where do you come from?"

"Tennessee."

"Your car has North Carolina plates."

She hadn't noticed that. Some detective she was. Not that it mattered. The story she'd initially given Marisa still held up. "It also has my ex-boyfriend's name on the title. I, uh, borrowed it when I left him."

Hector's laugh was bold and made half the people in the place look at him. "You *stole* his car?"

"He should have treated me better. Consider that fair warning."

"Yes, ma'am." He gave her a cocky salute. "You think he's looking for the car? Is that why Nomas seems a good place to stay a while?"

She shrugged.

"If he comes around, you let me know. My boys and I will take care of him."

"What do you mean by 'take care of him'?"

He leaned closer to her and lowered his voice. "Anything you want. We can persuade him to go away and forget the car or we can fix it so he'll leave you alone for good."

"You mean—" she swallowed hard, unsure whether she was doing it for effect or for real "—kill him?"

His expression didn't change. "You want him dead?"

"No."

"Then no, not kill him."

But that was exactly what he'd meant. She could see it in his eyes. How comfortable did a man have to be in his environment to make such an offer to a virtual stranger? Sure of himself, his friends, the local authorities…and sure of her? Sure that he could *take care of* her, as well, if circumstances so required?

"What do you do when you work?"

The question jarred her out of the cold of her thoughts. Grateful her hand was steady, she took a drink, then set the bottle on the table. "I've waited tables, tended bar, cooked, answered phones…as long as it's not too complicated, I can do it."

"Huh. Every fall I have a big party—grill some steaks, barbecue some brisket, plenty of booze. Practically everyone in the county comes. Maybe you can help me plan the next one."

"Maybe. What's the occasion?"

"Hector don't need no occasion to celebrate," he said in a mock growl, then shrugged. "It's a joint birthday party. Me and my brother were born just a week apart, plus seven years."

Bailey's breath caught in her lungs. "Will he be here for it?"

"If nothing happens between now and then. But we party with or without him. You interested?"

"Party planner. No, *event* planner. That'll look good on my résumé." Though it took every bit of her willpower, she stuck out her hand and didn't so much as flinch when he took it. "You bet I'm interested."

There wasn't much that could get on Logan's nerves quicker than watching Bailey smile at and talk with Escobar. At least they hadn't danced together again. If he'd had to watch the bastard take her in his arms, he would have…

Would have sat there in his chair and done nothing, he admitted grimly, just as he'd done the night before. Would have hated it and taken great satisfaction in the idea of pulling Escobar away from her and pounding him into a pulp but still would have sat back and just watched.

He'd bought four beers and nursed half of one through the evening, while Marisa polished off the others. They didn't talk much, and what conversation there was was idle chatter. He assumed she was still interested—she'd tried to get him to spend the night when he'd taken her home the night before—but she didn't bother flirting tonight.

Because it was obvious his interest lay elsewhere.

"She seems like a nice woman."

He glanced at Marisa. "Who?"

"Bailey. The woman you've spent two nights staring at. I told you, I'd be happy to introduce you."

"No, thanks." They would have to get naked, down and dirty to get to know each other any better, and that was something he wasn't ready for. Would never be ready for. No matter how much he wanted her.

"I can't figure what her interest in Hector is. He's just not the kind of guy who appeals to intelligent women."

"Isn't your sister intelligent?"

She gave him a dry look. "She married him, didn't she? Had kids with him. Stayed with him for four freakin' years. Does that answer your question?"

Logan acknowledged that with a nod, then asked, "You haven't heard from her in all this time?"

She shook her head sadly. "I think she's dead. I think Hector or those bastards who work for him killed her and I think they killed the twins, too."

"Maybe that's what she wants everyone to think."

"I'm her sister! I'm those babies' aunt! How could she want me to think they're dead?"

"Do you know a battered woman's chances of dying increase dramatically if she leaves the person who's beating her? Batterers don't like losing their targets. They'll track them down, try to get them back and often they kill them in the process." He wondered how his parents had reacted to *his* leaving. Had they looked for him? Or had they been satisfied to let him go as long as they still had Brady to torment?

He didn't know. And though he tried to tell himself he didn't care, it wasn't as easy to believe as it would have been a few weeks ago.

"Yeah, and a lot of battered women get killed before they get the chance to leave."

"That doesn't mean your sister's one of them. The best way to escape was to just disappear. Break off all contact. Let everyone think she's dead—including you, because you could inadvertently lead him to her."

"I'd kill him first," Marisa whispered, then she leaned her head back and closed her eyes. "Maybe you're right. Maybe she's just so scared…."

Logan didn't have a clue whether he was right. There could

be a thousand graves out there on Escobar's desert land that no one would ever find. He could have killed them at the house or anywhere on his property with no one the wiser and had his goons leave the car alongside the road to divert attention away from the ranch and suspicion away from him.

Sam's truck could be out there, too, with Mac's fingerprints inside it, possibly with Sam's or Ella's blood inside it.

His jaw clenched, he directed his attention back to the table near the door. Bailey was on her feet, and so was Escobar, but he was keeping his distance. They talked another moment or two, then she walked out the door. He watched her go with a too-admiring look, then took his beer and joined his pals at the center table.

Logan gestured toward the bottle in front of Marisa. "You gonna be okay to drive?"

She studied it, then sighed. "Yeah. I can't go to church tomorrow with a hangover. It tends to make the pastor a little cranky. I'll be going home before this one's gone."

"Good. I think I'll head on out now."

Her smile showed that she wasn't the least bit fooled. "You planning to arrange your own introduction?"

"Just planning to go back to the motel and get some sleep." He wasn't very convincing, though, if her look was anything to judge by.

"Like I said, she seems nice. Don't hurt her."

As if he could. Bailey was tougher than him, stronger than him, braver than him. She could walk away from a drunk twice her size and could not only face her family—and his—but enjoyed doing it.

"I'll see you around," was all he said before he eased from the chair and crossed to the door. He waited for three men to come in, then stepped outside, where he stopped for a minute to replace the stale smoke in his lungs with cool, fresh air. When he walked around the corner to the west side of the building, he abruptly stopped. The car was gone from its space. He took a quick look around, his heart rate jumping from normal to under fire, before the low rumble of a powerful engine coming from behind the bar caught his attention. As he headed that way, he could make out the Plymouth's front end in the deeper shadows there.

"Why'd you move?" he asked as he slid into the passenger seat.

"There were some guys standing in the parking lot. I drove off, circled around and came back here to wait." Switching on the headlights, she turned toward downtown, then took the first side street. "I missed something important in doing my research. Hector's and Mac's birthdays are only a week apart."

"And what's so important about that? Mine and Brady's are only three days apart." See? It had been easier to say his brother's name that time. Before long, if he wasn't careful, it would be as if they were regular brothers, living regular lives. Damn.

"Yeah, but you and Brady don't throw a big *joint* celebration. In October."

He and Brady had never done anything together except help each other survive their parents, he thought cynically. Then he realized what she was saying. Mac's and Hector's birthdays were next month, and they celebrated together, which meant…

"Mac will be here for the party?"

"Hector says they party with or without him. But if nothing happens between now and then, he should be here."

Jeez, Mac could be in town in a few weeks, maybe even just days. Logan had waited so long, and now the wait was almost over. This part of his life could be over in a matter of days. Sam and Ella would have the justice they deserved, and so would Mac. And Logan would have…he didn't know what, besides some measure of satisfaction. Some sense of closure. And a whole lot of nothing.

"And still more good news," Bailey went on. Slowing to a stop at the intersection closest to the motel, she looked at him. "Hector asked me to help him plan the party."

Chapter 9

"No."

Bailey's mouth tightened into a frown as she checked the street in both directions, then turned. He was so damned predictable. Any other client would have been thrilled that she'd gotten an in with Hector, that she would likely know as soon as he did whether his brother was coming to the birthday bash. But no, not Logan. All he wanted to be was difficult, and he excelled at it.

"I don't believe I asked for your permission," she said, her tone deceptively mild as she made the turn into the motel. "I was simply stating facts."

"Unless you can plan this party in public, you're not doing it. You're not going off alone with him."

"You're not my boss." He wasn't even her client. And catching Peter MacGregor wasn't her job, except in a roundabout way, which did sort of make him her boss, in an even more roundabout way. But it would be a cold day in hell before she admitted that to anyone.

"Thank God for small miracles," he muttered.

She gave him a sharp look before parking in her usual spot. "My boss adores me."

"I find that hard to believe." Then, without pausing, he added, "You're not working for Escobar."

Ignoring him was the best solution, she decided. She got out of the car, climbed the steps and unlocked the door, then went inside. Her purse landed on the coffee table as she passed. She left her sandals in the middle of the bedroom floor, the jean jacket hit the bed with a whoosh, then she closed the bathroom door behind her and leaned against the counter, concentrating on breathing.

The man just couldn't be grateful, she thought as she began removing her makeup. Planning Hector and Mac's party was the perfect excuse to ask more questions about Mac, and the perfect opportunity to find out when he was expected in town. Logan could contact the proper authorities, and they could be waiting the moment he showed his face, and it would all be over except the trial. Logan should be happy.

But he wasn't.

A knock sounded behind her as she rinsed the cleanser from her face. Wiping the residual suds with a damp washcloth, she turned and opened the door.

Logan stood there, still wearing his jacket and scowling. "I'm going out to Hector's place. Do you want to come?"

She didn't. She wanted to change into more comfortable clothes, fix herself a bowl of ice cream with chocolate syrup, curl up on the couch and watch television before going to bed. But she would never be able to relax, what with worrying about where he was and what he was doing and if he would make it back… Stifling a sigh, she said, "Give me a few minutes to change."

He nodded once and returned to the living room.

Shucking her shirt, she pulled on a long-sleeved T-shirt, then traded her snug-fitting, hip-hugging jeans for a more comfortable pair, adding a belt to hold the holstered .45. As soon as she tied her hiking boots, she returned to the bathroom to apply her moisturizer, stuck out her tongue at her un-made-up face, then left.

The drive through town passed in silence. Logan was still scowling, as if his face had frozen like that, and she didn't care. Really, she didn't.

"Hector's still at the bar," she commented as they drove past.

"According to Marisa, he and his boys will close it down sometime around three unless he gets lucky."

"That's a scary thought." Though most of the women she'd noticed in the bar hadn't seemed nearly as repulsed by Hector as she and Marisa were. Some didn't care about his reputation; others were no better than he was; and for still others, Hector's having money far outweighed what he'd done to get it.

"What are we going to do at the ranch?" she asked since Logan had quit glowering for the moment and was talking again.

"I want to have a look around."

"What are we looking for?"

He shrugged.

They parked at the garbage dump again, locked the car and headed along the road. The sky was clouded over, meaning no moon to make them visible in the night, but also meaning the walk was harder, especially once they left the roadside. The trail Logan blazed sloped steeply down into the valley. More than once they slid from one bit of footing to the next, and at one point she found herself slipping out of control in a shower of loose dirt and rock. If he hadn't grabbed her by the waistband of her jeans, she would have fallen and, with her luck, sprained something.

"Be careful," he murmured, his fingertips cool against her back as he steadied her.

"Oh, gee, there's a thought that hadn't occurred to me," she replied snidely, pushing his hand away, adjusting her clothes.

When she looked up, his mouth was twitching as if it wanted to smile, but he didn't. With only the faintest of starlight touching his face, he looked like some long-ago desperado, all hard lines and shadows. Add an incredibly sexy mustache like his brother's, and the picture would be complete. *I'm the man your mama warned you about.* Yes, indeed.

Her breath was tight in her chest, and it had nothing to do with the climb or her near fall. She covered the last few yards to the desert floor, then dragged air into her lungs, forcing them to expand.

"What if—" In spite of the breath, her voice still sounded dazed and insubstantial. She tried again. "What if he has people watching the place?"

"According to Marisa, he doesn't do anything illegal here. The land's been in his family a long time, and he doesn't risk losing it. Odds are, if he does have anyone watching, it's at the house, and I'm not interested in it."

"What exactly does he do?" All the research she'd done before coming hadn't told her a damn thing about the real source of Hector's income, and neither had the few people she'd spoken to in town.

"It's hard to say. Some people think it's drugs. Based on a few things Shelley said, Marisa thinks it's people."

As they set off across the desert toward the ranch buildings, Bailey shivered. "They think he's trafficking in *people?*"

"There are a lot of people desperate to come to this country. They pay smugglers to bring them in and then they're virtually held prisoner—forced into jobs that pay nothing, living in substandard conditions and kept there by the fact that they're here illegally."

"They kick up a fuss, the bad guys threaten them with Immigration," she murmured, and he nodded. "Modern-day slavery. Jeez."

"I wonder how much Escobar could get for you."

She would have smacked him if she hadn't needed all her energy to match his pace and most of her concentration to do so without breaking her ankle or her neck.

They came upon the occupied area of the ranch before she was ready. At the first barbed wire fence Logan stopped and crouched, and she did the same. There were a few lights on in the house but no vehicles parked outside. The pole lamp dimly illuminated the barn and the other buildings, where everything was still. It definitely looked as if no one was home.

When Logan pulled out the night-vision scope, she sat down, letting her muscles relax and her breathing even out. She was in good shape, but hiking across the desert in the dark with someone else setting the pace was a new experience, one she hoped she wouldn't have to repeat in the near future.

At last he deemed it safe enough to go on. They climbed through the wires, angling toward the rear of the barn and away from the house. He'd said he wasn't interested in the house. So what *was* he hoping to find?

Maybe Sam's pickup. Not that it mattered to the old man anymore, but better to have it someplace—anyplace—else than in the hands of his murderer's brother.

They cut through several more fences before reaching the back of the barn. Gesturing for her to stay put, Logan disappeared into the shadows.

Crouching with the weathered barn boards at her back, Bailey huddled into a tight ball—to combat the chill, she told herself. To control her sudden trembling, she grimly admitted as the reality of the situation sank in. They were trespassing on the property of a man who had plenty to hide, who some suspected of murder, whose brother was definitely a killer.

Sure, they were armed and they could look out for themselves, but they were still at a distinct disadvantage. For one thing, there were only two of them, while Hector had at least four men at his beck and call, probably more. For another, she and Logan were law-abiding citizens. Violence wasn't a way of life for them as it was for Hector.

For another, she was scared spitless.

Eyes closed, she concentrated on listening, but all she heard was the pounding of her heart and the rushing in her ears. Finally she picked out the scrape of a footstep an instant before a hand touched her. She choked back a shriek but couldn't stop the jump that made her land on her butt on the cold, hard ground.

Despite the darkness, she was positive Logan was scowling again as he pulled her to her feet, then leaned so close that his mouth brushed her ear. "There's nothing in the barn except junk," he whispered. "I'm going to check the other buildings. You want to come or stay?"

"Come." Without a doubt.

He led the way to the east end of the barn, peered around the corner cautiously, then they climbed a wood fence encircling bare earth that had once been a corral. They climbed out again on the far side, then ducked behind a rusted tractor to reach the first shed. Swinging open the door, Logan cupped his hand to block most of the light, then shone the flashlight inside. "Jeez, this guy never throws anything away."

There was a path down the center of the small structure, but the rest of the space was packed to the rafters with boxes and bags, none of them labeled. Spilling out of one box was the corner of a quilt, yellow gingham offset by white squares embroidered with nursery-rhyme characters. "Not a very sentimental father, is he?" she whispered.

Logan's only response was a grim shake of his head.

The third building had a padlock hanging from the hasp, looking as if it had rusted in the open position. It was twice the size of the shed, had a loft and was also stuffed full. Many of the boxes were original packaging, bearing photos of a toaster, a microwave, a computer, a cradle, but gave no hint what they now held.

There was no way a pickup truck could be concealed in either building.

"I don't suppose you know how to fly a plane," she remarked.

He glanced at her. "I've jumped out of one a few hundred times, but no, I never learned to fly. Why?"

"I was just thinking it might be worth our while to rent a plane and fly over the property and see what other buildings there are or if Sam's truck is just out in the open somewhere."

He didn't say good idea or bad but simply nodded once before stepping outside again. She followed, slamming into him as he stopped short. Reaching back, he caught hold of her, steadying her with a firm hand and a warning "Shh."

She peeked over his shoulder and saw twin beams of headlights illuminating the night. A moment later another pair appeared, then the engines shut off, doors slammed and voices carried on the still air.

Logan backed up, pushing her with him, pulling the door up behind him. "The loft," he whispered, and she turned toward the stairs that ran alongside the east wall. With his hands on her shoulders, able to make out little besides shadows and shapes, she was almost there when she stumbled into a stack of boxes. A grunt escaped her, but she didn't slow. Once her foot touched the first step, she picked up speed, hurrying to the top of the stairs, using the tiny beam of her penlight to locate a likely hiding place. It was in the distant corner, a long, narrow space between the wall and a stack of boxes.

She was looking for cobwebs, spiders or bugs when a creak came from downstairs, followed by a huge crash. Muttering a curse, Logan grabbed her arm and dived into the space, yanking her in on top of him. "What the hell was that?" she whispered, but he placed his fingers over her mouth.

It was okay—she knew. The boxes she'd fallen against had taken their sweet time about it, but they'd finally fallen to the floor and, by the sounds of it, taken out one or two of the other unsteady towers with them. She closed her eyes, embarrassed by such a careless mistake. No doubt Logan would point out to her soon that if she couldn't even avoid a stupid accident when the bad guys were *this* close to catching them snooping around, then she damn sure couldn't be trusted on her own scamming Hector. The worst part was, he might be right.

Even though her heart was pounding wildly, she could still hear the thudding of running footsteps. The door downstairs was flung open, bright light shone into the room. "What the hell…?" That was Hector, and he wasn't alone.

"Do you see anything?" a second voice asked excitedly.

Footsteps entered the building, echoing on the wooden floor. Closing her eyes, Bailey pressed her face against Logan's shoulder. She'd gone through a short phase when she was a kid of believing that if she couldn't see someone, they couldn't see her either. Now more than ever she wished that was true.

Logan's heartbeat was steady, maybe increased a few beats per minute but nothing like hers. Of course, he was more accustomed to danger than she was. Two years at war had taught him that. She matched her breathing to his, tried to match her heart rate to his. She wasn't in this alone. She could take care of herself, and if she really needed help, he would be there.

The footsteps made a circle of the building, stopping again near the door. "Looks like some boxes fell over," voice number three said.

"Boxes don't just fall over." That was number two again. "Something *made* 'em fall."

"Hell, Tommy, look at the way they're stacked. A rat farting could probably knock 'em over." Hector sounded annoyed—because Tommy wasn't the brightest bulb in the box? Because his adrenaline had gotten pumping over nothing? "Just to be safe, check upstairs, then lock this place up."

Lock it up? Bailey grimaced at the thought of being trapped inside, then Hector's first words penetrated. *Check upstairs.* Oh, God, oh, God, oh, God.

Two pairs of steps went outside while the third started up the stairs. Logan twisted onto his left side, depositing her on her right side in the cramped space, the wall hard against her back. He maneuvered his pistol out of its holster, thumbed off the safety, then waited. He was barely breathing—and she was close enough to know. That was fair enough, since she couldn't fill her lungs either.

The light came closer, lighting up the rafters, bouncing down to cast eerie shadows. Finally the footsteps stopped and the light made a quick trip around the loft. "Check upstairs," Tommy muttered. "Hell, like anybody could hide in all this mess? The place ain't fit for pigs. If he wants someone pokin' around up here, he can damn well do it himself."

Still mumbling, he clomped back down the stairs. A moment later the door closed with a bang.

Bailey heaved a great sigh. "Oh, thank God."

"Maybe you didn't notice, but he's locking us in here."

"Locks we can deal with."

"Oh, yeah? Then you damn sure didn't notice the padlock hanging on the latch outside when we came in."

Okay, so it wasn't a simple matter of turning the knob and walking out. She was so grateful to have not been caught that she didn't care. "We'll manage." She started to push herself up, but he pushed her back down.

"We're not going anywhere yet. He may be gone, but when Escobar realizes he couldn't have done a thorough search, he might be back."

She settled in again. Now that the danger was mostly past, the space wasn't nearly as comfortable as it had been a few moments earlier…or maybe it was entirely too comfortable, and that was what made her *un*comfortable. They were touching chest to thigh, and his knee was between hers. The only way they could possibly get any closer was to take off their clothes, and no matter the reason, she found such intimacy…well, *intimate*.

Not that he seemed to have noticed.

"I'm sorry," she murmured.

"For what?" His breath, smelling of dark beer, tickled her temple.

"Those boxes fell over because I bumped into them."

"Maybe. Or maybe a rat did fart."

She had expected snideness, criticism, scorn. His careless dismissal surprised her…and touched her. He could have made her feel really crappy, but instead he minimized her mistake. He really might be human under that arrogant shell, after all.

"So…" She shifted to ease the pressure where her pistol pressed into her hip and found pressure of a different sort, where the beginnings of his arousal pushed against her. She cleared her throat. "So…you, uh, jumped out of airplanes."

"Yes, ma'am."

"I d-don't like to fly."

"Me, neither. But you can't skydive without getting up into the sky."

Though it was chilly outside and not much warmer inside, her body heat had started a steady climb. Wishing for a window to open, she tugged at her jacket, trying to slide it far enough down to free her left arm. She stopped wriggling the instant Logan's hand settled on her hip.

"Please don't do that." Even in the darkness she could see his eyes were closed, his expression pained, and she could feel…oh, man, could she *feel*.

She tried to smile but couldn't. "Th-there's something about adrenaline, i-isn't there?"

He made a choked sound that she thought he might have intended to be a laugh. "You think that's adrenaline?"

Before she could form a reply, he slid his arm around her, sliding her onto her back, settling himself above her, and kissed her. It was a good kiss—a great one. Not too demanding, not too gentle, greedy and hungry and all tongues, nipping, tasting, teasing. He nudged her knees apart and settled between her thighs, his erection hard and hot where she was damp and hot, and he settled his hand on her breast, stroking and pinching her nipple to an aching peak.

Finally, when she needed air so badly she might die, he ended the kiss, lifted his head an inch or two and stared hard into her eyes. "Are you ever gonna make love with me?"

The words themselves, the husky, raw tone of his voice, the plaintiveness that underlay it—all were a tremendous turn-on, but even combined they couldn't make her forget the decisions they had each reached earlier: that he'd be a great one-night stand. That all he wanted from her was one round of sex. One great orgasm, and so long, it's over. She would have to be a fool to agree…and a bigger fool to refuse. He could be her best one-night stand ever, and if she found herself in the morning wishing for something more…wouldn't the doing be worth the regret?

"Kiss me like that again, and I'll do it right here, right now."

He ducked his head to nuzzle her breast, mouthing her swollen nipple through her shirt, then suddenly levered himself to his feet. "Not here, not now. Let's see if we can find a way out of here."

For a time she just lay there, suddenly cold and lonely. She wanted to pull him back down, wanted to kiss him longer and harder than he'd just kissed her, wanted to get lost in that kind of kiss. Instead, with a sigh, she accepted his hand and let him help her to her feet, brushed the dust from her backside and followed him carefully down the stairs.

The front door was securely padlocked, and there was no back door. Logan made his way over piles of junk to the outside wall and shone his light the length of it. "There's a window back here," he said, carefully moving toward it. "Pray it opens so we won't have to break it out."

If broken glass was added to the fallen boxes, even stupid Tommy would realize there had been an intruder. And with Bailey and Logan the only strangers in town, and all her questions about both Hector and Mac… She sent up a silent prayer for a clean getaway, finishing just seconds before Logan said, "It does open. Can you get over here without—"

"Knocking anything over?" she sarcastically finished for him.

There was a moment's silence before he quietly said, "Without using your light? This window is a clear view from the entire back of the house."

"Sorry," she said between clenched teeth. She shut off the penlight and stuck it in her pocket, then began a tortuous trip, squeezing between boxes, stepping over cartons, sliding across a table, and the whole time she tried not to think about the dust, the spiders and webs she was disturbing. There would be another hot shower for her tonight, another scrubbing to clean Escobar germs from her skin.

And then what? Hot sex with Logan?

If he was still interested.

She felt the cool night air before she reached Logan. He'd already raised the window and was intently watching outside as he held out one hand to help her over the last obstacle. "Take cover behind the shed," he commanded as he lifted her feetfirst through the window.

The instant her feet touched ground, he let go, and she crossed the few yards to the shed with long strides, all too aware of the feeble starlight and the stronger yard lamp. When she ducked behind the shed into shadow, relief washed over her.

Logan eased out the window, closed it as much as he could, then moved noiselessly to join her. It was just a few steps to the old tractor, a few yards in the open, then the corral. He led the way, this time circling behind the corral instead of across the middle. It took longer but gave them the added protection of the five-foot-tall board fence.

They were creeping along the back of the barn when Bailey laid her hand on his shoulder. "Listen," she whispered. Voices sounded from the vicinity of the house, moving in their direction. They both stopped short, and she frantically looked about for a hiding place. There was nothing but scrub and the occasional outcropping of rock, and none of it near enough to be of any use at all.

Taking her hand, Logan eased to the corner of the barn and looked around. She couldn't see but could tell the voices had stopped near where the vehicles should be parked.

"…going back to Pat's," number three said. "What about you?"

There was a pause, then cigar smoke drifted on the cool air. "I might," Hector said.

"Or he might go to the motel looking for that girl," Tommy bragged, as if discussing his own exploits.

Logan's fingers tightened painfully around her hand. She squeezed back, and he eased his grip. She got the message, she grumbled silently. It wasn't a game. Hector was a dangerous man; she was risking a lot every moment she spent with him. She knew all that. But hearing his friend talk so casually about his going to the motel.... She had felt *safe* there. She hadn't once imagined him coming looking for her—and finding her and Logan.

Hector's response to Tommy's comment was a snort. "It'd be a waste of time. She wants to *get to know me*. Like I'm gonna be her damn boyfriend?" Another snort. "I just want to—" He finished with an obscenity that made his friends laugh and her skin crawl.

"So why don't you just blow her off?" number three asked.

"Because Hector don't walk away from a challenge." This time he did the boasting himself. "If she wants to get to know me, she will. *Real* good. And she'll be happy she did."

After a moment's silence, number three asked, "So…you comin' or stayin'?"

"I think I'll go check up on the boys. See if everything's in place for the next shipment. Then I might drop in."

They said their goodbyes, then pickup doors slammed, an engine started and the vehicle drove away. A moment later another truck door closed, another engine revved to life and Hector followed in their tracks.

Logan turned back and looked at her. She felt the intensity, but it was too dark to read anything—anger, smugness, jealousy, concern. She swallowed, looked away, then raised her chin and met his gaze head-on. "See? I was right," she said in a low voice. "Hector fancies himself a ladies' man, and I fancy myself a lady."

"A lady he wants to—" He repeated the same profanity. Somehow it didn't sound nearly so vulgar in his husky voice.

"Hey, he's interested and he's talking to me. That's what we needed."

"He's interested in getting you naked."

"So are you," she retorted.

"There's a difference."

"I know." She listened for any sound that didn't belong and

heard nothing, then took a step out of their cover before she turned back. "Hector's not going to succeed."

Then she strode quickly, almost giddily, toward the first fence.

There was a reason Logan didn't deal with women on a long-term basis: they didn't hold his interest, they flat-out bored him or they drove him crazy. Bailey was driving him absolutely crazy. Sometimes he couldn't wait to be free of her, other times he couldn't imagine going back to life without her, and always he wanted her. Even now, when all he should *really* want was to shake some sense into her.

He followed her across the desert floor, not the least surprised when she led him straight back to the spot where they'd descended the slope earlier. If she were his typical woman, she would have gotten lost a half-dozen times. Hell, if she were his typical woman, he never would have considered taking her out there with him and she never would have considered going.

Bailey wasn't *anyone's* typical woman.

But she just might be the right one for him.

They made it back to the car in good time and drove straight to the motel. There was no sign of Escobar's big truck anywhere in town or, thank God, around the motel. If he changed his mind, if he did show up there…

Bailey would handle it. She was doing a pretty good job of keeping the bastard under control. She was capable, and if she ever went looking for a hero, she wouldn't look Logan's way.

But she was looking to him for sex.

By the time he'd locked the cabin door behind him, she had removed the jean jacket and her belt and pistol. "I'm going to take a shower," she announced before disappearing into the bathroom.

Take a shower. Get naked. It was too easy to picture her wet from head to toe, her skin slick, her hands gliding over her body….

With a groan he made sure all the windows were locked, the curtains closed. Leaving only a dim lamp burning on the end table, he sprawled on the couch and turned on the television, but it was impossible to concentrate with the sounds of the running shower in the distance and the faint scents of Bailey that clung to the pillow beneath his head.

Finally the water stopped. He closed his eyes and found it all too easy for his imagination to supply what he couldn't see—the curtain sliding back, those long, long legs appearing first, leading up to nicely rounded hips, a narrow waist, breasts that could make a man hard without so much as a taste. She would dry her hair first to stop its dripping, then rub the towel slowly, caressingly, over every bit of her skin before wrapping it around her and—

"Your turn."

He gave a start, his eyes popping open. She stood in the doorway, her hair dripping tiny rivulets, and instead of a towel that was barely decent, she'd wrapped a bedsheet around her. It left her shoulders bare and pooled on the floor around her feet and still looked incredibly sexy.

"M-my turn?" he repeated blankly.

"To shower. No Escobar cooties allowed here."

Oh, yeah. Shower. He'd intended to do that. He just needed a minute to think how to go about it—not easy when all the blood was rushing from his head to lower parts of his body.

She picked up a bottle of lotion from the end table, then sat in the glider and propped one bare foot on the coffee table. "Go on. And make it quick."

He watched her squirt sweet-scented pink lotion into her hand, then rub her palms together before she started smoothing the stuff over her leg, starting at her ankle and working her way up. About the time her hands slid above her knee, he gave himself a mental shake and managed somehow to get to his feet, even though the only thing he wanted in the world was to sit there and watch her.

Not true. More than that, he wanted to touch her. Kiss her. Hold her. Screw her, have sex with her, make love with her— all the same act, with all their variations. Sleep with her. Stay with her. Over and over.

He showered in record time and even shaved. He dried off just as quickly, combed his fingers through his hair and wrapped the towel around his middle—for all the good it did when he was harder than he ever could remember being. Finally he left the bathroom.

All the lights were off except for a frilly thing on the night table that showed an empty bed. Its illumination filtered through the open door into the living room, weakening the farther it went, but it was enough to see the sofa was empty, too. Enough to absorb into the white sheet she wore like some kind of Grecian goddess while she gazed motionlessly out the front window.

He crossed the room silently, not stopping until nothing but the sheet and a wish separated them, and laid his hand over hers where it held the curtain back. "Anything out there?"

She didn't startle or tense but instead seemed to relax comfortably with his presence. "No. One o'clock and all's well."

"If he comes looking for you…"

"I'll handle it." She sent a brief look over her shoulder, half smile, half regret. "He sees me as a challenge because men always want what they can't have."

He left the curtain to her and rested his hands on her shoulders, ducking his head to brush his mouth along the elegant line of her neck. "But sometimes we get lucky and we get what we want."

With a *mmm* of pleasure, she tilted her head to the side, giving him better access. She smelled of soap and shampoo, of flowers and sweet lotion, and she tasted fresh, clean, unspoiled. For a time he focused on that part of her—shoulder, neck, delicately shaped ear—until she suddenly shivered and sank back against him. With that encouragement, he slid one arm around her, coaxed her to turn her face to him and thrust his tongue into her mouth. She tried to twist in his arms, but he held there, her bottom pressed snugly against his groin, her breasts an erotic weight pressing against his arm, and kissed her long and hard, thoroughly tasting every part of her mouth.

In some still-rational part of his mind, he knew he should ask her if she was sure she wanted this. Their adrenaline had been pumping when he'd started it back at the ranch; now that they were safe, she might have changed her mind. But he wasn't going to ask, because she might *have* changed her mind, and he was already in enough pain. He didn't need to add disappointment to it.

Besides, he knew *willing,* and everything about Bailey was definitely willing.

For tonight, at least.

He would deal with tomorrow when it came.

She reached back, blindly groping, and discarded the towel around his waist. Before she could do more than brush his erection, he caught her hand and laced his fingers with hers, keeping it a safe distance away. He'd waited too long, wanted too much, to risk her torturous caresses.

When his lungs threatened to burst, when his heart was pounding and perspiration slicked his skin, he ended the kiss and dragged in a sweet breath. "Hey, Bailey," he said, his voice so harsh it was almost unrecognizable. "Want to—" He repeated Escobar's profanity and received a wide, sexy-as-hell grin in return.

"You bet. Just follow me."

He let go of her, and she started toward the bedroom, every movement graceful and fluid and making him throb harder. With one easy flick she loosened the knot that held the sheet in place, and it drifted to the floor as she continued to walk, giving him an amazing view of the long line of her back, the shapely curve of her bottom, the long, lean legs....

"Sweet damnation," he cursed—pleaded—before he started after her.

The frilly little lamp showed that the bedcovers had been turned down and that her pistol was on the nightstand, along with a handful of condoms. She had come on this trip prepared. So had he. Once hers were gone, he would dig out his stash. And then tomorrow...

She met him at the foot of the bed, wrapped her arms around him, sought his mouth, and the entire concept of *tomorrow* went out of his head. Now...that was all that mattered.

They kissed a long time, his tongue in her mouth, her tongue in his, their hands everywhere, until he couldn't stand it anymore, until she whimpered with every touch, until he couldn't tell whether the raspy *please* was coming from him or her. Quickly he fumbled a condom in place, settled between her thighs, then slowly, so damn slowly it hurt, he slid inside her, stretching her, filling her. When she'd taken every inch of him, he closed his eyes, his breathing little more than pants, and for a moment just concentrated on how hot and tight and wet and incredibly good she felt.

Then she began moving—not much at first, just a tightening of muscles, a shift of her hips, a clenching—and, grinding his teeth, he couldn't help but respond. He eased out until only the tip connected them, then sank in slowly again, out and back in, a little faster, a little harder, each time, until they matched in a frantic rhythm, the heat burning out of control, the need growing, consuming, the pleasure easing into pain that was all too erotic and back again.

A groan tore through him as he came, his muscles rigid, his breathing harsh, his entire body throbbing. Dimly he was aware of her own orgasm, helpless little cries that cut right through him, tight little spasms where her body held his, increasing his own shudders, making him groan again.

Muscles twitching, skin damp, breathing settling into ragged gasps, he rested against her for a moment. Just a moment—that was all he needed. Despite his release, he was still hard inside her, still needed more, still needed *her.*

As the tension slowly seeped from her body, her hands eased their grip on his shoulders, becoming a gentle caress instead of a desperate lifeline. She gave a great sigh, then smiled, eyes closed, in his direction. "Wow."

And as her hips thrust slightly against his, as she guided his hand to her breast, then brushed a kiss across his mouth, he could think only one thing.

Damn straight.

Chapter 10

*W*ow.

It hadn't been Bailey's most articulate moment ever, but it might have been her most heartfelt. She'd been a hundred and ten percent right when she'd thought Logan might be the best one-night stand in existence. She felt…incredible.

Incredibly greedy.

He lay on his stomach beside her, head pillowed on his arms, the sheet pulled up to his hips, and he was watching her with an expression she couldn't begin to read. It was serious, measuring…questioning. But questioning whom? What? Why he'd done this? What she would expect of him now? Whether he'd made a mistake?

She hated feeling insecure, especially when every part of her body was warmer, heavier, lazier, more satisfied than she'd ever experienced before. She'd had a variety of lovers before, from good to indifferent to appallingly selfish, but Logan was different.

Because the way she cared for him was different.

She wasn't falling in love, she hastily assured herself. But she could. If she was foolish enough. If she wanted to hand him her heart and say, *Here, break it.* She could convince herself that his kissing more than made up for his arrogance and bossiness. She could admit that life with him was certainly better than life without him. She could wake up in the morning with his body warm and hard against hers and believe that this was the way she wanted to start every morning for the rest of her life.

She could love him.

If she was foolish.

She lay on her side, both pillows stuffed under her head, the sheet pulled over her breasts. It had been a futile gesture, though, because the way the fabric gapped, he could still see them, all the way down to her still-sensitive nipples. He could still slide his hand under the sheet, which he did, and cup her breast in his palm, his fingers rousing her nipple to a crest that ached for his mouth.

"Hey, Madison." He sounded hoarse and sated and, yes, smugly pleased with himself. That was okay, because she was pretty damn pleased with him, too. "Did I tell you you're beautiful?"

She wore no makeup, her hair had probably dried going every which way and she'd just recently been sweaty, panting and flushed all the way to the tips of her breasts, to say nothing of getting quite crudely vocal. If he could still say she was beautiful, the least she could do was believe him. "No, but feel free to."

"I'll keep that in mind," he said with a careless shrug, making her grin.

"You're beautiful, too," she said, catching her breath as he gently pinched her nipple, then rubbed away the sting. "Actually I believe *gorgeous* is the word Marisa used and I agreed with."

"Uh-huh. Tall, dark and scarred—that's me."

She scoffed. "Those scars have zero influence on your opinion of yourself."

"Nope," he agreed. "They're just another part of me, like my arms and legs and—"

Sliding closer, she pressed her fingers to his lips. "And everything else." She paused a moment as he slid lower in the bed to suckle her nipple, letting her eyes close and sensation wash over her. Finally, though, she opened her eyes again, stroked her fingers through his hair and feigned carelessness as she said, "I didn't know Brady had his own scars until you told me. I've never seen him without a shirt, not even when we're all swimming in his pool."

Logan flicked his finger across her nipple, sending quivers of pleasure through her breast. "He's afraid of the water. Our father damn near let him drown when he was trying to teach him to swim."

If there had been some emotion in his voice—anger, bitterness, hatred—it wouldn't have affected Bailey the way it did, but he spoke so matter-of-factly because such incidents had been a daily part of his and Brady's lives growing up.

"Brady's more…sensitive, I guess," he went on. "He cared more about people, about things, than I did. I can imagine he would hide the scars."

While Logan didn't exactly flaunt his, he certainly didn't hide them. That first night in the Dallas motel, they'd known each other all of a few hours, yet he hadn't hesitated to strip down to his boxers and turn his back to her. When she'd gasped, he'd given her a look that challenged her to say something, anything, and he'd won—she had kept her mouth shut.

"Have you ever wanted to go back to them and say, 'I'm alive and well and living a normal life, so screw you'?"

Using just the tip of his finger, he traced feathery light patterns over her breast, making the skin ripple, before he leaned forward and took her nipple between his teeth. The gentle bite sent shock waves through her, especially between her legs, and made her pant softly before he let go.

"No. They mean nothing to me. I don't even think about them—at least, I didn't until I met you. That part of my life is over. Nothing can be changed, nothing can be made right, so why bother with it?"

"Your relationship with Brady can be made right." She said the words carefully, holding her breath as she awaited his response. It didn't come for a long time as he played with her instead, but finally he glanced up into her eyes.

"Maybe."

One brief, guarded word that filled her with hope—not just for Lexy or Brady but mostly for Logan. He needed family more than anyone she knew…and if he connected with *his* half of the Marshall clan, then *her* half would keep her filled in about him when he was gone. It wouldn't be like saying goodbye to him forever.

Though close.

Finally he shifted onto his side, moving snugly against her, fitting his arousal in the vee of her thighs, and nuzzled her jaw. "You have any more condoms over there, or do I need to get mine out?"

She fumbled on the nightstand and found three empty packets before finally coming up with the final one. "Lie back," she said, giving his chest a push. "I want to do the honors this time."

For once, he didn't offer even the slightest of arguments.

She moved to straddle him, bending low over his chest and mouthing first one nipple, then the other, into a hard bead. Leaving them wet and swollen, she placed openmouthed kisses across his ribs, dipping into the hollow beneath the sternum, gliding across his abdomen, his hips, the muscular ridges of his thighs. He was hard, throbbing, as she tore the package open, fished out the latex ring inside, then placed it over the tip of his arousal. Slowly, teasingly, she eased it down, one millimeter at a time, following it with her mouth, taking what she could as she unrolled the sheath to its full length.

With a groan Logan tangled his fingers in her hair, holding her head close, then let them fall limply to his side. His hips arched, thrusting uncontrollably, then abruptly he grabbed hold and pulled her up his body. "Not in your mouth," he said, grinding out the words. "Inside you…"

Wrapping her fingers around his hard, hot length, she guided him into place, then sank down until he filled her snugly, so hard, so hot.

It was fast and greedy and over too soon…or maybe just soon enough, she amended when she lay damp and breathless in his arms again. She'd built to her orgasm in record time, every nerve ending in her body sizzling, every beat of her heart pumping liquid fire through her veins. Her body had never been so sensitized, her arousal so raw, her satisfaction so incomplete. Four shattering orgasms, and she still wanted more.

Later. When her skin stopped rippling with sensation. When her lungs could take a full breath. When her body heat dropped below molten.

Later. If there *was* a *later* for them.

She fell asleep in his embrace and woke up sometime later on the edge of the bed, one foot dangling off the mattress, the covers pulled up to her nose. The sun was up, dispelling the nighttime gloom, showing her clothes in a wad on the dresser, her pistol on the night table and four empty condom wrappers…as if she needed an external reminder of how they'd spent a good part of the night. All the reminder she needed was in the tenderness between her thighs and in the comforting warmth of complete and utter satisfaction that weakened her muscles and made it impossible for her not to smile goofily.

She didn't need to look behind her to know that Logan was already up. Because he didn't need any more sleep? Or didn't want any more sex? Was he looking for a way to put some distance between them, to make sure she understood what he'd said before about not wanting sex with her more than once?

Her smile faded as she sat up. She shoved her hair from her face, then combed her fingers through it. She understood just fine. She had come into this with her eyes open, with the expectation that they would have one night, nothing more. It was all right with her. Truly.

Untangling the sheet, she wrapped it around her like a shroud, grabbed clean clothes from the dresser and disappeared into the bathroom. She would be better able to face the day fully dressed, with her hair combed and her teeth brushed, as if it were merely any normal day.

When she came out a few minutes later, Logan was waiting in the doorway between bedroom and living room, leaning against the jamb, wearing nothing but jeans that rode low on his lean hips. He held a mug of coffee in both hands and looked at her as if…as if he was sorry she was dressed. As if he wanted her. And as if he didn't know what to say to her.

Fair enough. In that instant she didn't know what to say to him either.

He figured it out first. "About last night…"

She was prepared for the brush-off, for the damn-it-was-fun-but-it-won't-happen-again, so why did that sudden surge of emotion flooding through her feel so much like disappointment? Why did her stomach knot at the prospect of hearing him say he didn't want to repeat the episode? "You don't have to—"

A knock at the door interrupted her. Both their gazes shifted that way, then met again briefly before he moved to the night-stand on his side of the bed. He left the coffee there, picked up his pistol, then returned to the bedroom door, where he nodded for her to move.

Swallowing hard, she crossed the living room in a few long strides, peeked out the window, then gave a relieved sigh as she opened the door to Faith.

"Good morning," the motel owner said with a cheery smile, her arms clasped around a load of linens. "I hope I didn't wake you."

"No, I was up."

"I'm making my rounds before church. Are you sure you don't want maid service even once while you're here? I'd be happy to change the sheets and vacuum."

"I'll take the sheets, but you don't need to vacuum. Everything's pretty clean."

"I don't mind at all."

"Neither do I, and you've got plenty of cleaning to do without adding me to the list." Bailey took the linens from her but didn't move away from the door for fear the woman would take it as an invitation to come inside.

Faith did peer past her, a sly grin on her face. "Is Mr. Handsome asleep back there, by any chance?"

"No," Bailey replied hastily, then managed a smile to soften her tone. "That was a, uh, one-time thing." No lies so far. Logan wasn't asleep and he'd been about to remind her of the one-night-stand agreement when Faith had interrupted.

"Too bad…though, under the circumstances, it's probably a good thing. I hear Hector's got his eye on you, and he doesn't like to share."

"Where did you hear that?"

"Oh, honey, Nomas is a small town. Everybody knows everybody else's business. My husband's cousin's sister-in-law waits tables at Pat's Place, and she says Hector thinks you're all that."

"He's been…friendly."

Faith snorted. "That's one way of putting it. He's been known to throw a woman over his shoulder and carry her off to his cave—sorry, his ranch. Well, not really, but close. He thinks he's God's gift. The important thing is, do *you* think he's God's gift?"

Bailey managed a casual shrug. "I don't know him well enough to decide. We're working on that." She paused a moment, then said, "I heard about his wife and kids disappearing. What do you think happened to them?"

The friendliness faded from Faith's expression, replaced by a somber look. "Everyone's got their theories. Some believe she's dead. Some believe she ran off. Back when they first started dating, Shelley thought she could change him. After four years of a lousy marriage, *she* was the one who changed. I think she admitted defeat, ran off, changed their names and settled with the kids in someplace Hector will never find them."

"So the only other close family he has is his brother."

"Good ol' Mac. We'll probably be seeing him around before too long."

"You don't sound like a fan."

"Nope. Not many people are." Faith looked away, her gaze lighting on the cleaning cart. "Sure you don't want me to vacuum while I'm here?"

"I'm sure. Have a good time at church."

"I'm the organist. I can't help but have a good time playing music. See you later."

Bailey closed the door and leaned against it. The bedroom door was still open, and Logan was still out of sight...but his size-twelve boots weren't. They rested on the floor, clearly visible from her point of view. Had they been from Faith's, as well?

Rolling her eyes, she carried the linens into the bedroom and dumped them on the dresser. "Next time you hide, hide your boots, too."

Logan's gaze went to them immediately, then flickered back to her. "Did she see them?"

"I don't know. She didn't act like she knew I was lying." She rested one hand on top of the fluffy white towels, the other on her hip, and waited for him to pick up where Faith had interrupted him. *About last night...*

He didn't. "If Escobar's the jealous type, maybe you should keep your distance."

From him or from you? she wanted to ask but didn't. "We already knew Hector's the criminal type, and I haven't been keeping my distance. Jealousy is no big deal."

"Yeah, tell that to Shelley Escobar. According to Marisa, he controlled virtually every aspect of her life."

"Well, I'm not Shelley. I'm not going to sleep with him. I'm not going to marry him. And I'm damn sure not going to let him think he owns me."

"You think you're so tough."

She grinned. "That's what Hector said last night. Gee, you two think alike. There's a scary thought."

He scowled in response. "Only when it involves you, sweetheart."

Silence fell between them, one moment, then another.

Though she tried, she found it impossible to keep her gaze locked on his face. It kept sliding away, over his unshaven throat, across his broad naked chest, to the snug denim that hugged his hips and, just for a change of pace, to the unmade bed behind him. It would have taken Faith only a glance to guess that Bailey hadn't been alone in that bed the night before—the sheets were pulled loose and wrinkled, the blanket was on there sideways and the spread was wrong side up. The entire scene had a rumpled, great-sex look about it.

Great sex. For one night. Damn, she was going to miss it!

Finally she cleared her throat. "You want to make the bed or start breakfast?"

He turned to look at the bed, motionless for a long time, then he opened his mouth, closed it again, then said, "I'll take the bed."

After nodding, she left the bedroom before she gave in to the temptation to ask him to rumple the sheets with her one more time before calling it quits. In the kitchen she pulled out the makings for a real breakfast. Except for their breakfast in Las Cruces the day before, they'd opted for convenience during their stay—cereal, toast, coffee. This morning she intended to fry bacon and eggs, make biscuits and gravy. Comfort food. Not that she was in need of comfort, mind you.

The bacon was draining on a pad of paper toweling, the biscuits were browning in the oven, the eggs were sizzling in one skillet and she was stirring the gravy in another when Logan finally came in from the bedroom. He could have made ten beds in the time he'd taken. It must have been climbing over those mountains of regret that slowed him, she thought with more bitterness than she had any right to.

"Smells good."

She glanced his way with a taut smile but didn't speak.

"Did your mother teach you to cook?"

For a moment she stirred the gravy, watching the bubbles rise, then burst. "Cooking didn't rank high on my interests when I was a kid, not when I could be climbing trees or playing baseball instead. I learned in college. I couldn't afford school *and* eating out all the time. I didn't learn to really enjoy it, though, until the last few years. I've gotten pretty good, if I say so myself."

"Ella taught me." As the timer beeped, he took the spoon from her so she could remove the biscuits from the oven. "She believed everyone needed to know the basics of cooking, cleaning and laundry, regardless of gender. I was the only one in my squad in basic training who knew how to do laundry. I had to teach everyone else."

"She was a smart woman."

"Yeah. She quit school in the ninth grade to go to work and help support her family, then married Sam not long after, but she was damn smart." His voice turned cynical. "My mother, on the other hand, graduated from Bryn Mawr and was still ignorant in all the ways that counted."

"My mother didn't go to college. All she ever wanted to be was a wife and mother, and she didn't need a college degree for that. As soon as we were all out of the house, she got married again, to a man with grown children of his own, and moved to Illinois. Now she's a doting stepmother and step-grandmother with the close-knit, loving family she always wanted, and we see her on holidays. Sometimes."

Using a pancake turner, she removed the eggs from the skillet, placing one on her plate, two on Logan's, then gave him an uneasy glance. "That sounded bitter, didn't it? I'm not, really. I love my mom, but she's got her limitations. After our dad went to prison, she fell apart. Neely pretty much raised us, even though she was just a kid herself. I'm really glad that Mom's got her husband and his family and I'm really glad that I've got my sisters and their families."

"But you choose to live hundreds of miles away from them."

"There's not much need for a private investigator in Heartbreak or Buffalo Plains." While he poured the gravy into a bowl, she carried the plates to the table, then returned for the biscuits. "I don't have to live in the same state with them to be close, just as you don't have to be hundreds of miles apart from someone to be distant." There was a fair amount of distance separating them, even though the real physical space was only a few feet.

They talked little while they ate, except for grudging-sounding compliments and similar thanks. When there was nothing left but empty dishes, Logan sat back in his chair, a determined look on his features. "About last night…"

It took more strength than she'd known she had to pull off a totally careless shrug and smile. "Hey, I understand. You don't have to spell it out for me. Don't worry." Rising from her chair, she gathered a handful of dishes and carried them to the sink. While the water heated, she returned for the rest, but he caught her wrist.

"You understand what?"

"The agreement. That it was just one night, no strings, no demands. That was all either of us wanted. Right?"

For a long time he just looked at her, the expression in his dark eyes impossible to read. Then abruptly he released her wrist and quietly, darkly said, "Yeah. That's right."

"So it's not a problem." With another shrug she collected the rest of the dishes and went back to the kitchen. Not a problem at all…except that one night hadn't been enough for her. A hundred sounded like a nice start, a thousand even better. Maybe then she would be satisfied and ready to move on.

Or maybe not.

But he hadn't looked relieved that she wasn't going to ask more of him. Her assurances hadn't particularly assured him. What if…was it possible that *he* had wanted more?

A glance his way didn't offer a clue. He was just sitting at the table, fingers laced around his coffee mug, looking a million miles away.

Maybe she should have kept her mouth shut—should have let him say whatever it was he'd wanted to say. Maybe instead of feeling rejected, she would have been pleasantly surprised. Maybe…

She was a pretty straightforward person. She didn't usually try to guess what people were thinking. There was no reason to start now. All she had to do was give him the opportunity to say what he'd wanted…and hope he would take it. And if he didn't? Then she might never know and she would have only herself to blame.

"Logan—"

Before she could go on, before he could do much more than glance her way, there was another knock at the blasted door. Swearing, Bailey grabbed a towel to dry her hands as he headed silently for the bedroom. When she reached the door, she glanced to see that his boots were gone. There was nothing to indicate she wasn't alone in the cabin.

The woman waiting on the stoop was a stranger, dressed for church, Bailey guessed, and looking put out. She balanced a vase of flowers in both hands while tapping one foot impatiently. The instant the door opened, she asked, "Bailey Madison? These are for you."

The flowers she thrust at Bailey were beautiful fall colors, lush and richly scented, with a small white card practically hidden in the mass. "You deliver on Sundays?" she asked.

"Not as a general rule," the woman replied curtly, already on her way back down the steps. Her car, parked behind the GTX, was still running, and three children waited inside.

"Thanks," Bailey called before retreating into the house again. She set the vase on the coffee table, then fished the card from its envelope. *My favorite color is blue, my favorite food is steak, the rarer, the better, and my favorite music is country. I'm Catholic, I love tough girls with long legs. And my birthday's coming up soon. Wanna make it a happy one?*

A bold arrow pointed to the back, and she flipped the card over. *Dinner? Tonight? My house? I'll pick you up at seven unless you'd rather drive. Call for directions.* Beneath that was scrawled Hector's phone number.

She was gazing at the card, bemused, when strong, dark fingers plucked it from her grip. Logan read it, his mouth tightening with every line, then crumpled it in his hand. "You're not going."

She'd already reached that conclusion, but his bossiness raised her hackles anyway. "And how do you think you'll stop me?"

A smile touched his lips but not his eyes as he leaned closer to her. His expression, his voice, his very presence radiated danger, but she couldn't come up with the command to make herself move away. "Oh, sweetheart, I've got ways. Trust me."

"You can't stop me from doing my job."

"Of course I can." There was nothing boastful in his words—just a simple statement of fact. She didn't doubt that he could, indeed, stop her. Heavens, he could make her forget all about Hector and Mac if he tried.

"It's just dinner."

"Alone. At his ranch. If you never came back, no one would know or care."

"You would know." She wasn't so sure he would care, other than in that broad sense of guilt he'd taken on when he'd accepted responsibility for other people's actions. But on a personal level, a man/woman/temporary-lovers level…

"Yeah, I would know…and what good would it do you?"

"I could learn something about Mac."

"Nothing you can't learn the next time you meet Escobar in public."

That was true. And it was pointless to argue with him when she didn't *want* to go alone to Hector's house.

Prying the card from his fist, she smoothed it as she went to the phone. She dialed the numbers, all too aware of Logan's gaze boring into her back, and counted the rings. Hector answered on the third.

"Hi, Hector, it's Bailey. I wanted to thank you for the flowers. They're lovely."

"No lovelier than you," he replied, and she made a face at the wall. "Can I hope you're calling to ask for directions to my house?"

"You can always hope," she said sweetly. "But I'm afraid I'll have to turn you down this time. However, I would like to meet with you tomorrow to discuss the plans for your birthday party. Would you be available?"

A floorboard creaked behind her, drawing her attention from Hector's answer. She refused to turn, even though every nerve in her body warned her that Logan was coming closer. She could feel it in the charged air that touched her bare skin, in the tiny hairs on her nape that stood on end, in the increased rate of her heart and the heat that spread through her body. She felt his own heat an instant before he stopped, his body so close behind hers that, real or imagined, she felt the brush of cloth against cloth, the whisper of breath against skin.

Silence on the phone called her attention to the fact that Hector had stopped talking and was awaiting a response from her. Blinking, she recalled what few words had registered: *busy…morning…meeting at lunch…free…afternoon…two.* "Um, how about two o'clock at the drugstore? I'll let you treat me to a banana split."

"The drugstore? With that damn Marisa? How about two o'clock at the café catty corner from the courthouse? Maria's Home Cooking."

"All right." Her voice sounded breathy—maybe because her lungs had tightened so that she couldn't manage a full breath—and higher-pitched than normal. "I'll see you then. Goodbye."

She hung up, missing the cradle the first time, then let the florist's card flutter to the table. She should move away from Logan, should confront him, should wrap her arms around him and kiss him one more time, long enough and hard enough to last. But she couldn't do anything…until he touched her arm. It wasn't an intimate touch—just the tips of his fingers brushing against her upper arm, casual, careless, innocent—but it made her shudder and sent tiny shivers of awareness ricocheting through her. A similar touch on her other arm brought a similar response, then he slid his fingers down, increasing the contact as they went—first the tips, then the fingers, then the palms. Clasping her wrists, he turned her to face him, then guided her arms around his waist before sliding his hands down to cradle her bottom against his arousal.

"About last night…"

Twice before he'd said the same words. Twice before she'd interrupted him. This time all she could manage was a dazed, "Yes?"

"I was wrong. One night wasn't enough."

"No." Little sounds, breathless, more a whimper than anything else.

He bent closer to her, softening his voice. "Another night won't be enough."

"No." This time she managed no sound, just a puff of air.

Closer still, softer still. "We're adults. We can have what we want."

She nodded, or thought she did, the instant before his mouth took hers in a hot, hard, hungry kiss. Then she stopped caring, stopped thinking, stopped everything except feeling.

They didn't make it far, just to a bare portion of wall, before he tugged off her jeans, opened his own jeans and thrust inside her. He took her there, smooth, cool wall against her back, hard, heated body against her front, with greedy kisses and frenzied caresses that made them both come, fast and hard. From there they moved to the couch, where they both stripped naked, where he sprawled back and she sat astride his hips, riding him at a torturous pace until he slid his hand between their bodies to find that swollen, ultrasensitive spot. His talented fingers pushed her over the edge, sending shudders through her, making her gasp with pain and pleasure before he filled her again.

Afterward, when they were stretched across the bed, sweaty and damp and temporarily sated, she thought about the condoms, or the lack thereof. As if reading her mind—or more likely entertaining his own concerns—Logan glanced at her. "I haven't had sex without a condom since I was eighteen."

"I was nineteen. My first time. I guess my date didn't think he'd get lucky."

"*All* men think they'll get lucky. He was just an idiot." He turned onto his side to face her. "In the service, you get tested regularly. I'm clean."

Bailey's cheeks, still flushed from the exertion, heated a bit more. "Gee, thanks. I hadn't yet gone past 'Oh, God, I could get pregnant' to 'Oh, God, I could catch something' or 'Oh, God, I could die.'"

"You won't catch anything from me."

Except maybe morning sickness. She relied on condoms and the infrequency of sex in her life for birth control; taking the pill seemed pointless unless she was involved in a steady relationship, which she hadn't been in ages. She'd had more sex in the last ten hours than in the past two years.

"So if you get pregnant…" Again his expression and his voice were totally unreadable. She couldn't tell whether he had even the slightest paternal gene in his body, whether fatherhood held any kind of appeal to him or if the idea repulsed him into utter emotionlessness. "We'll deal with it."

"I appreciate the 'we,'" she said drily. "But if I got pregnant—" *God forbid* "—*I* would handle it." She was a grown woman. She knew the potential consequences of unprotected sex, even if she *had* lost all capacity for reason at the time. She wouldn't marry a man because they'd both suffered from temporary insanity. Marriage was tough enough when two people loved each other and wanted to spend the rest of their lives together. It stood little chance when the only reason was an accidental pregnancy.

His gaze narrowed in warning. "I don't turn my back on my responsibilities."

"My body, my baby," she said with a shrug.

"My mistake, my sperm, my baby."

"You don't even want kids, do you?"

"Neither do you," he retorted.

That was true…so far. But if she got pregnant, she would have seven or eight months to change her mind—and she *would* change her mind. Not wanting and not having was one thing; not wanting and having anyway meant you damn well *learned* to want.

"Don't worry about it," she said, achieving the carelessness she was aiming for. "I've been lucky so far. But—" she gave him a lazy, wicked smile "—you might want to dig out your condoms…just in case."

* * *

The only time Logan had ever given any thought to becoming a father was when he was eighteen—that last time he'd had sex without a condom. His girlfriend had come to him in a panic a few weeks later because her period was late. Images of himself forced into marriage with a girl he didn't love, forced to play father to a kid he didn't want, had ensured that he'd never made the mistake of unprotected sex again. He'd had no clue what kind of parent he would be—just the overwhelming sense that, with the role models he'd had, he didn't want to find out.

But he'd taken that chance with Bailey—twice. Careless. Stupid. He still had no desire to find out if he would suck as badly at fatherhood as his own father had. There were enough kids in the world, enough lousy parents. He didn't need to make himself one, too.

But there had been something…appealing about not using a condom. About trusting a woman enough to forgo the protection. About wanting a woman enough to forgo it. About it being just him and her, nothing between them, filling her so that the act had the potential for more than the mere pleasure of the moment.

He needed his head examined.

It was nearing five o'clock on Monday afternoon. Bailey had been gone three hours, and he'd spent much of the time looking out the window. There were fifty-four channels available on the television, but none of them held his interest—not the talk shows or the soap operas or the sports shows or the cartoons. He'd settled on a music channel and wished like hell that she would come back safe and sound.

Not that Escobar was likely to screw with her in the middle of Maria's Home Cooking. Surely the townspeople weren't so intimidated that they would stand by and watch while he forced a woman to leave against her will…or maybe they were. But Bailey wouldn't go quietly and she wouldn't hesitate to pull that pistol from her purse or, he hoped, to use it.

She was safe. She could take care of herself. She didn't need him.

Funny how a feeling could change. He was used to not being needed. He deliberately cultivated that in the people around him and he'd always been satisfied with it…until now. Some stupid part of him *wanted* Bailey to need him. *Wanted* her to want him. To depend on him.

Stupid.

It was one of the rare moments when he wasn't at the window that the GTX's engine broke the stillness. He crossed the room in three strides and watched as she pulled into the space in front of the cabin. A quick look showed no one else around— no burgundy extended cab following her, no busybody motel owner hanging about for the chance to talk—so he opened the door about the time she reached the stoop.

She came inside, smelling of cigar smoke, and laid her bag on the armchair while he closed the door. He leaned against it and watched her. "Three hours to plan a damn party?"

Turning, she gave him a sarcastic smile. "And hello to you, too."

"Hello. Three hours to plan a damn party?"

"It's not just a party. It's the social event of the year for this part of the state. Last year he had over five hundred guests. Friends and business associates come in from all over, probably including a fair number of *America's Most Wanted*." She began unbuttoning her blouse, a simple black cotton shirt that shouldn't have looked more than serviceable but did. The black bra she wore underneath it was a hell of a lot more than just serviceable, with its lace trim and tiny satin bow right between her breasts.

Logan forced his gaze up from the bra to her face. "Then it's a good thing you won't be around for the party."

"Maybe I won't. Maybe I will." Wadding the shirt, she went into the bedroom, tossed it on the dresser, then took off her boots. When she pulled down her jeans, revealing panties that were also black and lacy and just barely there, he stifled a groan and set his jaw stubbornly.

"You're not going to that party." Too late he remembered her typical response to his declarations—pure stubborn mule-headedness—and hastily raised one hand to stop her argument. "Surely you have to get back to work sometime."

"This is work."

"I mean your real job, where you get paid."

"I'm getting paid."

"By yourself." He could offer to pick up the tab. He had the money, and she *was* helping him, and Lexy *was* his brother's kid, for whatever that was worth. Though it hadn't occurred to him until that moment, he probably *would* offer...after Escobar's party, if they failed to find Mac before then.

She shoved the jeans past her knees, then kicked them off before looking at him. "You are so damn hardheaded."

"Funny. I was just thinking the same thing about you."

"No, *I'm* dogged and determined. You're just plain stubborn. You're not my boss, my protector or my hero. Remember that." With a toss of her head she went into the bathroom, closed and locked the door. A moment later the shower came on.

He wasn't anybody's hero. He'd never wanted to be.

Until now, that voice of utter stupidity whispered slyly in his head.

He sat down on the bed, then scooted back until the pillows were behind him and waited for her to come out again. It didn't take long. Ten minutes, and the water shut off. A couple minutes after that the door opened and she emerged wrapped in a towel that started under her arms and ended a millimeter past decent. She collected clean underwear and a T-shirt from the dresser, ducked back into the bathroom, then came out again wearing the clothes and minus the towel.

If a flimsy bra, a deep-purple thong and a snug shirt that ended at her waist could be called *clothes*.

She sat down at the foot of the bed, propped one leg up and began rubbing lotion into her skin. "I asked Hector if he could put me in touch with Mac. I told him I needed to know Mac's likes and dislikes if I was going to make the party really special. He didn't give me a straight answer to any of my questions. When I asked where Mac was right now, Hector said he's 'around.' When I asked what he does, he 'keeps busy.' When I asked to talk to Mac, he said maybe I could."

"If Mac was your half brother and you knew what he was capable of, would *you* give straight answers to anyone asking questions?"

"If he was my half brother, I would have turned him in to the cops a long time ago."

"Really. And here I thought family was so important to you."

She gave him a dry look. "I wouldn't protect family who broke the law. I would get them a good lawyer and visit them in jail, but I wouldn't protect them from the consequences of their actions."

He believed her. Which meant she wouldn't hesitate to turn *him* in once he'd finally found Mac. He wasn't even family—just family of family, though that meant something to her, too. He wouldn't need her help with a lawyer—he could afford the nation's best—but would she visit him in prison? Or would that constitute cruel and unusual punishment?

Prison. If he succeeded at his mission, there was a good chance he would spend the rest of his life there. That would definitely take care of Lexy wanting to know him. It would also ensure Brady would never come around. And Bailey, who wholeheartedly believed that he intended to turn Mac over to the authorities as soon as he found him…she would be disappointed by his lies and would hate him for using her to kill a man. She would wish she'd never met him. Never helped him. Never made love with him.

And if he didn't go to prison, if he bought his way out of a conviction…she would despise him for not facing the consequences of his actions. Not that she should be surprised. As he'd told her and she'd learned all too well, he was nobody's hero.

"I haven't planned a party since Kylie graduated from college," she went on, switching legs, perfuming the air with the lotion's sweet fragrance. "I doubt we had more than forty people at that. Setting aside the facts that Hector's a no-good snake and I'm just using him so we can get his brother arrested and sent to prison for the rest of his worthless life, this is actually kind of fun. Money is no object. He insists on the best food, drink, entertainment. I could get used to spending someone else's money."

"Dirty money," Logan reminded her. "He makes that money off people's suffering."

The easiness left her expression, replaced by somberness. "Maybe we can get him, too, for harboring a fugitive. That carries a decent penalty."

Or maybe he would try to protect his brother and get killed in the fallout. Logan could live with two more deaths on his conscience.

But not with letting Mac continue to live while Sam and Ella were dead.

Even if it meant prison.

Even if it meant making Bailey hate him.

Finished with the lotion, she was about to get up when Logan caught her wrist and pulled her down on the bed beside him. If he gave himself a moment, he could get turned on by her warmth, her scent, her softness, by *her,* and he could get lost inside her and stop thinking, at least for a while. But instead of pulling her against him, kissing her, touching her in the ways that touched *him,* he slid his arm over her, pressed his face against her damp hair and just held her. There was nothing sexual about it. It was just…intimate. Warm. Sweet.

And he needed it more than he ever could have imagined.

Because he was starting to need *her.*

More than he ever could have imagined.

Chapter 11

After supper, Bailey hauled out her laptop and signed online to check her e-mail. There was the usual spam, notes and funnies from her friends in Memphis, a couple of notes from Lexy and one from her boss asking when she would be back in the office. She also had an e-mail statement from the bookkeeper asking for the next payment on Lexy's account. It wasn't a huge amount, but it was another drain on her dwindling savings account. If she could just convince Logan to take a break for a quick trip to Oklahoma… It wasn't likely he would miss Mac; the next time the man showed up in Nomas, he was expected to stay for several weeks at the least. And spending a few days in the company of his brother and nieces would have to be better than the restrictions he faced here in Nomas.

But if she did convince Logan to live up to his end of their bargain ahead of time, then what? She still wouldn't be free to return to Memphis and start making money instead of spending it, because she hadn't yet lived up to *her* end of the bargain. And she could hold on a few more weeks. Surely Mac would come to his own birthday party, and Logan would contact the New Mexico state police, and as soon as Mac was taken into custody, they would leave for Oklahoma.

Then it would be home to Memphis and hello to work for her. And goodbye to him.

After sending a few brief e-mails to Lexy and friends, she signed off, then opened a photo and graphics program. She was in the process of designing a party invitation when the phone rang. Finishing up with the dinner dishes, Logan glanced at it, then her, but didn't move away from the sink. Sure it would be one of her sisters or maybe Reese, she answered with a cheery hello.

"Is this Bailey Madison?" an unfamiliar male voice asked. He had no recognizable accent, just flat sounds in a flat tone.

"Yes, it is. Who is this?"

"I'm the better-looking of Ellen MacGregor's two boys. Peter MacGregor, better known as Mac. Hector tells me you wanted to talk to me about this party we're having."

She swallowed hard, not easy when her throat and chest were tight. He sounded so…*normal*. Not like a cold-blooded murderer at all.

Or *exactly* like one.

"So…" Her voice was breathy. She forced herself to breathe a time or two as she shifted chairs at the table so she faced Logan. "Should I call you Pete, Peter or Mac?"

The cup Logan was rinsing slipped from his fingers and into the sink, splashing soapy water over his shirt. He didn't appear to notice but dried his hands and came across the room, sliding into the chair she'd just vacated.

"If you're half as pretty as my brother says, you can just call me *darlin'*."

"Oh, I'd like to think that I'm twice as pretty as your brother says." Her face was warm, and her fingers were knotted tightly around the receiver. If it were any more cheaply made, it would be at risk of disintegrating in her grip. "I take it this phone call means you'll be here to celebrate with us."

"I can't let Hector have all the fun by himself. I surely will be there. I might even come early, before the vultures descend."

"The vultures?"

"Hector's buddies. They like pretty women. Once they've gotten there, the pickin's get pretty slim."

The image that formed in her mind was enough to make her skin crawl, but she put a lot of energy into pretending otherwise. "Gee, that paints a pretty picture," she said drily, drawing a laugh from him. "The party's on the tenth. When do you think you might get here?"

"Oh, I don't know. You'll see me when you see me. Hector said you have this thing about getting to know people."

"A new experience for him, huh? I get the impression he'd rather just throw me over his shoulder and haul me off to his cave."

"Aw, he'd ask your name somewhere along the way. Me, I'm more of a gentleman than that. I approach every woman as if she just might be the love of my life."

Gazing at the tabletop, Bailey brought his image to mind— fair skin, auburn hair trimmed and neat, clean shaven, glasses that gave him a studious look. Asked to guess his occupation based on nothing more than his photograph, she would say minister, schoolteacher, accountant. It was the roundness of his face that hinted at softness, teddy-bear-ness. A dangerous man should look harder, sharper, more angular. Like Hector.

Like Logan.

"And has that happened yet?" she forced herself to ask lightly. "Have you met the love of your life?"

"Not yet. At least—" his voice took on a teasing tone "—not in person."

Once again she swallowed hard. She'd thought before that he might charm a woman's feet out from under her. No doubt he'd done just that plenty of times. He might not be the handsomest man around, he might have all the bad-boy appeal of the cuddly teddy bear she'd thought of earlier, but he thought he was pretty damn special, and women responded to that. *She* could respond to it…if she didn't know better.

"So...where will you be coming from?" she asked cheerily.

"Here or there. Where are *you* coming from?"

"Tennessee."

"Hiding from an ex-boyfriend."

"More like hiding his car from him. I see Hector's told you about me. No fair. He's said very little about you."

"He's afraid you'll fall for me instead of him."

"You two often compete for the same women?"

"There's no competition. They take one look at me and forget he exists."

Across the table Logan was scowling at her. His hands were knotted in the dish towel, tightening the fibers to their limit, though he looked as if he'd rather have them around Mac's throat...or maybe hers.

Mac must have charmed Ella and Sam Jensen. He would have flirted with her and showered her with compliments, while showing Sam nothing but the utmost respect...and then he'd killed them with horrifying brutality. How cold, how irreparably broken he must be.

"Hel-loo. Are you there?"

She gave herself a mental shake. "Sorry. I was just thinking.... Shall we discuss your party?"

"Oh, yes, let's," Mac replied in a bad British accent that got the snobbish part down right. "I do so like entertaining and being entertained."

She asked a few fairly pointless questions—his tastes in food and drink; if there was anyone he wanted to add to the guest list; if he had any particular requests to make. He gave fairly pointless answers—he wasn't picky; he would eat and drink whatever was set in front of him; he would issue his own invitations; and his only request was for a little one-on-one time with her. She could make his birthday *very* happy, he told her in a voice that must have been accompanied by a leer and a waggle of eyebrows.

"Can I call you back if I have more questions?"

"Oh, I'd be happy to check in with you in a few days just in case."

He was probably calling on a damned cell phone. It wasn't as if knowing the number would tell her where he was…though with the latest cell phones equipped with global-positioning-satellite chips, maybe it would.

Gritting her teeth, she said, "Then let's make a date. Why don't you call me on Wednesday at— What time is it where you are?"

"It's the middle of a dull, boring evening. Of course, if you were here…"

"Where is 'here'?"

"Halfway between the middle of nowhere and the end of the line. Why don't I call you about this time on Wednesday?"

"Why don't you," she agreed. "I'll be waiting." Before he could say anything else, she hung up. She practically had to peel her fingers loose from the receiver, then she shoved her chair back, went to the sink and washed her hands. It was silly—it couldn't possibly wash away the revulsion that had settled over her—but she felt better for it anyway.

When she turned, Logan was standing in front of her, holding out the towel. "You didn't have to flirt with him," he said stonily as she dried her hands.

"I don't know. I think it's better that our cold-blooded murderer likes me than doesn't."

"His liking you won't keep you safe. He liked Sam and Ella. Just not as much as he likes killing."

A shiver skittered down her spine, making her hug herself tightly. "Can we go for a walk?" She needed fresh air, no walls around her, just the cool night and the stars and Logan.

He nodded, and they both got jackets and their pistols. The sun had long since set, and the temperature had dropped twenty degrees. Around the motel office, flood lamps buzzed, but all was in shadow around their cabin. They circled behind the building and set off across the desert, the distance between them far greater than the silence suggested. She would have liked to feel his arm around her or to hold his hand, but she couldn't reach out. Not yet.

They'd gone a few hundred yards when she finally glanced his way. "Do you think Sam and Ella were his first?"

He didn't look back. "I don't know. He killed people in battle, of course, but... I don't know."

Mac's criminal record as a kid had been mostly petty stuff—shoplifting, vandalism, brawling. He'd never used a weapon, never done any real harm to anyone...as far as the authorities had known. Had war taught him to enjoy killing or would he have graduated to murder regardless?

"He liked fighting," Logan said quietly. "He was more gung ho about going to Iraq than anyone else in our company. He never seemed to feel a moment's remorse over killing anyone. It got his adrenaline pumping, got him all psyched up."

But Logan, she would bet, *had* felt remorse. No matter how justified it was, no matter that it was kill or be killed, killing didn't come naturally to him. It was necessary, vital to his survival, but not a thing to enjoy.

"He'll come on to you when he gets here," Logan said flatly.

She nodded but kept her gaze on the uneven ground.

"He comes on to all women, and the fact that his brother saw you first won't slow him down."

"I can keep him at a distance."

"Most women don't."

"Then it's time he meets one who does. He'll probably be intrigued by it, like Hector."

Logan fell silent for a time before finally cautiously asking, "Once he shows up in town, will you leave?"

She could. Their deal had been that she would help him find Mac. She would have fulfilled her obligation. As to whether he fulfilled his...that wasn't her responsibility. It wouldn't reflect badly on her if he failed.

But if she left, Logan would have to go it alone. What if Mac saw him before the authorities arrived? He'd killed the Jensens to stop them from reporting the theft of their beat-up old pickup and seventy-eight dollars. He wouldn't hesitate to kill Logan to stop him from turning him over to the cops, not when he was facing the death penalty.

She couldn't risk that. Even if it meant facing danger herself.

"Don't you think it would make both Mac and Hector suspicious if I suddenly disappear?"

"You could always tell them your ex tracked you down."

"Hector would know there wasn't anyone new in town."

"You could say he called and spooked you. That you're afraid it's just a matter of time and you're getting out while it's safe to go."

She shook her head. "I'm not a quitter."

"Sometimes the best measure of intelligence is knowing when to quit."

"You won't quit."

"I can't."

Up ahead a boulder loomed large in the darkness. Pulling the penlight from her pocket, Bailey shined it over every inch of the surface, then, satisfied there were no snakes curled up there, sat down. "Bringing Mac to justice won't bring back Sam and Ella."

"I know that. But seeing him dead will at least bring…closure." He said the last word with some bit of mockery, as if he wasn't comfortable with such a touchy-feely term.

"Are you so sure he'll get the death penalty?"

He gave her a startled look, then bent to heft a chunk of rock that he sent sailing off into the distance. "We're talking about Texas," he said uncomfortably. "They don't like people going around slaughtering their elderly citizens."

He didn't like the idea of Mac being executed—was that the reason for his discomfort? He'd known all along that Mac faced the death penalty when captured; he'd even told her so. Maybe now, with Mac due in town any day, it finally seemed *real*.

"Mac's death won't be your fault," she said quietly.

That made him look sharply at her. After a long time, he offered a poor excuse for a smile. "We all make choices. I have to live with mine, and he has to die with his."

A simple statement of fact. He had to live with the fact that he'd brought Mac into the Jensens' lives. She was sure that was what he'd meant. Nothing else. Nothing more sinister.

So why was there a tiny cold place forming deep inside her?

* * *

Logan had never lived under such restriction in his life, and by Wednesday evening he was chafing with it. Sure, his parents had kept a tight rein on him and Brady, but they'd gone to school, visited their grandmother and roamed the property at will. In basic training, the Army had kept him on a rigid schedule, but he was always going somewhere, doing something.

All he could do here was wait. And worry.

If he was a smart man, he would be planning a dozen different scenarios for taking out Mac. He would cover every possible contingency, would decide whether to turn himself in when the deed was done or disappear, as Mac had done.

But he couldn't plan. He was too preoccupied.

This evening Bailey was waiting with him. She'd spent both Tuesday and Wednesday afternoons with Hector, showing him the different invitations she'd created on the computer, drawing up menus, discussing the merits of a live band versus a DJ— actually treating this whole party as if it was important. Even now, she was curled up on the couch, a legal pad on her lap with lists of foods covering the page.

And waiting for Mac to call.

"You have a picture of Lexy?"

The surprise on her face was echoed inside him. He'd had no clue before the words had come out that they were even inside him. He wasn't particularly interested in this daughter of Brady's. The kid had grown up just fine without knowing him, and considering the future that awaited him, she would continue to do just fine without meeting him. He wasn't curious at all about her…though the sly, stupid voice in his head disputed that.

Bailey laid aside the legal pad, then slid to sit on the floor between the sofa and coffee table, where her laptop was humming quietly. With a few clicks of the mouse she opened a program, then gestured for him to join her. He did, sitting shoulder to shoulder with her, leaning back against the sofa.

The electronic photo album she opened was filled with family pictures. She clicked on one thumbnail to enlarge it, then glanced at him as the photo of a teenage girl filled the screen. Her age was impossible to guess in that way teenage girls had today. Her hair was brown, her eyes clear, her smile happy. She wore twelve or fourteen earrings divided between both ears, along with a stud in her nose, and looked…happy. Normal. Quite an accomplishment for a kid whose life had been touched by Jim and Rita Marshall.

Bailey chuckled as she gazed at the image. "When she first came to town, she had spiked purple hair and a bar through her eyebrow. She wore shirts two sizes too small—the better to show off her belly ring and tattoo, of course—and skirts six inches too short with combat boots. She certainly stood out in the little town of Buffalo Plains."

How had Brady greeted that sight? Logan wondered. His brother had never been the rebellious type—had always avoided attention when he could. Living with a long-lost daughter whose mere appearance screamed *Look at me!* must have been an adjustment for him.

When he didn't say anything, Bailey clicked to the next photo—Lexy holding a little girl. "That's Brynn. She looks like her daddy, acts like her mama and loves her sister dearly."

She was a pretty baby, not even a year old, with dark hair and skin and surprisingly blue eyes. Brady's eyes. Logan's eyes.

"Hallie," Bailey announced when the next photo popped up. "My little sister."

Beautiful, blond, hazel-eyed. Neely, in the next shot, was beautiful, with light brown hair and hazel eyes. So was Kylie.

"Mom and Pop Madison hit the jackpot," he remarked. "Four beautiful daughters."

"Beautiful and talented," Bailey said immodestly. She shuffled through the next photos, identifying Neely's husband, Reese, their mother and stepfather, friends and extended family, before finally stopping. Drawing her hand away from the mouse, she sat back and looked at him.

While he looked at Brady.

They'd always shared a strong resemblance, and time hadn't

changed that. Black hair, dark skin, blue eyes that knew too many secrets… Brady was probably still a few inches taller and definitely still fifteen pounds heavier, but except for the mustache, their faces were still very much the same. Nineteen years, and he still looked the way Logan remembered him. Strong. Solid. Dependable.

While Logan had been wild, reckless and unreliable.

Nineteen years. More than half of their lives. Brady had been his closest friend, his only confidant, the only one who knew the full extent of the nightmares going on in the Marshall house. They'd stood up for each other, cried in each other's arms, kept each other going…until Logan had ended it. *Logan.* Not Brady. His brother had done nothing that night that he hadn't done countless times before. It had been Logan who couldn't bear it, who couldn't forgive it.

Who couldn't forgive himself.

Damn Bailey for being right about that.

The photo had been taken at a backyard party; Hallie, Neely, Lexy and Brynn were in the background. Brady hadn't been aware the camera was directed his way, and he looked more relaxed than Logan had ever seen him. More than just happy—contented, the bone-deep kind most people never found. That Logan had never found.

They'd both left home, cut off contact with their parents, created lives that suited them, but Brady had gone one step further. He'd found himself a family and friends. Not just buddies, not just acquaintances thrown together by the luck of a duty assignment, but honest-to-God friends. He *should* feel damned contented. If anyone ever deserved to, it was him.

Logan never would have thought he could envy his brother. He'd liked his life—at least, until Mac had screwed it up. He'd liked the distance between himself and everyone else. Ella and Sam had filled any need he might have had for emotional closeness. He'd been satisfied.

But his career was gone, his buddies were gone and Ella and Sam were cold in their graves because of him. And what did he have to replace that? A burning need for justice, for vengeance.

And Bailey.

For the time being.

After a time, she clicked on an icon on the screen, then leaned back beside him as the pictures began advancing automatically, each getting its five seconds of viewing time before another flashed into place. Thanksgiving, Christmas, Easter, Mother's Day, a backyard barbecue, the Fourth of July—a normal family celebrating holidays with normal get-togethers, with hugs, food, laughter and smiles.

He'd never had that and couldn't remember ever wanting it. Even in his earliest memories, he'd known his relationship with his parents was unnatural. He hadn't wanted their love and affection; he had wanted only to survive them. To escape them. And eventually he had.

Thirty-four was a hell of an age to start regretting what he'd never had.

When the original photo of Lexy came on the screen again, Bailey stopped the program, then bumped her shoulder into his. "You're not going to make me take you to Buffalo Plains in the trunk of your car, are you?"

"I told you I would go." Told—and lied. Was probably lying even now. Once he'd taken care of Mac, he had only two options: to turn himself in or to go on the run. Neither was an ideal setup for a family reunion.

"Just making sure you haven't changed your mind." She rested her head on his shoulder for a moment before quietly stating the obvious. "Mac's late."

Logan glanced at the computer's clock. Mac had said he would call about the same time as before, which had passed more than two hours ago. "Maybe we got lucky and he pissed off the wrong guy." Even as he said it, he knew it wasn't likely. Someone else killing Mac would be too lucky indeed.

"Maybe he suspects something."

"More likely *he* got lucky, either at cards or with a woman."

She tilted her head back to give him a seductive smile. "You want to?"

"Play cards?" he asked innocently and received an elbow in the ribs in response. "Honey, I get lucky every day."

For now. But that would soon change. It was a good thing he was so skilled at adapting to change, though this time might be harder than the others.

Getting to his feet, he offered her a hand, pulled her up and into his arms, then headed for the bedroom. Halfway there, the phone rang. Though he wanted to keep walking, he stopped, scowled at her, then turned and carried her back across the room. As he let her slide down his body to the floor, she picked up the receiver and said, "You're late." Then she added, "Oh. Sorry, Reese. I was expecting someone else."

Logan's muscles unknotted as he left her to talk and began turning off the lights. He double-checked the lock on the door, idly listening to her end of the conversation.

"You know I shouldn't discuss cases with you any more than you should discuss yours with me… You're not my boss *or* my protector. I can take care of myself… I know these guys are scum. That's why I'm keeping my distance…." Then phony sweetness entered her voice. "Yes, you worry, and that's only fair, because I worry about you and Brady. But you guys are qualified for your jobs and I'm qualified for my job—and don't you dare snort at that. I *will* be up there in Oklahoma when I'm done here, and I *will* make you sorry. I'm not doing anything dangerous here."

Except risking her life every time she saw Escobar.

She talked a few minutes more before sending her love to her sister, then hanging up. When she saw Logan watching her, she smiled faintly. "Remember I asked Reese to run those license tags? Being the curious sort, he also ran a criminal history on those guys, and guess what? They all had one." She widened her eyes in mock surprise, then shrugged. "He doesn't have a lot of faith in my ability to do this job."

"It's not that. Of course he's going to worry about you."

Logan caught her hand, turned off the last light and pulled her into the bedroom. There he repeated some of her own words back to her. "Men still have some old-fashioned notions about women. They want to take care of them, to protect them. *Not* because they're weaker or not as smart or capable but because that's the way the world is."

"Well, I don't need to be taken care of," she said grudgingly.

"Probably not. But you like it sometimes, don't you? You even expect it sometimes, like when a drunk cowboy is hitting on you." When she'd been disappointed in him for not inter-vening. He didn't regret letting her handle it, but he did regret that it made her think less of him.

Though he couldn't tell it by the way she snuggled close to him when they got into bed.

"I've decided you did the right thing that night," she an-nounced, her cool, delicate fingers gliding over his skin, spread-ing heat and tension with every feathery touch. "It was good for my self-confidence to find out that I could handle a real-life situation."

"It convinced you that you couldn't count on me."

She didn't deny that—they both knew better—but shrugged instead. "I'm counting on you now, just like you're counting on me. We're partners."

Partners. He'd never wanted a partner of any kind before. He liked doing the loner thing. But there was something in-triguing about a partnership with Bailey. Something that could give a man a sense of satisfaction, that bone-deep contentment that most people never found.

Too bad he hadn't been looking for it.

Even worse that he couldn't hold on to it.

Not with the future he was planning.

Bailey spent most of Thursday morning on the phone—with caterers, a party-supply outfit, a management company for local bands and florists, all in Las Cruces. Hector wasn't con-cerned about supporting the local businesses with his party plans; he did that all year round, he boasted. He was Nomas's life blood—a claim she imagined most of the people in town would take exception to. His bogus ranch operation didn't make a dint in the local unemployment and his real work didn't seem to employ a lot of people beyond those she'd seen at his ranch.

But he could brag all he wanted. Maybe one day soon he would be doing it from jail. A harboring charge probably wouldn't keep him there long, but hopefully it would be long enough for his business to fall apart so he would have to start over again when he got out.

She had a meeting with him again in an hour. For a man who said he wanted control of the party plans, he had little interest in them when they met. Instead he asked questions about her, volunteered information about himself, invited her to dinner, to a movie, a concert or other diversion—said with a wink and a smile—in Las Cruces. He promised to be the perfect gentleman; why, he would even get two hotel rooms since, of course, it would be too late to drive back to Nomas when the evening was over.

The mere thought of spending that much time alone with him made her skin crawl. A few hours in Maria's was all she could bear at one time.

She finished getting ready, then walked into the living room. Logan was sprawled on the couch with the television tuned to CNN, but his attention was on her. "You're early."

"I thought I'd stop by the drugstore and see Marisa first." She felt a need to talk to someone other than Logan and Hector, to someone with a woman's perspective. "Afterward I need to pick up a few things at the grocery store. Any requests?"

He shook his head.

"Then I'll be back in a few hours." It was a relief to step outside the cabin, into the bright sunshine and fresh air, out of the murky gloom and tension. She knew it must drive Logan nuts to be trapped there, but he was a good soldier. He didn't complain. But ever since Mac's phone call on Monday, his nerves had seemed to ratchet tighter and tighter. Anticipation? Guilt? Dread? Probably a combination of the three.

There was little traffic on her way downtown. She parked directly in front of the drugstore, then went inside and climbed onto a stool at the fountain. Marisa finished waiting on the customer at the checkout before approaching her warily.

"Does Hector know you're consorting with the enemy?"

Bailey gave her a chastising look. "It's none of his business what I do."

"Ha. He thinks everything's his business."

"Not me. How are you?"

With a shrug Marisa picked up a cloth and wiped the already clean counter. "I haven't seen you around…though I hear Hector has. Every day."

"I'm helping him plan his birthday party."

"I was hoping he wouldn't see another one."

Bailey didn't respond to that. She wouldn't wish death on the man. Just a miserable life in prison. "What does he do for a living?"

"I told you, he has a ranch."

"That doesn't appear to have any livestock."

Marisa's gaze shifted uneasily as she bluntly changed the subject. "What can I get you?"

Bailey studied the menu on the wall behind the counter, then said, "I would order a banana split, but I've been told I don't need any more of those. How about a root beer float?"

Color stained Marisa's gaze. "When I drink, I tend to say things I shouldn't. I—I'm sorry."

With a wave of her hand Bailey dismissed the apology, then rephrased her earlier question. "Where does Hector really get his money?"

Marisa concentrated on scooping ice cream into the goblet, filling it with root beer, wiping the splashover from the sides and sliding both a spoon and a straw down into the froth before setting the glass in front of Bailey. "There are some things you're better off not knowing."

"Do *you* know?"

"I've heard talk."

Of course, in a small town, there was always talk, often untrue. But just as often, Bailey would wager, at least part of it was true. "I've heard it involves smuggling."

Marisa didn't meet her gaze.

"Is it drugs? Guns? People?"

Still no response from the other woman.

"Come on, Marisa. I'm just trying to get a handle on this guy. Help me out."

Finally she did look up. "If criminal activity bothers you, then stay hell and gone from Hector. That's all I can say."

After taking a long drink from her float, Bailey idly asked, "Is his brother a part of it?"

Nothing.

"He's coming back to town soon."

Still nothing.

"Jeez, getting people to talk around here is like pulling teeth."

Marisa leaned across the counter and hotly whispered, "Because talking about the wrong thing can be dangerous."

"You think Hector's dangerous?"

"What have I been telling you ever since we met?"

"What do you think he'll do to me? Kill me?"

"Oh, no. If he got that pissed off with you, he would probably just sell you instead." Abruptly she clamped her jaw shut and turned away. "I've got work to do. The float's on the house."

Before Bailey could say anything else, she disappeared into the back of the store.

He would probably just sell you instead. It was Logan who had brought up the idea that Hector might traffic in people. She'd seen stories about it on television before, about people, particularly girls and young women, smuggled into the country and forced to work under slave conditions. They spoke little English, were allowed no contact with outsiders and were too afraid to ask for help if they could.

Smuggling drugs and guns was despicable enough. But to sell human beings as if they were animals, as if he had the *right*...

Too sick to finish her float, Bailey pushed it away, laid a dollar and a nickel on the counter, then stood up. As she turned, a man on the street caught her attention. There was nothing unusual about him—he wore jeans and a T-shirt like most of the other men she'd seen. He was average height, average build, with a feed-store gimme cap covering his hair. He did seem unusually interested in the car, but that was a man thing. All that power seemed to touch a chord in their testosterone-laden genes.

She waited for him to move on—she didn't want to talk about the car—but instead of doing so, he glanced up and down the street, then turned and looked straight through the plate glass at her. Removing his cap, he pushed his glasses up onto the bridge of his nose and gave her a broad, benign, couldn't-hurt-a-fly grin that made her heart stop beating in her chest.

Oh, God.

Peter MacGregor had come to town.

Chapter 12

He was waiting when she summoned the courage to walk out the door and toward the car. The grin grew, stretching from ear to ear, as his gaze slid lazily all the way down to her toes, then back up again.

He waited until she was only a yard or so away before speaking. "You must be Bailey."

"Why must I be?"

"Because I've spent enough time in Nomas to know that you don't live here. Besides, Hector told me you were hot." He stuck out his hand. "Peter MacGregor, but everyone calls me Mac."

She resisted the childish urge to hide her hands behind her back. If merely talking to him on the phone made her feel unclean, what would actually touching him do? But she offered her hand, forcing it to hold steady, hiding the tremor that was sweeping through her.

His hand was warm, his palm callused, his grip strong. It was likely this right hand that had held the knife he'd plunged into Ella Jensen's frail body seven times, that had swung the firewood that crushed Sam's skull. Without a doubt, he could kill *her* with this hand—without a doubt, he would try if he ever suspected her real reason for being there.

She let go as quickly as possible, crossed her arms over her middle, the right hand tucked out of sight, and clenched her fingers tightly. "You didn't call last night."

"I didn't see any reason to, since I knew I'd be seeing you today." He glanced from her back to the Plymouth. "Is this your car?"

She nodded.

"You don't sound like you're from North Carolina."

"I'm not."

He stepped off the curb and started a slow circuit around the vehicle. "I knew a guy had a car just like this once. *He* was from North Carolina."

"Really." The word squeezed out through the tightness in her throat. It had never occurred to her or Logan that Mac might recognize the GTX. Just how well had he known the car? Was there anything in particular about it that could help him identify it for sure?

"Wouldn't it be something if this was the same car?" He gave her a look over the roof that suddenly didn't seem so benign. It wasn't anything particularly substantive—just a hardening of his gaze, a cooling—but it made her cold all the way to her toes.

"Hector says you stole this from your ex. He got a real kick out of that—leaving the poor slob but taking his prized possession. What's his name?"

"I usually refer to him as Rat Bastard," she said, hoping she sounded more casual to him than she did to herself. "Most people call him Mike. Mike Cadore." Easy enough to remember—the first name of her first serious boyfriend and the last name of the last one.

The key to a believable lie, claimed Charlie, back in the office, was details. Giving a careless shrug, she provided them. "I met him at a bar in Nashville. Should have left him there.

And I didn't exactly *steal* the car. After living with him, cleaning up after him and supporting him for three years, I took it as payment for services rendered."

"Not the same guy I knew." Mac finished his perusal of the car and joined her on the sidewalk again. "I understand you're hooking up with Hector over at the café. Come on. I'll walk you over."

Bailey was surprised by how badly she wanted to say no, thanks, but instead she nodded and turned toward the courthouse down the street.

"You said you've spent time here," she remarked, gazing in the windows they passed so she wouldn't have to look at him. "Where do you live?"

"Around. I'm too restless to stay in one place for long."

Was that why you deserted your unit in Iraq? she wanted to ask. *Why you killed Ella and Sam? Because a year was too long to stay in one place?* What a sad, sorry reason for their deaths.

Instead she said, "You should try it sometime." *Like in prison.* "Your brother's lived all his life in Nomas and seems happy enough."

"Some people are stayers. Others, like you and me, are goers."

She shuddered inwardly at being lumped into the same category with him.

An hour ago the idea of greeting Hector with relief would have struck her as absolutely impossible. But when they crossed the street to Maria's and she saw him sitting in his usual booth, relief was exactly what she felt. After all, Hector *might* be evil, but Mac definitely was.

Wishing for any excuse to suggest that they move to a table, she did the next best thing and waited until Mac slid onto the empty bench, then drew a chair from the nearest table and seated herself at a right angle to both men. They exchanged grins. Pulling the legal pad from her bag, she flipped it to a clean sheet, then looked from one to the other. "Guest lists," she said expectantly.

Hector raised up enough to pull a pad of folded papers from his hip pocket. It was a database printout, six pages of names and addresses. He didn't look like the kind of guy who could even define *database,* much less set one up and use it. The fact that he could made her wish for access to his house and time alone with his computer. What other interesting things might she learn?

As she smoothed the creases in the pages, she asked, "Did your wife do all the planning when she was here?"

Hector and Mac traded looks, then Hector replied, "Nah. We didn't start celebrating until she was gone."

Simple words. Simple chill creeping along Bailey's spine. What in hell was she doing sharing a table with a known murderer and a man who might have killed his own wife and children? Staying in the office and dealing with crooks only by computer wasn't really such a bad way to do her job. A little dull, sure, but safe and sane, while there was nothing sane about playing games with these two.

But she was doing it for Logan, she reminded herself. He needed closure and would never find it as long as Mac remained free and unpunished. He needed to know that he'd gotten justice for Sam and Ella, and she was his best bet for doing that. It wasn't *really* dangerous, no matter what Logan and Reese thought. She wasn't taking any unnecessary risks.

Even if sitting in the café in broad daylight with them did feel terribly risky.

"Hector says you're from Tennessee."

She slid the computer printout into the back of the legal pad before gazing at Mac. "Yes, I am. Memphis."

"What'd you do there?"

"Waited tables. Cooked. Worked as a barmaid. I did a little data entry, but I don't really like working with machines that are smarter than I am."

"How long did you live there?"

"Eight years." Truth—easy to remember.

"And you supported the rat bastard for two."

"Three. Three wasted years." His deliberate mistake made her stomach muscles tighten. Though his manner was casual, just making conversation, there was something about his eyes, some little bit of hardness…distrust. Was he thinking it too much a coincidence that her fictitious ex had owned a car identical to Logan's or did he meet all strangers with that suspicion?

"You seem too smart to settle for being a waitress or a barmaid."

She raised one brow. "Don't have much respect for the service industry, do you?"

"Someone's got to do jobs like that, but it damn sure isn't gonna be me."

It took a lot of gall for a man who couldn't settle down because the police were after him, who stole and murdered and did God knew what else, to look down his nose on the people who waited on him. "Well, like you said, someone has to do it. I don't mind. It's an honest living."

Another degree of hardness, another notch up on the suspicion scale.

With some effort she directed the conversation back to the party and, with a lot of effort, kept it there. Hector was more interested in flirting, and Mac was more interested in…

It took her a moment to characterize what he was doing: feeling her out, looking for reasons to trust her—or more likely to *dis*trust her. Since the easy solution to dealing with someone he distrusted was murder, she brought the meeting to an end the first chance she got, packed up her notes, said her goodbyes and escaped out the door. Aware that they were watching her, she strolled down the street instead of dashing. She acted as if she couldn't possibly have a care in the world beyond making Hector's party the best ever, at least until she'd reached the relative safety of the car and driven out of sight. Then she pulled to the side of the street and surrendered to the uncontrollable tremors rocketing through her.

Though the afternoon wasn't overly warm, sweat beaded on her forehead and trickled down her spine, and her palms stuck damply to the steering wheel. She couldn't let go of the wheel, couldn't force her fingers to uncurl or her lungs to expand for a badly needed breath. All she could do was let the delayed re-action run its course.

When the shaking finally stopped, when the heaving of her stomach had settled and her heart had resumed something close to a normal rhythm, she pulled back onto the street and drove the short distance to the motel. Faith, outside Cabin 1 with the housekeeping cart, waved, and Bailey weakly returned it be-fore parking in front of number seven.

Logan was dozing on the couch when she walked in and locked the door behind her. Instantly alert, he grabbed for the pistol on the coffee table as he sat up, then let it slide back onto the wooden surface with a clunk. He took a long look at her face, then flatly said, "He's here."

She nodded. He didn't look triumphant, excited or any of the things she might have expected. Instead his expression was one of utter grimness.

"Did you talk to him?"

"Oh, yeah. He sat in on the meeting with Hector." Laying her purse aside, she went to stand in front of the air conditioner. The air cooled her heated skin, dried the sweat and raised goose bumps on her arms. She hugged herself as she faced Logan. "I actually ran into him on the street. He was very interested in the car. Said he knew a guy back in North Carolina who had one just like it. How familiar is he with your car?"

Before she finished speaking, Logan was shaking his head. "He reported to our company two weeks before we left for Iraq. He saw it three, maybe four, times."

"Well, he remembered it."

"So…you think he suspects something?"

"I think he suspects everybody of something. It's the best way for a man like him to live." Then she sighed quietly. "I think he bought the story I told him." *Think.* As in, *possibly, maybe, but not sure.*

In the silence that followed, she studied Logan. In jeans, T-shirt and bare feet, his hair mussed from his nap, he looked almost harmless…except for his eyes. They were icy-hard-blue, unforgiving, determined. This was a man who needed justice, no matter what the cost.

"Now what?" she asked softly.

For a time it seemed he hadn't heard her. He just continued to stare off at nothing, his thoughts a few miles distant. Then he blinked and focused on her. Her breath caught in her chest, and her stomach knotted painfully as she amended her earlier thought.

This was a man who needed vengeance.

No matter what the cost.

Now what?

Logan knew what Bailey wanted him to say. *Now we call the state police. We notify the Army where their deserter can be found. We turn him over to the cops and we get the hell out of Dodge.*

Could he lie to her? Could he tell her what she wanted to hear, then go ahead with his own plans?

Why not? He'd been lying to her in one way or another since they met. He'd never intended to let Mac walk away from their reunion, or to travel to Oklahoma with her to meet Brady's daughter. Deception had stood him in good stead so far. Why stop?

"I'll call the authorities in the morning. You get in touch with Mac and invite him over here tomorrow night."

She nodded solemnly. "Then they'll arrest him and we can get out of here."

He nodded, too, though guilt prickled along his spine. There would be no authorities, no arrest. He would be the only one waiting when Mac walked through that door. The element of surprise, along with months of bitter hatred, would be on his side, to say nothing of the fact that he would be armed to the teeth and ready to kill.

But not in front of Bailey. He would take Mac out into the desert miles from the motel, where no one would hear the gunshots, where the chances of his body being found before the carrion was finished off were between slim and none. He would dispose of Mac's car and then he and Bailey really would get the hell out of Dodge.

She would hate him forever.

But he could live with that.

A shiver rippled through her, and she rubbed her hands briskly over her arms to warm them. "Wow. It's almost over."

In more ways than one. His search, their affair, Mac's life, a part of his own life… For months he had lived with the need for vengeance. Nothing else and no one else had mattered. He hadn't planned for the future because as long as Mac was out there free, he wouldn't have one, not after he'd brought his old buddy to justice. He had accepted that. Hadn't cared at all.

Now, as he looked at Bailey, her arms once again wrapped around her middle and her expression cold with worry, he cared. She looked as if she needed someone to take care of her, to hold her and protect her and assure her that everything would be all right, and damned if he didn't want—need—to be that someone.

Too bad their definitions of *all right* differed so wildly.

Finally she moved away from the air conditioner, passing Logan to go into the bedroom. "Lexy's going to be so excited," she said as she stopped in front of the dresser to take down her braid. "I won't tell her we're coming. We'll just show up and surprise her."

He watched her loosen each tightly woven strand of hair and tried to ignore her words. He didn't want to think about how disillusioned she was going to be, how betrayed she would feel, how much she would hate him. He didn't want to think at all about Brady's daughter, fifteen and looking for a normal relationship with a normal uncle. According to Bailey, Lexy was no stranger to disappointment, but that didn't make it any less wrong to heap more of it on her.

Jeez, right now he didn't want to think of anything—not the past that was pushing him, the future that held nothing for him or the present that threatened to drown him in guilt. He didn't want to think about the knot that had settled in his gut when

Bailey had walked in the door, or the sick feeling that left him cold inside and out, and he damn sure didn't want to think about the doubt. Killing Mac was right. Everything Sam and Ella had given Logan—a home, support, love, acceptance—demanded it. No matter how much it cost him.

Killing Mac was the right thing to do. The prudent thing. The safe thing. He would never hurt anyone else, never destroy anyone else's life.

And Logan was prepared to pay the price to make sure of that. Later. Not just yet.

He crossed the few feet to stand behind Bailey. Her hazel gaze met his in the mirror, her expression soft with sympathy. "It's almost over."

It would never be over. But he didn't say that to her—didn't say anything at all to her. Instead he wrapped his arms around her, rested his cheek against her hair and just held her.

The evening passed quietly, slowly. They fixed dinner, then both picked at their food. They cleaned up the kitchen together, watched television without really seeing it, then finally went to bed, but neither was in the mood for sex. After going months without, he'd been in the mood ever since he'd met Bailey. But tonight, when things were about to end—badly—and she didn't know, it seemed wrong.

Before dawn Friday morning he slipped out of the cabin and retrieved one of the gun cases from the trunk of the GTX. He slid it under the bed, then crawled back under the covers with Bailey, snuggling close behind her. She shivered when his cold skin touched hers, murmured restlessly, then sank back into a deeper sleep.

The case held a Galil MAR assault rifle, a nice little weapon for mowing down the enemy. It would be his backup weapon, in case Mac tried to make a run for it, though that wasn't likely. The case also held a half-dozen large cable ties to use as handcuffs and a roll of duct tape. A few circles of that around his ankles, another piece over his mouth, and he would be pretty subdued.

Logan intended to use the .45 for the actual shooting. He wouldn't make Mac suffer the way Sam and Ella had. He wouldn't beat him until he was unrecognizable, wouldn't slice through his tissue, nerves and muscles. One bullet to the brain. Quick, easy, far too painless, but it would be enough.

The sick feeling started in his stomach again, nausea rising, an uncomfortable ache spreading. He did his best to ignore it, to convince himself it meant nothing. It wasn't an indication that he'd made a wrong decision. It was just anticipation. Nothing more.

God help him, it couldn't be anything more.

"Call Mac. Invite him over."

Bailey looked up from the computer screen where she was once again working on the party menu. Between them, Hector and Mac had managed to veto about two-thirds of what she'd presented the day before, even though the menu had been created entirely from Hector's list of likes and dislikes. She suspected he was being difficult because he could, because it kept her coming around—at least for the time being. Heaven willing, the *time being* was very short, indeed. She intended to say goodbye to Nomas for good sometime tonight.

"You call the state police first."

"I already have. While you were in the shower."

Pushing the computer back from the table's edge, she brought both feet onto the seat and wrapped her arms around her knees. "What did they say?"

"They made sure there was a warrant issued for Mac—there were a half dozen, in fact, from various states—and they said they would be here to pick him up this evening."

She studied him for a long time, but he didn't look back. His attention instead was focused on the guest list Hector had given her. Checking to see if any of Mac's old Army buddies were listed?

Something about his manner stirred an uncomfortable niggling in her stomach, but she couldn't put her finger on exactly what. He was a little edgy, but that was to be expected under the circumstances. His tone of voice had been relatively normal, and his words were perfectly normal—exactly what she would expect the cops to say when offered up a double murderer and deserter.

Was the niggling because he wasn't looking at her? Or maybe because of that look in his eyes yesterday when they'd talked? That vengeance-driven look that had made her so cold?

"I got out of the shower two hours ago," she remarked casually, "and you're just now telling me?"

Color darkened his cheeks. "I was preoccupied. Sorry."

Preoccupied with what? she wanted to ask. The events leading to Mac's arrest wouldn't involve him. *She* was the one who would invite Mac out. *She* was the bait to lure him into the trap. All Logan had to do was stand back and watch as the state police slapped the handcuffs on him.

If that really was the plan.

She hated doubting him. Hated thinking that he might be using her to set up Mac so he could…could… The word wouldn't even form in her mind without effort on her part.

Kill.

So he could kill Mac.

Her exhalation was heavy and ragged, and what air she could drag back in was insufficient. This was silly. Logan wasn't a cold-blooded killer. He'd said so himself that first day, and she believed him. She *knew* him, knew he wasn't capable of murder.

Though he probably didn't think of it that way. Likely he saw it as payback, justice, the natural consequences of Mac's actions. She couldn't even completely disagree. She thought death was the only just punishment for what Mac had done to the Jensens…but *after* he'd gone to trial. *After* he'd been convicted by a jury of twelve citizens. *After* he'd been sentenced to die. That was just.

Killing him now was murder, and Logan *wasn't* capable of murder…was he?

He nudged the phone in her direction, but she didn't pick it up. "When will the police be here?"

"In time to set up."

"When is that? Six o'clock? Five? Four?"

"I don't know and I didn't ask. They said they would be here, that they would come straight to the cabin, and I didn't ask for details." He still wasn't looking at her, even though he'd finished flipping through the database pages and was starting again.

"Why don't we leave before they get here? They don't need me to open the door to Mac. They don't need us to identify him."

Finally he did meet her gaze. His eyes were shadowy, cold. "I need to be here."

Maybe so. After all the time he'd spent looking, maybe he needed the satisfaction of seeing Mac handcuffed and taken away. Maybe he needed Mac to know that *he* was responsible.

Or maybe he needed to be there because there weren't any cops coming.

"Mac and Hector are family, with all the loyalty that implies. Do you think Hector will sit back quietly while his brother's arrested for murder? He won't go after the cops, but he very well might come after us."

"We'll leave when the cops do." Once more he pushed the phone closer. "Call him."

She laid her hand on the receiver, her fingers curling tightly around the hard plastic, but instead of lifting it and dialing, she fixed her gaze on him. "Logan…you do intend to hand him over to the authorities…don't you?"

Once again his color heightened—not a lot, just a tinge of bronze in his cheeks. Once again he couldn't look her in the eye.

Something—disappointment, fear, dread—settled hard in her stomach. "You didn't call anyone this morning, did you?"

Once again he had no answer.

"Oh, Logan…" Her chest tightened and a knot formed in her throat that choked her voice. "I can't help you with this. I can't be a party to murder. I know you loved the Jensens and you blame yourself for bringing the cause of their deaths into their lives. But killing him isn't right. It won't bring them back. It won't ease your grief or your guilt. You'll just be letting Mac destroy you, too, because you can't live with murdering a man. I know you!"

"No, you don't," he said quietly. Numbly. "I'm not interested in easing my grief or guilt. I'm looking for justice, and any way you look at it, *this* is justice."

"Any way you look at it, it's murder, and I won't be part of it." Though she already had been, she realized with dismay. She had led Logan to Hector, had insinuated herself into Hector's world, had put herself in a position to pass on information about Mac. Any halfway decent prosecutor could make a case that she'd been a coconspirator to commit murder, no matter that she hadn't had a clue. God, she'd been naive!

"So leave." For the first time since the conversation had begun, his voice showed some emotion. It was harsh, cutting, dismissive. "Pack your bags and get the hell out. Marisa would be more than happy to give you a ride to Deming. But first call Mac and invite him over here."

"No. You want him so damn bad, you call him." Letting her feet hit the floor with a thump, she shoved the chair back so hard it fell, then swept across the room and into the bedroom. She jerked on the jean jacket she'd been wearing the past week, realized it was Logan's and jerked it off again, then shoved her feet into a pair of loafers.

Her intention was to make a grand exit, stomping across the living room, slamming the door behind her, but that became impossible when he blocked her way, looking harder and more immovable than she'd ever seen him. "One damn phone call, Bailey," he said, his jaw clenching tightly on each syllable. "That's all I'm asking of you."

"All?" she echoed shrilly. "*All?* I've already done enough to make me guilty as hell, because I was stupid enough to trust you! Now you expect me to lure a man to his death and you have the gall to say that's *all* you're asking of me?" So angry she had to hit something, she chose his shoulder, smacking him hard, making him stumble back a step. "How dare you use me and betray me like this? How dare you do this to your brother and your nieces? And how the hell dare you desecrate Sam and Ella's memory this way?"

Instead of smacking him again, she used both hands to shove him out of the way. He lost his balance, scrambled over the coffee table and landed on the couch, but she didn't care. She didn't slow in her rush for the door, which she slammed behind her with tremendous satisfaction.

She was halfway down the steps when she realized she didn't have the car keys with her or any money or even her cell phone, but she couldn't bear going back just yet. She needed to plan, to think, but at the moment all she could think was that Logan was going to kill Mac. He was going to ruin his life, to break Brady's heart and Lexy's and hers.

It wasn't anger that had made her smack him, she realized as she stalked along the drive that curved past the next six cabins, but fear. Fear of what he would do. Fear of the lives he would damage or destroy. Fear of what she had helped him do.

And, yes, anger, too, that he'd lied to her from the beginning. He'd involved her in a major felony with no regard for her safety, her honor, her moral code. He'd used her to fulfill his need for retribution without a care about how she would cope with the consequences.

He'd *used* her. He didn't love her. Didn't need her. Didn't want her. Didn't care about her. He'd said the right words, told the right lies and had gotten her services as a private investigator, to say nothing of her sexual services, while *she'd* paid her own fees.

God, she was a lousy P.I., suckered by a handsome face. All this time she'd thought she was so capable, when she'd been too gullible to recognize the lies she'd been swimming in. Being used, getting her heart broken—she deserved it for being so damn stupid.

When she reached Cabin 1, she kept walking, bypassing the drive that led to the highway for the open desert. There would be plenty of time for scolding herself later. Right now she needed a plan. Make a phone call, Logan had said, and that was exactly what she intended to do. She would call Reese and Brady and tell them what was going on. Reese would contact the New Mexico authorities, and Brady, she was sure, would be on the next plane west. The cops would be there in no time, and Brady soon after, and Logan wouldn't have the chance to carry out his insane plan. He would probably hate her for interfering, but that was okay. She was doing a pretty good job of hating him at the moment.

At least, until she remembered that she had actually thought she might be falling for him.

Stubbornly she forced her thoughts from that direction. Now that she had something of a plan, her first priority was to get to a phone. She would go back to the motel office and borrow Faith's phone and then she would go back to the cabin and keep an eye on Logan until the cavalry arrived, to make sure he didn't do something stupid.

With a plan in place, the tension in her chest eased a bit, allowing for easier breathing as she spun around and marched back the way she'd come. Her gaze was on the uneven ground—the last thing she needed was a broken ankle—until she became aware of the hum of a powerful engine. The GTX? she wondered, jerking her head up. Had Logan come looking for her? Or was he going looking for Mac?

Her feet stopped so abruptly that her body swayed forward before coming to a halt, as well. The engine didn't belong to the Plymouth. No, this was a burgundy extended cab pickup truck. Hector sat behind the wheel, grinning broadly, and Mac was climbing down from the passenger seat. "We were looking for you."

She swallowed hard, estimating the odds of making it to the motel office or back to the cabin or even to the highway before they caught her, and coming up with the same answer: zero. Instead of running, she stood her ground and did her very best to appear innocent. "I wasn't aware I was missing."

One hand still on the open door, Mac gestured with the other. "Come on. Let's go for a ride."

"No, thank you."

"'No, thank you,'" he mimicked. "So proper. Doris Irene must be proud of you."

Her blood ran cold at the mention of her mother by name. She took an involuntary step back and once again considered her options. The men and the truck were between her and the cabin, between her and the office. If she ran for the cabin, they would likely catch Logan off guard. If she went for the office, Faith would be in danger, too, and maybe her kids, if they were home. And the road…they could travel much faster on its paved, flat surface than she could.

"So you learned my mother's name," she said, faking a calm she didn't feel. "If you'd asked, I would have saved you the trouble of finding out."

"It was no trouble. Did Hector ever mention that the sheriff here is a cousin of his several times removed?" Mac reached behind him with his free hand and drew a pistol. "Come on. Let's go for a ride."

"Do you know the p-penalty for k-kidnapping?" she stammered even as she began moving reluctantly in his direction.

"It ain't got nothin' on the penalty for desertion and murder. Of course, you know all about that, don't you? My good buddy Logan told you, didn't he?"

He couldn't have seen Logan…but he could have asked Hector's cousin the sheriff to run the license tag on the GTX. He could have asked about any strangers in town besides her and heard about Marisa's tall, dark and handsome friend at Pat's Place.

Apparently he'd asked a lot of questions—and gotten a lot of answers.

As soon as she got close enough, he grabbed hold of her wrist and shoved her into the truck's backseat with enough force to send her sprawling. He climbed into the front, then twisted around to catch her wrists in one hand and wrap a wide strip of duct tape around them. Before resettling in his seat, he did the same to her ankles.

As Hector followed the drive toward the highway, he met Bailey's gaze in the rearview mirror. There was no sign of the man who'd flirted relentlessly with her for the past week. The grin still remained, cold enough that it made her cold, and there was an unholy light in his eyes. "You know who I am and what I do and what my kid brother's done, and now I know who you are and what you do. So what do you think, sweetheart? Do we know each other well enough for you to go home with me?"

She stared back at him, concentrating hard on keeping the fear from her expression—not an easy task when she was consumed by it. No doubt, they intended to use her to lure Logan out of the motel and then they planned to kill them both. She was going to die in some nowhere place in the New Mexico desert, and on her first case, no less. Her boss had been right to keep her shut up in her office. She'd screwed up this case from the moment she'd laid eyes on Logan. She hoped he felt damned guilty about it before they killed him, too.

Tears blurred her vision. She was going to *die*. It would break her sisters' hearts, and poor Lexy! She would blame herself, when none of it was her fault. Her sisters would have to clear out her office and her apartment and dispose of her belongings, and Doris Irene… God, how awful would it be for their mother to have to bury her second daughter?

Damned if she was going down without a fight. She didn't know what she would do, but by God, she would do *something*. Mac and Hector might have the devil himself beat when it came to evil, but she had intelligence on her side.

And Logan. He didn't want to be anybody's hero, but he'd do it for her.

She hoped. Prayed.

Believed.

Chapter 13

For a long time Logan stayed where he'd fallen, head tilted back, eyes squeezed shut. His lungs were so constricted that he could barely breathe, and his gut was still knotted. It wouldn't take much to send him to the bathroom for a case of the dry heaves—just an easing of his control. But he didn't ease it. He kept a tight hold on himself to keep himself from falling apart.

Bailey's disappointment and anger had been everything he'd expected. Worse, she had been right about Sam and Ella. What he was planning *was* disrespectful to them. They'd been good, kindhearted people who'd helped anyone who needed it. He wasn't the first one they'd taken in over the years and he hadn't been the last. They had lived their lives according to the Good Book and they would be so appalled by the choice he'd made. Not angry—they'd never gotten angry with him, no matter what he'd done. Because of that, their shame and disappointment had been so much harder to bear. He'd worked damned hard not to disappoint them.

Until now.

Finally he sat up to look at the clock. He didn't know what time Bailey had left, but it must have been at least fifteen minutes ago. She'd gone off on foot with nothing but the clothes she was wearing. Her purse still sat on the table, the car keys beside it, her cell phone hooked to the strap, her pistols inside. She was probably at the motel office, cooling off with the owner or, as angry as she'd been, she might have made it all the way into town to vent to Marisa. She would be back soon.

The assurance didn't do anything to ease the knot in his chest.

He looked out the window and saw no sign of her. Stepping out onto the stoop for a better view, he watched Faith come out of the second cabin with the housekeeping cart. So much for Bailey cooling off with her.

Back inside, he went to the phone and the slim directory on the kitchen counter. Marisa answered the drugstore phone on the second ring. "Hey, Marisa, it's Logan. Have you seen Bailey this morning?"

"Log— Oh, tall, dark and handsome. I didn't realize you were still in town. I haven't seen you at Pat's in nearly a week."

"Yeah, I've been busy." Making love with Bailey. "Have you seen Bailey today?"

"No. I saw her yesterday with Hector's snake of a brother, but not today. Why? Is something—"

He hung up before she could finish. He didn't want to hear that final word, but he couldn't avoid it. *Wrong*. Something was damned wrong. He could feel it in his gut. Bailey wasn't off somewhere getting over her anger and disappointment or plotting ways to stop him. Something had happened to her, and it was his fault.

He didn't realize his hand was still on the phone until it rang. Startled, he jerked his fingers away, then stared at it. Who knew to call Bailey there? Marisa. Escobar. Mac. Her brother-in-law, Reese. No one, other than Marisa, who should know that *he* was there.

The phone rang six times, went silent a moment, rang six more times, stopped, then started again. It could be Escobar or

Mac…but it could also be Bailey. That persuaded him to pick up the receiver, though he said nothing.

"Hey, buddy."

It was Mac.

Logan's fingers tightened until the tips went numb. For a moment he couldn't breathe, couldn't see through the red haze that clouded his eyes, couldn't feel anything but pure, burning rage…and fear. Mac was the *something wrong* that had happened to Bailey. Logan felt it in his soul.

"No greeting for the man who saved your ass more than a few times?" Mac asked. "You wound me, Marshall. I hear you've been looking for me. I hope you don't have some crazy idea about turning me over to the cops. You know me, man. I don't like staying too long in one place. That makes prison kinda hard, you know?"

His chest burning, Logan realized he'd stopped breathing. He forced in one breath, then another, and the ache eased. The fear didn't.

"I don't intend to go to prison," Mac said, his tone conversational but underlaid with steel. "That's why I got me a little insurance. We're out here at my brother's ranch. You come on out, and I'll let her go, and you and me—we'll settle this privately. Sound like a plan to you?"

Finally Logan found his voice. "Sounds like a setup."

Mac laughed. "Aw, don't you trust me anymore? And after all we've been through together…"

All they'd been through… Mac *had* saved his life a time or two, and Logan had returned the favor. Now he intended to take it from him. Even if it meant dying himself.

Anything, so long as Bailey walked away unharmed.

"You know the way this plays out. You come alone. No cops, no friends, no help. This is between you and me. Understand?"

"You and me and Hector and his friends?" Logan asked sardonically.

"A lesser man would be insulted by your lack of trust, Marshall. See you . . . oh, let's say in an hour."

Before Logan could ask for more time, the line went dead.

One hour to prepare to walk into an ambush and find some way to get Bailey out alive. The odds weren't good, but damned if he was going to live—or die—with her death on his conscience.

One hour, and the clock was ticking.

The ride to the Escobar ranch had never seemed so long, but then Bailey had never made it trussed up like a prisoner in the back of someone's truck. Bracing herself on the bumps was practically impossible, and the skin on her wrists and ankles was already starting to chafe in reaction to the duct tape. When Hector finally parked beside the house, she gave a sigh of relief and wriggled into a sitting position just in time for Mac to grab her by the ankles and haul her out the door. Instead of setting her down and removing the tape, though, he hefted her over one shoulder and strode toward the barn. She watched the ground pass bumpily before closing her eyes to stop the vertigo rising inside her.

Hector went ahead and slid open the wide barn doors to reveal a piece of ancient farm equipment—she couldn't begin to guess at its purpose—and piles of junk. Mac dropped her to the ground in front of the equipment, with its tall, fat tires and rusted implements, then took a few steps back. "Get comfortable, sweetheart. Now we wait."

She struggled to sit up, a piece of machinery at her back for support. "How am I supposed to get comfortable with my wrists and ankles taped? I'm allergic to adhesive, you know."

"Yeah, right."

"Really. Look." She thrust out her hands to show the redness that had formed at the edges of the tape. "Can't you take this off and just tie my hands? Surely a ladies' man like Hector has a good supply of rope around."

Hector glanced at her, offended by the suggestion he needed rope to have his way with the ladies, then at Mac, who shrugged. Pulling a knife from his pocket, Hector bent and cut through the duct tape, then ripped it off and threw it away before going to get a length of rope.

She really was allergic to adhesive and spent a moment vigorously scratching the hives starting to form around her ankles. The more she scratched, the worse they would look and the more quickly. If they looked bad enough, maybe she could persuade him not to tie her ankles, and once Logan arrived, she would have a shot at doing something…not that she had a clue what.

When Hector returned with the rope, he started to loop it up high around the machinery. "Oh, come on," she said scornfully. "You expect me to sit here with my hands above my head? Do you know how uncomfortable that will be? I'm one unarmed woman against two bigger, heavily armed men. What are you afraid of?"

"Certainly not you, sweetheart." He didn't relent completely, but he did loop the rope instead around a bar that would allow her to rest her hands in her lap. Once he finished securing it around her wrists, he sat back on his heels and grinned. "Don't want you to be too uncomfortable. You and I still have business to finish."

That wolfish grin made it clear exactly what that business was and made her swallow hard. She couldn't think of anything much more repulsive than having sex with Hector—maybe having it with Mac—but it beat what seemed the only alternative. As long as she lived, she could fight.

"What makes you think Logan will come?" she asked Mac, standing near the doors and gazing out.

He glanced over his shoulder, somehow still looking so damn harmless. "I killed his surrogate parents and now I've taken his woman. He'll come."

"I'm not his woman. I'm a private investigator working a case with him."

"Yeah, yeah. Whatever you are, he'll come for you."

"He'll come for *you,*" she pointed out. *To kill you.* She had to admit that at the moment Logan's plan to kill Mac was looking better. Was she so self-centered that her moral values changed when the dilemma involved her? No, her morals hadn't changed. The situation had. What Logan had been planning was cold-blooded murder. Now their lives were on the line. If he didn't kill Mac, Mac and Hector would kill both of them. Now she didn't care whether Mac got the justice of the legal system or the justice he deserved.

As long as she and Logan came out of this alive.

The feel of hands on her feet jerked her out of her thoughts and instinctively she kicked out. Hector scowled at her. "Knock it off. I just need to tie this."

She scowled back. "Look at my ankles. They're already swollen from the damn tape. Besides, what do you think I'm going to do? Walk off dragging this—this thing behind me?"

He did look at the welts ringing her ankles everywhere the tape had touched, shrugged and tossed the second piece of rope aside. He didn't move away, though, but continued to watch her with a look that made her skin crawl. She was tempted to kick him—hard—but that would surely result in her getting trussed up again. Gritting her teeth, she gave him a sarcastic smile, then turned back to Mac. "Why did you kill the Jensens? They opened their home to you. They showed you kindness and compassion. They wouldn't have hurt you even if they could."

"They would have called the cops on me for taking their truck and their money."

"No, they wouldn't have." Logan had gotten caught stealing from them years ago, but instead of calling the sheriff, they'd taken him in, fed him, given him a home. Obviously Mac had been beyond that sort of help, but she doubted the Jensens would have wanted him arrested for taking their property. More likely they would have written him off as one they'd tried to help but failed.

Mac shrugged as if her argument was pointless. "I made sure they couldn't tell anyone." There was no remorse in his voice, his expression, his affect. He didn't regret what he'd done to the Jensens and wouldn't regret what he intended to do to her and Logan. He had no conscience, no humanity. The world would be better off with him dead.

"What about you?" She shifted her attention to Hector. "Do

you kill people on the off chance that they might cause problems for you?"

"Nah. I leave that to him."

"Did he kill your wife and children?"

A startled look came into Hector's expression as his gaze darted to Mac. Surprise. Doubt. Distrust. He had complained to his brother about Shelley, had probably talked about getting rid of her, of being better off without her, and right at that moment he was wondering if Mac had taken him seriously.

This time Mac glowered at both of them. "I was in Korea when the bitch disappeared, remember?"

"Yeah, and planes fly back and forth every day," Bailey said helpfully.

"Jeez, Hector, Shelley was your problem, not mine. If you'd killed her, I'd've helped you get rid of the evidence, but I sure as hell wouldn't have bothered to do it myself. For God's sake, stop listening to the woman. She's just trying to cause trouble." Then to Bailey he said, "Shut the hell up or I'll make you shut up."

She would have liked to have the nerve to make some smart response. The problem was, she believed he really would shut her up.

Permanently.

It was all Logan's fault.

If he had called the state cops that morning, as he'd told Bailey he had, they never would have argued, she never would have gone out alone and Mac would have had to go through Logan to kidnap her. If he had called the state cops, they might even already be in town or at least on their way. But it was too late for regrets now. It was up to him and him alone to rescue her, and he didn't have a clue how.

He worked methodically, assembling his small arsenal, loading each weapon, sliding extra rounds and magazines into his pockets and backpack, which held the binoculars, as well. He concentrated fiercely in an effort to keep his mind off Bailey and what she was thinking, how afraid she must be, how hopeless she must feel. After all, in her opinion, he was no kind of hero. She wouldn't expect him to even try to save her, and wouldn't expect him to succeed if he tried.

He clipped the .45 onto his waistband in back, then slid the .40 into the shoulder holster he wore. He didn't bother with a jacket to hide it; Mac expected him to show up armed. After strapping a dagger to his right calf beneath his jeans leg, he picked up the backpack by its straps, the assault rifle by its strap, and strode across the living room to the door.

Eleven minutes had passed since he'd gotten off the phone.

After a quick stop in town, he drove out to the Escobar ranch, bypassing the garbage dump where they'd parked before, leaving the car in the middle of the road while he moved stealthily to the outcropping of rocks that offered a good view of the ranch below. The big truck was parked next to the house, which appeared silent and closed up. The barn doors were open, though, and sitting on the ground just inside, her hands tied to some kind of farm equipment, was Bailey.

Relief surged through him as he studied her with the binoculars. It didn't appear that they'd hurt her. Her position didn't look particularly comfortable, but there were no bruises, no cuts or other visible injuries.

Relief was joined by admiration as he saw the defiance mixed with fear in her expression. She was a strong woman. If Mac and Escobar expected tears, hysteria and submission from her, they were going to be disappointed. Judging by the look she wore, the bastards were wise to keep her restrained, or she would do them serious harm.

He would do them serious harm for her.

Before rising, he scanned the area for any sign of his targets. There in the shadows of the barn, far enough from the doors to avoid the sun beating down overhead, a pair of feet were propped on a stack of wooden crates. He couldn't see the body they belonged to, whether it was Mac or his brother or one of Escobar's men. It didn't really matter. He would take care of them all once he got down there.

After putting the binoculars back in the pack, he returned to the road and jogged east, past the car, the Escobar driveway and the tilted mailbox, to the end of the road and under the barbed wire fence. The lay of the land was better for concealment on the east side than on the west, where he and Bailey had approached the ranch together Saturday night. Gentle hills, gullies and heavier undergrowth gave him better odds of reaching the house and its outbuildings unseen. From there he would circle behind the sheds, come up on the barn and…rescue Bailey. Save her. Protect her. Somehow.

God help him, he would succeed…or die trying.

"He's late," Mac announced flatly, leaving his comfortable seat in the shadowy coolness of the barn and coming to stand in the doorway again. He cradled his rifle in both arms as he scowled at the unchanged scene outside, then turned to scowl at Bailey.

She scowled right back. The sun was directly overhead, and she was hot, dirty, sweaty and thirsty. She needed to go to the bathroom, her ankles and wrists itched like hell and her butt was going numb from staying in the same position on the hard-packed dirt for so long. "Why did you think he would come? For me? I told you, I'm a private investigator helping him on a case. I'm not his girlfriend, not his partner, not even his friend. He's got no reason to walk into an ambush just because I'm here."

Even as she said the words, she desperately hoped they weren't true. If he didn't come, Mac would surely want to kill her anyway—after all, he didn't like to leave witnesses alive—while Hector was already talking about the money she could earn him. He'd given enough broad hints to confirm the rumors Marisa had mentioned—that he did traffic in people. Though the idea repulsed her, it beat the hell out of dying there in the dirt. He would have to keep her alive and relatively unharmed to maximize his profits, and as long as she lived, she would have hope.

Leaning back on a couple bales of ancient hay to the left of and behind Bailey, Hector chuckled. "I told you to just give him a half hour."

"Shut up, Hector," Mac said irritably.

"An hour's long enough to come up with a plan. A half hour, he wouldn't have had much more than the time needed to drive out here."

"And what kind of plan you think he's gonna come up with in an hour? Going to the sheriff? Bringing in reinforcements? The sheriff would laugh at him, and he'd need a hell of a lot more than an hour to get reinforcements into this godforsaken place." Mac kicked a clod of dirt and sent it rolling away in a dozen smaller clumps. "The son of a bitch isn't coming."

"Impatient, aren't you?" Bailey asked, forcing cheerfulness into her voice. "How late is he? Three, four minutes?"

Mac turned a sour look her way. "Maybe you don't understand. If he doesn't show up, you die."

"You want to kill me if he doesn't show up, you want to kill me if he does and Hector wants to sell me to some disgusting criminal type with no ethics, no morals and no mercy—"

"But plenty of money," Hector interjected with a grin.

She finished with a shrug. "So it doesn't matter much to me either way."

The instant her last words were out, the rumble of an engine broke the desert stillness and the GTX turned off the dirt road into the driveway. Her muscles tightened, and both relief and disappointment swept through her. She was grateful Logan had come—she'd had no doubt that he would—but she had expected him to come sneaking across the desert, taking them by surprise, turning their ambush against them. But to drive right up to the barn—which he was doing very, very slowly—didn't bode well for their escape. He wasn't even trying for the element of surprise. Maybe he intended to come out of the car shooting. Maybe he didn't care what happened to her or himself as long as Mac died.

The car eased to a stop thirty feet away. The noon sun glinted off the windshield, making it impossible to see inside. The tension in the air was so thick that Bailey swore she could actually feel the engine's grumble as Logan sat there, unmoving.

"Why isn't he getting out?" Hector asked, sitting up straight and lowering his feet to the ground.

"Like I know?" Mac snapped back. He took a step toward the car, a step that brought him right into the doorway, and shouted, "Turn off the damn engine!"

A moment passed, then the motor went silent. The quiet was so sudden, so profound, that it seemed eerie, sinister. The utter stillness inside the vehicle magnified the sense of foreboding. Swallowing convulsively, Mac looked back at Hector, on his feet now, then moved forward once again. "Get out of the—"

The butt of a rifle smashed into his face as Logan stepped around the corner of the barn. Blood spurted from Mac's nose, and his glasses went flying, the lenses shattered. Another blow, this one to the back of his neck, sent him sprawling in the dirt, scrambling to lift his weapon into firing position.

Hector rushed to his brother's assistance, his own gun drawn. Bailey shoved one foot into his path, tripping him, then gave him a good kick with the other foot to send him crashing down, his pistol landing between them. He grabbed for it just as she kicked again. She connected with his fingers, making him yowl in pain, then caught the gun with enough force to spin it far out of reach across the ground.

Enraged, Hector lunged for her. Grateful for all the miles she'd run and the workouts she'd put herself through, she kicked again and again, landing blows wherever she could, the hardest, most vicious blows her loafers would permit, in his kidneys, his stomach, his chest, his jaw. She was losing ground, though, as he slowly moved closer, blocking the movement she needed to give strength to her kicks. He crawled over her, wearing that soulless grin, and dealt her a bone-jarring blow, snapping her head back against the metal, making her vision go blurry. Her cheek burned and tears filled her eyes even as the taste of blood filled her mouth. For one endless moment she couldn't see, think, move, do anything but hurt.

Then the ringing in her ears faded, replaced by a dull buzz, and the burn spread from her face into her chest as her lungs struggled for breath. He'd wrapped his hands around her throat, she realized too late, and was squeezing the life from her. She tried to claw at his fingers but couldn't lift her hands, tried to wriggle out from beneath him, but couldn't do more than think the thought. He was going to kill her, and there was nothing she could do—

The gunshot was deafening, reverberating through the barn, through her very body. Hector stiffened, then slumped forward against her, his hands loosening around her throat. Bailey dragged in a few sweet breaths before the blood seeping across the back of his shirt registered. Realizing that he was dead or dying, she frantically shoved at him, desperate to get him off her, to put as much distance between them as possible.

A few yards away Logan and Mac were on the ground, both bloody and battered, as startled by the gunshot as Hector had been. If it hadn't been Logan who fired, then who....

The door to the GTX stood open, and Marisa was slowly walking toward them, Hector's gun shaky in her hands. She came close enough to nudge his body with her foot. When she got no response, she turned toward the other men. "Get out of the way, Logan, and I'll kill him, too," she said calmly, politely.

He shoved Mac back, then got unsteadily to his feet, his breathing heavy, dripping blood from a gash on his forehead. Bailey waited, once again barely breathing, silently pleading with him to turn down Marisa's offer. He looked at her, his gaze searching, then turned back to Mac, subdued on the ground. "I appreciate your offer, Marisa," he said, gently taking the gun from her. Once more he glanced at Bailey. "But he'd rather die than go to prison. Being locked up in a cell the rest of his life is the worst punishment he can imagine. Let's let him have it."

Bailey slumped back against the machinery, her shoulders rounding, suddenly becoming aware that her entire body was aching. She was still hot, dirty, sweaty and thirsty and she still needed to go to the bathroom, and if she didn't get away from the lifeless scum snugged up against her, she was going to be sick.

But she was alive. Logan was alive.

And Mac was alive. She'd never thought she would find a reason to rejoice in that.

Logan found the rope Hector had discarded and tied Mac securely, then crouched beside her, gingerly touching the swelling where she'd been hit. "Are you okay?"

All she could do was nod.

"I'm sorry." His fingers brushed light as feathers across her cheek, then her jaw, her throat. There was a look in his eyes she'd never seen before—not guilt, anger or bitterness. Not aloofness or iciness or indifference. It was…intimate. Heated. Possessive. Thankful.

And it was for *her*.

Though she hated to break the moment, she was still entirely too close to Hector for comfort. "Please," she said, her voice raw and ragged. "Get me away from him."

With a blink that look disappeared and Logan turned grim again. He pulled a knife from an ankle sheath and sliced carefully through the rope, put it up and helped her to her feet. When she was shaky, he lifted her into his arms and carried her through the double doors and into the sunlight and fresh air. She filled her lungs deeply with it.

He covered the distance to the house's front porch in long strides and lowered her to a shady spot on the porch. When he tried to straighten, she held on to him. "You asked Marisa for help."

"I was scared," he said simply.

"I thought you didn't want any help."

"I didn't know what I wanted."

"Thank you for not killing him."

Closing his eyes, he rested his forehead against hers. "For more than a year I thought I had no choice. What kind of man would I be if I didn't avenge Ella's and Sam's deaths? I owed it to them, and with them gone, I had nothing to lose—or so I thought."

She laid her palm against his left cheek, unmarked with blood. "You had plenty to lose—the things the Jensens taught you. Your honor and self-respect. Your family." *Me.* "And you were right. Mac doesn't deserve such an easy way out."

He held her a moment longer before lifting his head to meet her gaze. That look was back again, along with a hint of expectancy, a little fear, hesitancy. Just as he opened his mouth, though, the ring of a cell phone interrupted. They both looked as Marisa pulled the phone from her pocket and flipped it open. She listened a moment, then said, "It's over. Come on in."

As she slid the phone back into her pocket, she started toward them. "That's the state police," Logan murmured. "We called them on our way out here."

"You really did ask for help. I'm impressed." Bailey eased out of his embrace and met Marisa, hugging her tightly. "Thank you."

Subdued, Marisa nodded, then seated herself on the porch. "I think he's dead. Now I'll never know what happened to Shelley."

"He didn't kill her," Bailey assured her. "While we were waiting, I suggested to him that maybe Mac had killed her, and he seriously considered it. If he'd killed her himself or had someone do it, he would have blown me off. He didn't know where she is."

Hope lit Marisa's gaze, but dimly. "Then maybe she really is all right. Maybe if she hears that Hector's dead, she'll come back home."

Those were big *maybes,* but Bailey didn't point that out. After six years of not knowing whether her only sister, niece and nephew were dead or alive, Marisa knew just how little hope she had of finding them.

"I know a private investigator who's pretty good at finding people who don't want to be found," Logan said quietly, his gaze on Bailey. "Once this is all done, maybe she'll be willing to take on finding Shelley."

"I can't afford a private investigator. I've already spent all I can spare on that," Marisa said glumly.

Bailey bumped shoulders with her. "He's talking about me, and I'd be happy to do what I can for free. After all, you saved my life." She couldn't help smiling. Her first real case, and Logan thought she'd done a pretty good job. *Excellent* or *outstanding* would have been nice, but she wouldn't have believed either one. She'd made too many mistakes. But *pretty good*...that made her feel damned good.

The first state trooper turned into the driveway, lights on but no siren. Several other cars, including one that was unmarked, followed behind, with an ambulance bringing up the rear.

It was almost over, Bailey thought with a sense of relief that very nearly overwhelmed the uncertainty inside her. What had Logan been about to say when the phone call had interrupted? Where would they go from here? What would the future hold for them, if anything? What did he feel for her? If anything?

Too many questions.

Not enough answers.

Logan's muscles were taut, his stomach tied in knots, as he followed Bailey's little red car along a winding two-lane Oklahoma highway. He would like to think it was the prospect of seeing his brother and meeting his nieces within the next half hour that had him so tense, but he wasn't sure of that. He suspected it had more to do with the fact that in the days since the incident at the Escobar ranch he and Bailey hadn't yet talked. Not really. Not to each other.

They'd done plenty of talking to the authorities, giving the details of Sam's and Ella's murders, their search for Mac, their activities in Nomas, her kidnapping and the rescue plan. They'd talked to the paramedics, to the local prosecutor, and had done their best to avoid talking to the press. They'd talked to Marisa and to Faith, to Maria who owned the café and to Celia, the librarian. But all they'd done when they were alone was make love and *not* talk.

Once they'd finally been free to leave Nomas, they'd driven straight through to Pineville, picked up her car and, after a night's rest—restlessness for him, at least—had headed north into Oklahoma. She hadn't teased him about handcuffs or riding in the trunk; he hadn't given a thought to reneging on his promise. His seeing Brady and Lexy would make Bailey happy, and that was enough for him. Besides, it wasn't as if he had any-place else to go or anyone else he wanted to be with.

They had passed through Heartbreak a few miles back, where Neely and her husband, Reese, lived. It was a nothing little town— nothing big, nothing fancy, nothing much—but Neely and Reese were happy there, according to Bailey. When you were living with the right person, Logan supposed, you could be happy anywhere.

There were occasional houses along the highway, along with pastures, but mostly there were trees, their leaves starting to change color, adding interest to the rolling hills. The closer they got to town, the closer the houses came, until suddenly they were there. It was almost four o'clock, according to the sign outside the bank, and the temperature was a near-perfect sev-enty-two degrees.

And now the knots in his stomach really were because of Brady and Lexy.

Bailey turned just past the courthouse and pulled into a parking space in front of an antique shop. He parked beside her, got out and faced the old stone courthouse, which, according to the sign, also housed the Canyon County Sheriff's Depart-ment. So that was where Brady worked. Logan had to admit, he'd been surprised when she'd told him Brady was the under-sheriff. Public service might have been considered honorable elsewhere, but not in the Marshall household. But on further thought, it seemed a reasonable choice. Brady had always had that protective streak; looking out for others was second nature to him. Why not choose a job where he got paid for doing it?

Bailey touched his arm and gestured toward the shop. "Lexy works here after school."

The wide plate glass windows showed a variety of mer-chandise, most of it just old rather than antique. Pottery, frilly beaded lamps, sturdy furniture, knickknacks—they sold it all.

Lexy sold it all. Brady's daughter. His niece. His family.

He'd been beaten within an inch of his life and shot at more times than he could count. In Afghanistan and Iraq, getting blown up had been a constant threat. Last week Mac had been fighting to save his own life and to take Logan's. All of that had been easier than finding the courage to walk across five feet of sidewalk and through the shop door.

Then he looked at Bailey, watching him with that look—the same one she'd worn when he'd let Mac live. A quietly contented, trusting look.

He crossed the sidewalk, opened the door, waited for Bailey to precede him, then went inside. An electronic bell announced their arrival over the beat of music coming from the back. The voice that responded came from the back, too, a young, cheerful voice. "Be with you in just a minute."

It was one hell of a long minute.

They were standing near the cash register, in the middle of the store, when footsteps started their way from the storeroom in back. She came around the corner wearing a blue-and-white cheerleader's uniform—short pleated skirt, sleeveless fitted top, legs even longer than Bailey's. She was tall—only an inch or two shorter than him—and willowy, with her brown hair pulled back in a ponytail and a dozen or so earrings glinting in her ears. The stud in her nose was a tasteful gold ball, and the one piercing her navel, just visible under the short top, was blue to go with the uniform.

Her eyes were as blue as her father's, as blue as his own. She was pretty, young, and he thought he'd have to kill anyone who even thought about hurting her.

"Aunt Bailey!" she shrieked, throwing her arms around Bailey. "I'm so glad you came! Tonight's homecoming, and guess who got picked as sophomore class attendant? You should see my gown! I look *gorgeous* in it. Dad said I couldn't set foot outside wearing it, but Mom changed his mind. Why didn't you tell me you were coming?"

"I didn't know when I'd make it." Bailey pulled out of her embrace and, clasping her hand, turned her toward Logan. "I brought someone to meet you."

Lexy noticed him for the first time. There was no joyous shriek, no rush to embrace him. Just as well, because he didn't think he'd know what to do if she did embrace him.

Instead tears filled her eyes, and she pressed one hand to her mouth. "Oh, my gosh…Uncle Logan. You found him," she whispered to Bailey, and then to him she said, "You came. I can't believe you came." She crossed the few feet between them, sedately hugged him, pressed a kiss to his cheek, then suddenly held on so tightly that his breath caught in his chest. "I'm so glad to meet you."

Awkwardly he slid his arms around her and found it wasn't so awkward after all. He could get the hang of this uncle stuff— could even learn to appreciate it. "I'm glad to meet you, too," he said hoarsely.

When he looked over her shoulder at Bailey, watching them with a knowing smile, he realized just how much he meant those words. Lexy had brought Bailey into his life, and he owed her for that.

Now he just had to figure out how to keep her.

As the hour approached midnight, Bailey found a seat in an oversize chair in Hallie's family room and snuggled in. They'd gone to the football game as a family—Hallie, Brady and Brynn; Neely and Reese; Reese's cousin, Jace, and his wife; Reese's parents; Jace's parents; and Bailey and Logan. Family, Buffalo Plains-style. They'd watched Lexy in her evening gown, as gorgeous as she'd proclaimed, then come back after the game to visit.

Hallie slid into the empty space beside her—a tight fit, but Bailey didn't complain. "You're my best sister," Hallie said, hugging her close. "Thank you."

"Is Brady okay with Logan being here?"

"Are you kidding? He's thrilled…though I can see it might be hard to tell."

No kidding. *Taciturn* was a good description for the elder Marshall. He felt things deeply; he just didn't show them easily. He had embraced Logan when they walked into the sheriff's office, though it hadn't been an easy embrace. They'd spent much of the evening since then off to the side, sometimes talking quietly, sometimes saying nothing at all. Some of the tension had eased from Logan's features, though, so she presumed things were going well.

"Was he hard to find?"

Bailey tore her gaze from the two men to look at her sister, looking as innocent as Brynn…except for her smug smile. She suspected there was something between Bailey and Logan and would probably ask outright if given a chance. Too bad Bailey didn't have an answer to give her.

Back at the Escobar ranch that day, he'd looked as if he'd had something important to say to her, but they'd been interrupted, and he hadn't tried again. Things had gotten kind of strained between them. The case was over. All that had been left was the visit to Oklahoma, and then…then she was supposed to go back to her life in Memphis and he was supposed to go back to doing whatever he intended to do, and everything between them would be finished—the case, the time together, the sex.

That was the way it was supposed to go. But she didn't *want* to go back to her life in Memphis. She didn't want things between them to be finished. She just didn't know how to tell him so, or how to bear it if he didn't feel the same.

That look he'd given her at the ranch was the only indication that he might.

Then again, that could have been pure relief that she'd survived unharmed, because he was already living with enough guilt.

Deliberately she forced her attention back to her sister's question. "No, he wasn't too hard to find."

"Did it take you long to persuade him to come here?"

"No," she lied. Right up until the moment he'd decided to let Mac live, she hadn't believed he would willingly travel to Buffalo Plains. "I think he'd had enough of being so alone." Was that why he'd extended their relationship beyond the one-night stand they'd both agreed to? And now that he wasn't alone any longer, would he still want her?

"Does he know how you feel?"

Bailey tilted her head to one side to study Hallie. She was considered the pretty one, the flighty one, the one with more looks than substance, but there was much more to her than most people gave her credit for. With a wry smile Bailey shrugged. "I'm not even sure I know how I feel. I wasn't looking for a husband or a father for my children. I wasn't even looking for a lover."

"But you found one anyway. Sometimes when you're not looking, you find exactly what you need. Do you think when I came for a visit after my *third* divorce I wanted to fall in love and get married again? I was feeling like the biggest loser in the world. And then I met Brady." Her expression softened as her gaze sought him out. "Besides, finding the right guy doesn't mean you have to get married and have children right away. There's nothing wrong with just being together for as long as it's right for both of you."

And there was something terribly wrong with being apart because you didn't have the courage to take a chance. She and Logan had been apart long enough, at least emotionally. It was past time to tell him what she wanted, to find out what he wanted.

The others began leaving, and within minutes the house seemed empty. Brynn and Lexy were already in their rooms, Brady and Hallie were heading off to their room and Logan and Bailey were alone in the family room. For a long time they just looked at each other, then he came to sit on the hassock in front of her.

"How's it going with Brady?" she asked.

He shrugged. "He hasn't changed at all. He's still too damn selfless for his own good. I'm…glad."

"Glad you came?"

"You wanna gloat? Go ahead. Yeah, I'm glad I came. I never had any kind of normal family. I can see the appeal of it." He reached for her socked feet tucked on the cushion beside her and drew them onto the hassock, his strong fingers kneading them. "I never had any kind of normal relationship either, until you. I miss you."

"I'm here," she whispered.

He smiled faintly. "Not like you used to be."

That was true. Except for the times when they made love, there was so much distance between them. It had been easier before, when circumstances had brought them together, when neither had had much of a choice. Now, if they wanted to stay together, it would have to be a conscious decision on both their parts. If they both wanted it, great. If he didn't…it would break her heart.

"Last week at the ranch, I told you that I hadn't known what I wanted. That was true, except for one thing—you. I wanted you, for more than one night, for longer than it took to find Mac, for—for as long as I can have you." This time his smile was unsteady, his manner uncertain. "I never gave much thought to getting married or having kids. I never thought it was anything I'd want to do. I still don't know… All I do know is that I like my life with you a hell of a lot more than without you."

The relief that swept through Bailey was enough to make her light-headed. Pulling her feet free, she slid forward in the chair until her knees were between his, until her hands were resting on his thighs and her face was mere inches from his. "Better watch it, Logan. Keep talking like that, and before you know it, you'll be saying something like 'I love you.'"

He leaned closer, too, bringing with him heat and comfort and security. "I've never said those words to anyone before. You'll be the first."

"I've said them to several people before. You'll be the last."

Sliding his arms around her middle, he slid her onto his lap, snug against his body. "You saved my life, Bailey. Now I guess you're stuck with me."

"You saved me right back." As she twined her arms around his neck, he kissed her, a sweet, lazy, happy-to-do-this-again sort of kiss that melted her inside and out and made her lean heavily against him. When he finished and she found her breath, she laughed softly. "You really are some kind of hero, Logan."

"Oh, yeah? What kind?"

"The reliable kind. The forever kind." She gazed into his blue eyes and saw *that look* again. That intimate, heated, possessive, thankful look. And she would bet her fee on this last case that the same look was in her eyes. "*My* kind."

* * * * *

INTIMATE MOMENTS™

Don't miss this exciting and
emotional journey from

Michelle
Celmer

OUT OF SIGHT

#1398
Available December 2005

After a treacherous life in a crime family,
divorce counselor Abigale Sullivan finally
found a place to call home in the bucolic
wilds of Colorado. Her dream world came
screeching to a halt when FBI special agent
Will Bishop came after her and demanded
she testify against a brutal criminal. Now
she had a choice to make: flee again, or
risk her life for the man she loved.

Available at your favorite retail outlet.

If you enjoyed what you just read,
then we've got an offer you can't resist!

Take 2 bestselling love stories FREE!
Plus get a FREE surprise gift!

eHARLEQUIN.com

The Ultimate Destination for Women's Fiction

The eHarlequin.com online community is *the* place to share opinions, thoughts and feelings!

- Joining the community is easy, fun and **FREE!**

- Connect with **other romance fans** on our message boards.

- Meet your **favorite authors** without leaving home!

- **Share opinions** on books, movies, celebrities…and *more!*

Here's what our members say:

"I love the friendly and helpful atmosphere filled with support and humor."
—Texanna (eHarlequin.com member)

"Is this the place for me, or what? There is nothing I love more than 'talking' books, especially with fellow readers who are reading the same ones I am."
—Jo Ann (eHarlequin.com member)

Join today by visiting www.eHarlequin.com!

INTIMATE MOMENTS™

New York Times
bestselling author

MAGGIE SHAYNE

brings you

Feels Like Home

**the latest installment in
The Oklahoma All-Girl Brands.**

When Jimmy Corona returns to Big Falls, Oklahoma,
shy Kara Brand shakes with memories of a youthful crush.
He targets her as the perfect wife for him and stepmother
for his ailing son. But Jimmy's past life as a Chicago cop
brings danger in his wake. It's a race against the clock
as Jimmy tries to save his family in time to tell Kara how
much he's grown to love her, and how much he wants
to stay in this place that truly feels like home.

Available this December at your favorite retail outlet.

www.eHarlequin.com   SIMFLH

COMING NEXT MONTH

#1395 FEELS LIKE HOME—Maggie Shayne
The Oklahoma All-Girl Brands
When Chicago cop Jimmy Corona returned to his small
hometown, all he wanted was to find a mother to care for his
son while he took down a perp. Shy Kara Brand, who'd once
had a youthful crush on him, was the obvious choice. But
danger soon followed Jimmy to Big Falls, and only Kara
stood between his little boy and certain death....

#1396 MOST WANTED WOMAN—Maggie Price
Line of Duty
Police sergeant Josh McCall came to Sundown, Oklahoma,
for some R & R and fell for an alluring bartender with a dark past
and an irresistible face. Josh was determined to uncover Regan
Ford's secrets despite the distrust he saw in her eyes. Would
persistence and energy win this troubled woman's
heart...or endanger both their lives?

#1397 SECRETS OF THE WOLF—Karen Whiddon
The Pack
Brie Beswich came to Leaning Tree for answers about her
mother's tragic death. But all she found was more questions
and hints of an earth-shaking secret. The small town's handsome
sheriff seemed to know more than he was saying. As danger
loomed, could Brie trust this mysterious man and the passion
that threatened to consume them both?

#1398 OUT OF SIGHT—Michelle Celmer
After a treacherous life in a crime family, divorce counselor
Abbi Sullivan finally found a place to call home in the bucolic
wilds of Colorado. Her dream world came screeching to a halt
when FBI special agent Will Bishop came after her and demanded
she testify against a brutal criminal. Now she had a choice to
make: flee again, or risk her life for the man she loved.

SIMCNM1105